Praise for

Gladiators

Historicals very rarely pull me in as much as 'House of Simeon' did, and it is a testament to the quality of the story that it held me captivated from the first to the last page.
~ *Queer Magazine Online*

Total-E-Bound Publishing books by D.J. Manly:

Schism

Anthologies
Stealing My Heart: Stealing Rain

GLADIATORS
Volume One

House of Simeon

House of Phineas

D.J. MANLY

Gladiators Volume One
ISBN # 978-0-85715-407-1
©Copyright D.J. Manly 2011
Cover Art by April Martinez ©Copyright 2011
Interior text design by Claire Siemaszkiewicz
Total-E-Bound Publishing

Published in 2011 by Total-E-Bound Publishing, Think Tank, Ruston Way, Lincoln, LN6 7FL, United Kingdom.

Total-E-Bound Publishing is an imprint of Total-E-Ntwined Limited.

Manufactured in the USA.

HOUSE OF SIMEON

Dedication

To the memory of those who fought and died in the arena.

Chapter One

Gold

"This is very exciting, my dear," the master's wife loudly announced to her husband, ensuring all of the servants heard the conversation. "I hear Gold obtained the best price, and soldiers the lot of them, no common criminals this time." She checked her nails. "The crowd doesn't appreciate those sorts."

Gold wasn't really my name, however the master — or lanista, as he was more commonly called — had the right to call me whatever he chose. I had earned the name Gold when I became the lanista's champion in the arena. With twenty two victories, and no ties or defeats, I was the undisputed champion.

"He seems to have a good sense for slave buying," Gracia went on with her commentary. "It was very astute of you to send Gold to town to do the buying. If anyone knows gladiator stock, Gold does."

Gracia often talked about me as if I wasn't in the room. But then, I was not really a person to her at all. I was a slave, albeit a somewhat exalted one.

I didn't even bat an eye when Master Simeon replied with a sly smile, "Yes, and Gold even bested my rival in the auction. I have won six of the finest on the block, and that's not easy to do nowadays, given what we mostly have to choose from is Sparta's rejects."

I was one of those so called Spartan rejects.

"That horrible Phineas must be cursing the gods themselves today," Gracie giggled recklessly.

We were trailing the master as he walked on through the tablinum, the place where he kept an impressive array of written scripts and original paintings.

He paused, a scowl spread across his middle-aged face. He was extremely superstitious and very careful about not offending the gods. His reprimand was severe. "Woman, watch that vile tongue of yours. The gods are no joking matter. Do you wish to bring the entire house down upon us?"

"I am sorry, my husband." She lowered her head.

I hid a smile, noting some of the other slaves in the vicinity did as well. We'd all felt the effects of her tongue and her whip often enough. It was nice to see her get some in return.

When we reached the other side of the grand house, we waited in the atrium, which was really the most important place in the house. It was the room where distinguished guests were usually entertained, so I didn't get to be in here often.

The master considered this to be an important event, so the new slaves would be brought in through the main door which faced the street.

I glanced up at the high ceiling for a moment and stood with my legs apart. I knew the lanista was relieved to have a new lot of slaves who had some potential for gladiator training. We had lost over twenty gladiators in a short period of time, due to the lanista volunteering many of his best to pay homage to dead family members of prominent citizens. He had ambitions to be elected to the senate, and he was willing to go to great lengths to win favour— sometimes to his own detriment, I felt.

I looked straight ahead now as I heard the shuffle of chained men being herded inside and down the narrow passageway to the grand, sparsely furnished room where we waited. There were six new slaves brought in, all of whom had been warriors in various foreign militaries. They were robust men in their youth and considered a prize, even if I knew most of them wouldn't see the sun set for more than one more day.

They were naked, hands thrust behind their backs, chains on their wrists. The chains extended in one direction to a metal collar around their necks, and in the other direction to both ankles.

The lanista went to inspect the first one in line and lifted his head up high. He did the same to the next and the next, until he came to the last one in the line.

I knew he'd take extra time with this one. He was the one I had bargained the hardest for, perhaps paying far more than I should have. But I knew he was worth the price. It was true he had an attitude which had actually forced me to order the guards to gag him on the way back home. Attitude, however, could be a good thing if channelled correctly. And I would soon strip him of his defiance, as surely as he'd been stripped of his clothing.

As the master inspected him, the slave did not attempt to disguise the sneer on his face. He stood to all his six feet, almost as tall as I was myself, and glared directly at the master. I knew what was to come. The master, a man of no more than five feet six, and far smaller in stature than his new acquisition, doubled up his fist and hit him directly in the mouth.

The slave's head went back as if on a spring, and his mouth ran with blood. His expression however never changed. He didn't utter a sound. He had the makings of an excellent gladiator, and the lanista knew it because he turned to me and laughed out loud.

A gladiator was taught to face death without crying out for mercy, without acknowledging pain. This one would honour the tradition nicely.

"This one has big balls, Gold. You have done well. If he survives the initiation, he will make a fine addition to the ludi."

I nodded.

The master walked around the captive, inspecting his hard, well muscled body. He was a little lean—a bit more girth around the middle was a good thing. It protected the gladiator's organs if they were stuck in the gut with a sword. Fortunately, his weight could be easily remedied.

And although he was dirty and bruised, his body was sensational with muscles as hard as granite. His cock was almost the size of my own. I couldn't deny that from an aesthetic point of view, he was quite pleasing to the eye.

I heard Gracia take a breath as she studied the man. She examined him like a starving person might regard a tasty piece of meat. In a way, I hoped this one might become her new plaything when her husband was away. She'd never taken to Thad, the present champion, and I'd serviced the whore for long enough. Although, since I no longer fought in the arena, I had to admit, she no longer called on me.

"He reminds me of you when you first came here," the master announced, holding the man's chin in his hands again while he struggled. "This one could well give Thad a run for it. Don't you think?"

I nodded. Thad, the present acting champion, was as arrogant as the day was long. And given the average life span of a gladiator, we'd need someone to replace him eventually.

It was natural for Thad to be arrogant, I supposed, although I had never thought of myself that way. The citizens idolized their champions. And Thad had been a free man, a man of status once, but had given up all his rights and volunteered to be a part of the brotherhood. Personally, I thought him insane. I would have never volunteered for this life.

Now Thad had become high on the glory. He lived for the roar of the crowd. And it was his arrogance that would finally see him on his knees, offering his throat to his contender.

Thad's ultimate dream, of course, was to challenge me, to finally take me off my pedestal, to become the true champion of Simeon, but Lanista wouldn't allow me back in the arena.

"Very well," the master was saying now to the guards, "have them cleaned up, then give them double rations, and put them in their cells."

The men were quickly escorted out of the master's house, and I prepared to follow the guards.

"We shall arrange for a contest tomorrow," the master told me, indicating that he wasn't finished with me yet. I waited.

"I will have only this evening to give them some basic instruction." It wasn't a protest.

"It's enough. The people are dying for some entertainment. We'll make it a public event, in town. We'll invite the senators, of course. We'll even invite Phineas." He chuckled. "He will die with envy given he was unable to obtain any suitable slaves for the arena."

I doubted he would care. Phineas owned the biggest gladiator school in Rome. "Are they to be put against the champion?" I asked him. I knew his diabolical mind.

"I haven't decided that yet." He began walking back through the house. His wife stayed behind. She was allowed to view the slaves, but not permitted to be present when business was discussed.

We stood for a moment in the triclinium, which served as the dining room. I had been called to this room often in my time, to be fondled and admired by the master's high-brow guests.

I waited for instruction.

"Choose two of our finest, other than the champion, and use them for training with the newcomers."

"Weapons?"

"No. I want to see what they can do unarmed."

"We may well lose them all," I told him. "That's a lot of gold, Lanista."

The master placed a hand on my naked back. "You are always thinking about my welfare. Your loyalty will be well repaid in the afterlife by the gods."

I nodded my thanks to him as was the custom. I was not actually thinking of his welfare at all. I could care less about his supply of gold. It was his blatant lack of respect for human life which concerned me. Even though I'd seen him do this sort of thing time and time again — paying good gold for men just so they could be slaughtered for sport in front of a blood-thirsty crowd — it never ceased to amaze me.

"It is worth the gold," he waved an elegant hand in front of me, adjusting his tunic as he stood looking outside. "It's the pure sport I love, the smell of fear and of death, the pageantry and the bravery of the defeated. And if any of those slaves actually survive the arena tomorrow, they will be well worth training, will they not?" He looked at me for confirmation.

"You are right, Lanista," I said.

"Ensure that the new slaves are dressed like our enemies. We have lost a lot of good soldiers in this last war. The people need to have an outlet for their anger. Does them good to watch the enemy cut down. The ceremony will be in honour of the glorious Roman army."

Again I nodded. "Good choice."

Simeon paused, raked his gaze over me. I knew that look well. Gracia wasn't the only one I had been required to service in this house. In fact, the lanista took the most advantage of my lowly position. "I am feeling rather tense."

I inclined my head. "I am here for your pleasure, Lanista."

"But," he sighed, coming closer, running his fingers down my naked, scarred chest and pausing at the short loin cloth which concealed my groin, "you have work to do and so do I. I mustn't delay. I must make sure that all the best people are in attendance at the contest tomorrow evening. I must have scaffolding put up for the crowds, and special seats assigned for the senators and dignitaries. And you must train the contenders in the protocol. Also, choose two strong men to play the parts of Charon, the ferry man, and Mercury. We will need them to carry out the dead."

"I will see to it."

"I will tell you which gladiator I will put in the ring with the innocents later this evening." He smiled as if it was a secret but it was really just a game he liked to play with me. We both knew who it would be. "Tomorrow needs to be something the people will remember for a long time to come. And the senators need to be aware that I will spare no expense to pay tribute to our glorious Roman soldiers, who honour the great emperor."

I made my face a mask. I didn't want to give him the idea that I was relieved he had many things for me to do, things which didn't include pumping my seed into his flaccid ass. Not only did I detest his amateur hands pawing at me, it was almost ninety degrees in the shade today, and bodily contact was the last thing I needed.

I hoped it would be cooler tomorrow for the performance. I suspected that there would be nothing worse than being face down in the dirt in the heat when you were dying.

"I think in the morning, we shall have animal contests," the lanista was saying now, talking more to himself than to me, "and perhaps some comedy in the afternoon."

Yes, I thought, *barbaric blood-letting always went over better with a touch a humour.*

"A great banquet here in the dining room for the select few."

"Great idea, master," I said in a perfunctory way.

He looked at me. "You will be present at the party. To the senators, you are still the uncontested champion of this house, not Thad. I know they would pay great coin to see the two of you together in the arena."

I was ready. In fact, if I'd been a religious man, I would have prayed to the gods for the lanista to let me back into the arena. I longed to have my chance to die the glorious death, to end this miserable existence once and for all. But

I dared not say anything. I had tried once, pleaded with him to let me fight. And he had me chained to the wall and whipped me senseless. Just because I appeared to be exalted among the slaves, the lanista made sure I didn't forget my place when he thought I'd stepped out of it.

He waited to see if I would speak, and when I didn't, he turned his back to me, which was my signal to leave.

I made my way through the house again. Several naked female house slaves were in the compluvium, a small shallow pool, located directly under a square opening in the ceiling. This opening was called the impluvium. Rainwater drained through the opening from the slanted tiled roof directly into the bath below, which was lined with marble and surrounded by a mosaic floor.

For a moment, I longed to join them, to feel the warm scented water on my hot skin, but of course I was only allowed to use the bath in the main house upon invitation.

The slaves were required to bathe in this heat often. Gracie often complained that the foreigners smelt very badly when they perspired and would have her house slaves flogged if the smell got too bad.

I often used the river nearby to bathe. We had a bath inside the gladiators' quarters as well but I still preferred to use the river. The bath was used as therapy for injured gladiators and also to ease the aches and pains in the joints. However with the lack of rain recently, the water had become dark and the stench was enough to discourage me. I actually enjoyed the solitude of the trek to the river late at night, even if I was obligated to be accompanied by a guard.

I stood now out in the courtyard, looking over at the gladiators' quarters, hoping to catch a slight breeze. The house was equipped to handle at least seventy-five men at any given time. But the life span of these men was so short for all but a few of them, we often housed no more than twenty or so. Right now, we were down to far less than that.

As I approached, two guards languished outside. One of them spit on the ground as I got closer but when I raised my head and met his gaze, he looked away.

The Roman guards hated me. They'd met many of my countrymen on the battlefield during their required years of military service, and regarded us as the enemy of Rome. They also disapproved of the assumed freedom the lanista gave me, and of my power to tell them what to do when it concerned the gladiators. I was a rarity, a foreign slave who'd risen to celebrity status. That didn't sit well.

Thad was the much preferred champion in their eyes. He was a free man, and one of their own. I could understand that.

I ignored the guard, ducked my head and walked inside. There were five men in the main room, three sitting in the bath, trying to combat the heat, and two others, including the present champion, attired as I was, covered with a length of material draped around the waist and threaded between the legs. These two men were sitting on chairs in front of one of the long tables.

Due to the influx of new slaves, they'd been given a break from training today, a rare occurrence.

"Sorry lot of losers you picked, Gold," Thaddeus announced loudly as I entered. "What do you expect to do with them, dance?"

There was hesitant laughter. He was the only one who would dare to speak to me in such a disrespectful manner. Because of his status, he considered me to be his equal.

Thaddeus had defeated every one of Phineas' gladiators over the last two years. Sometimes when he got mouthy, I thought maybe I'd trained him too well.

It was stifling hot inside the brick structure. The sun beat through the open doors at the side which faced the courtyard. I wiped the sweat from my eyes and regarded Thad with half closed eyes. He was as anxious to get me into a ring as I was to be in there with him. I was the bane of his existence, the only thing standing between him and the crown of the true champion.

But we both knew that particular competition wouldn't happen any time soon. I had been the uncontested champion for almost ten years now, longer than any other gladiator alive. The lanista had told me out of the blue one day that the gods no longer wanted me to fight. "They have shown me your death in a dream," he told me. "They wish me to reward you for the honour you have brought to my name."

I was devastated. I believed I deserved to die the death of honour. I had earned it, and yet he was taking that from me. He was also taking away the right of any gladiator after me to claim that honour.

"You have done well, Gold," he told me. "You are a common enemy, a criminal, who rose above that stigma to win the hearts of the crowd. They love you — the young girls idolise you and the young men long to be you. Even the senators love the idea of you. You are too valuable to me to die."

"So you would deny me the right to offer my throat to the next victorious contender?"

"I need you. If you die, there will be no one to train the others. Ceden wishes to retire from the job, and he has served long enough to be given his freedom. You are now officially the trainer of the gladiators, with all the rights and respect that bestows."

Those so-called rights were very limited. "And my freedom?"

It was often the case that gladiators, even those who were common criminals, won their freedom if they survived five years in the arena. If I was not to die the glorious death, then at least I should have my liberty.

"Do not ask me that," came his response.

"But it is only just."

"I cannot," he hissed, "I will not let you go. One more word, Gold, and I shall be forced to strip the flesh from your back."

I had not been happy with the news. And of course I had made my feelings known, and felt the sting of the whip, much to the satisfaction of the guard who wielded it.

To the people, I would always be the undefeated one. But to some I was seen as a coward, asking for special favours from the lanista, as if I had asked the lanista myself not to put me back in the ring.

Thaddeus hated me for not allowing him to challenge me. Because of this, his title would always be precarious. And when he entered the arena, the crowd still chanted my name before his. If he thought he could have gotten away with it, he would have murdered me in my sleep. But that would have meant his certain death.

Thad was still making irreverent comments about my choices at the slave auction but I ignored him. I intended to go and check on Aden, and my thoughts suddenly turned to his welfare. He'd been gravely injured in his last contest, and I wasn't sure if he'd ever be able to fight again. "How is Aden?" I asked, cutting through the sniggering.

Silence loomed. Aden was well respected among us.

Phillip, who was the most sympathetic of the lot, said solemnly, "Not well. I fear he has not long for this world."

I walked through the room, feeling all eyes on me then turned down the corridor to the place where Aden lay on a concrete slab. Some greasy cream coated the open wounds in his chest and his breathing was laborious.

"Aden," I said, looking down at him. "Are you in much pain?"

He reached up his hand and I took it. "Yes, for now, but soon I will be able to fight again," he attempted a smile. "I am glad to see you."

I'd always suspected that Aden was enamoured of me, although I'd never given him any encouragement beyond the exchange of sexual favours which often went on in this house—late at night, in the bath. It was as automatic and necessary as eating or sleeping, a way to work off tension. I sometimes engaged in it myself, even though I knew the lanista would not have approved. He would have seen it as a waste of energy. It was pure lust, automatic, without sentiment. It meant nothing. "Rest now," I told him.

"What will happen if I can't fight again? Will I be put on the cross?"

"Of course not. You have honoured yourself in the arena. I will not allow that to happen." I turned away, and left to check on the new ones who waited in their cells.

Aden being put to death was, of course, always a possibility, especially if he was seen as a liability. More than likely, the master would find a better use for him. He had great respect for his gladiators, and Aden had always fought well, with honour.

It was a strange phenomenon really. We were still slaves, the power of life and death over us was held by our master, yet at the same time, we were beloved and revered due to our acts in the arena, like celebrities in a cage.

I knew as I left him that the medicine being administered to Aden was not working. The wounds were too deep. And if Aden would never be strong enough again to fight, it was better if Charon did come for him. If the master gave him a house job, it would be the ultimate humiliation for a gladiator. He would live out the rest of his life in disgrace.

The guard opened the door for me as I came to the row of cells. "Were they fed?" I demanded.

The guard nodded. "Double rations."

"And allowed to bathe?"

"Not yet."

"Put the others in their cells and take the new ones to the bath." I didn't want to mix them just yet. The gladiators would taunt and distract them, and I had a lot to do with them before tomorrow.

The guard gave me a disrespectful salute.

I walked past the cells, glancing at each of the men I'd purchased. Some may have once been my countrymen. Now, they were nothing to me except potential gladiators, or more aptly, fodder for the crowd tomorrow.

I stopped in front of the cage which held the man who, in my mind, stood the greatest chance of survival.

He was half lying on the straw mattress, his face covered in blood and dirt. He glanced at me lazily as I peered at him through the bars. "What do they call you?"

"Screw yourself."

"That's an odd name, and physically impossible."

"Is that your idea of a joke?"

"If you knew me, you'd know I'm not one who is prone to joking. Now, either tell me your name, or face my whip."

"You'd whip a man for not telling you his name?" His voice was filled with disbelief.

"I've whipped a man for less than that."

There was silence. I guess he realised I was serious because he said after a few seconds, "Samson. My name is Samson."

"Stand up, Samson. You'll be going to the bath." I stepped away from the cage as the guard came and opened it.

"Get up, you filthy Spartan rat," the guard yelled, sneering at me the whole time. "Aren't you a Spartan as well, sir?"

I didn't answer. If I had been a Spartan, that identity was long gone.

The prisoner gave me a sly glance on the way out of his cage. I stared at his broad back as he followed the others into the outer room. I even allowed myself the luxury of letting my gaze travel down over his back and settle on his hard, round buttocks. *Desire.* For a second, I almost actually felt something akin to it but then it disappeared as if it had never been. I'd long since taught myself not to feel anything, not anger, or pain, fear or humiliation, and certainly not desire. It wasn't even a word in my vocabulary anymore, but there it was, fleeting yet acute.

Not feeling desire, however, didn't mean I couldn't function in a sexual manner. When called to service someone sexually, like the master, or his wife, or even one of his very dignified guests, I performed exactly as I was directed. Anatomically, everything seemed to react in a predictable way but I felt nothing except lust. And that's why when my gaze moved over the length of this slave's body, it took me by surprise. The desire was in my mouth more than anywhere, and it was somewhat different than lust. It fascinated me.

A few minutes later, with that forgotten, I stood in front of the six newcomers. They were sitting in the bath, quietly washing the debris from their bodies, and trying to cool off.

Two guards taunted them with their swords for a few minutes, poking at them until I told them to stop.

This was met with hostile glances but the guards obeyed and drew back against the wall.

"I am called Gold," I announced. "You are all the property of Simeon of Tiber, the master of this house. He has purchased you and saved you from the gallows. As a result, you owe him your gratitude, your lives and your loyalty. Tomorrow, you will face a gladiator in the arena. If you survive, you will be kept here and trained to be one of the glorious warriors in the brotherhood of gladiators. Are you all familiar with the contest?"

There were some mumblings but not much else. I wasn't sure that they all understood what I was saying, given I heard various dialects, but I was positive they'd all seen a contest before. "I will say this once and only once. Listen well. Tomorrow you will be dressed in the garb of Rome's enemies and led into the ring where you will face the gladiator. The fight is to the death. If you are at the point of death and the referee decides there is a tie, or takes mercy, the crowd will be asked to vote on your fate. Thumbs down and you will die. If you want to die with dignity, you will hold up your finger and offer your throat to your executioner. If by some miracle you survive, you will be rewarded, kept here, and trained to be one of us."

One of the prisoners raised his hand. "May I speak?"

"Feel free," I nodded.

"Will we have weapons?"

"No. You are prisoners at this time. This is your test. But today I will try to give you some basic training that will give you a chance of survival."

"This is bullshit," a deep, male voice announced suddenly.

I narrowed my eyes and looked over at the one called Samson. It didn't surprise me that the outburst came from him.

He stood, water dripping off his chest and between his thighs. Even with the bruised and spilt lip, I realised now that I could see his face, that he was handsome.

The guards stepped forward, ready to grab him out of the water. I put up my hand. "Let him speak freely."

"This Roman slave owner puts us in the arena to be cut down like dogs, without weapons. And we are supposed to be grateful? Where is the glory in that?"

"You are a captive of war, and the master has the right of life and death over you. Your opinion is of no importance."

He wasn't to be put off. "And what is the reason that we are not given weapons?" He looked directly at me, demanding an answer.

"I have already told you," I placed my hands on my hips.

"But the gladiators will have weapons," he insisted. "And they are well trained. A weapon would at least give us a fighting chance."

"Yes, it would. You are at a disadvantage. Your point is?"

He laughed harshly, his mouth twisting as he said something under his breath.

"I suggest you sit down." I told him, my mouth hardening. I looked at one of the guards. "You will find these men the garb of the Semite, a scutum, an ocrea, and a galea with a large crest and plume." The Samnites were a tribe from Campania which the Romans had fought. They were traditionally the prototype for Rome's professional gladiators. If not the Samnites, then the Gauls, or Thracians, two other tribes the Romans had defeated.

"At least we are to have helmet and shield," Samson called out again, seeming immune from the threats of the guards.

As a military man, he understood very well what I was saying. A *scutum* was a large oblong shield, and a *galea* a visored helmet with a large crest and a plume. There were many in storage from the warriors who had been captured before them.

The Samnites also wore a leather or metal grieve on the left leg, which was called an ocrea. This afforded some protection from the sword although I certainly wasn't optimistic about its efficacy.

"How fucking noble," Samson muttered aloud. For his comment, this time he received a hit to the diaphragm from the guard.

"Take them outside," I instructed. I went to get Phillip and Gabien, who I decided would help with their training.

When one of the guards saw the three of us appear outside, he smirked. "Not Thad? You might put the mouthy one in with him tomorrow, and watch Thad rip that grin off his smug face. The people have a right to see their champion."

I had no intention of using Thad to train the newcomers because I knew the master would use him tomorrow in the main event. Even though putting these poor slaves in the ring with Thad tomorrow would be more than cruel, the master would think it genius. One man against six. The crowd would eat it up. Thad would be more exalted in the eyes of the senate. That exaltation would distract them from their continual insistence that Simeon put me back into the arena, which was getting harder for the lanista to defend.

I went to the other side of the house and stared up at the sky for a moment. It had cooled a little because the sun was going down. The sky would turn pink and orange in the horizon soon, warning of another scorcher tomorrow.

The crowd could be particularly vicious when the humidity settled in, showing no mercy when mercy was called for.

It was time. I walked back through the house and out into the courtyard. I observed the six men for a moment while they stood in a row and waited for instruction.

"Come at me," I motioned to them with my hands.

The men looked at me in surprise, then at each other, not sure what to do, thinking that possibly I'd lost my mind.

"Come at me," I repeated the command, louder this time.

The one called Samson of course was the first to take me up on my offer. He charged me, perhaps thinking that his fury would make him strong enough to knock me off my feet.

I braced for his attack. He was almost as large as I was, but I'd had ten years in the arena. I knew how to fight, how to survive, and he was a long way from being able to best me.

I lowered myself as he ran and poised my hands to slide down between his thighs and lift. I heard him grunt as my forearms smashed into his groin and I threw my entire body back, spring-boarding him into the air. He went down hard in the dirt. For a moment, I thought maybe I'd broken his back, but after a few seconds, he shook himself and got to his feet.

He charged me again with a furious cry. This time he attacked me from the side. I swung around and slammed my body into his, hard. He almost managed to stay on his feet until I gave him a second blow to the shoulder and he went to his knees in front of me with a groan.

I reached down and took his chin firmly in my hand. I could feel his resentment for me radiating from deep inside. I tilted his head back, withdrew my sword slowly, and placed it strategically across his throat. The indentation drew blood. "You would be dead now if this was for real."

His eyes were blue, bluer than the sky at sunrise, and the look in them was one of defiance, in spite of the sword at his throat. He needed to hold onto that rage of course, but that alone wouldn't be enough to ensure that he survived tomorrow. He had yet to learn that rage alone would only postpone the inevitable, but I wasn't sure that there was time for me to teach him that.

"Do you want to live?"

"Let my fate be in the hands of the gods," he practically spat at me.

"Fuck the gods," I replied with blatant irrelevance. I owed the gods nothing. In spite of what the lanista said, the gods had never favoured me. I lived now only because I had learned to fight better than every man I faced in the arena. "If you want to live," I told him, removing my sword from his throat, "then swallow your pride and pay attention to what I tell you. If anyone will survive this contest tomorrow, it will be you, but only if you lose that arrogance long enough to accept I may have something to teach you."

"You call me arrogant, you who are heralded as the unrivalled champion of the Gladiators who holds onto his title only because he hides behind his master and refuses to enter the arena?"

I narrowed my eyes. "You presume to know much about me, slave. You have seen me in the arena then?"

He gave me a faint smile and got to his feet. "Yes," he picked up the helmet, and dusted himself off, "I have seen you, battered and bloodied. I know that you never showed any mercy to your competitor. Your title is unrivalled, and so is your thirst for blood. What is your real name, Gold, or have you completely forgotten it?"

That was a definite slap in the face. I almost struck him but I held back. Anger. That was one emotion I had learned to control, except in the arena where I let it consume me. But right now looking at his face, mocking me, I felt that emotion full force.

He laughed a little, sensing he'd hit the right nerve.

I backed away from him, my fists clenched at my sides. "Then let your blood run in the arena tomorrow if that's what the fates have in store for you," I muttered then looked over at the two gladiators I'd chosen for the training session. "Engage them all in contest," I called out, "one by one. Be tough on them but leave them in shape for the contest. We need them alive for tomorrow."

I walked off for a moment. I needed to retain my composure. No one had made me this angry in a long time. I didn't like feeling out of control. Personally, I was not at all confident that a few hours of training was going to do anything more than bruise them a little, but I would do what I could to give them the illusion that they would have a chance in there.

Some time later when I had come back to observe the training, Gabien came up beside me. He wiped the sweat off his brow, and guzzled some water. "Who will be put into the arena with them tomorrow?"

Phillip had already put two of the men on ground and was waiting for them to get up again.

"I'm sure it will be Thad that will meet them in the arena tomorrow but that has not yet been confirmed to me."

Gabien laughed out loud. "It will be a short contest."

I gave him a sharp glance. "It is your job to make sure the contest lasts a little more than a few minutes. The senators will expect a show. Go on," I said, giving him a push forward, "go back to work now. We haven't much time left, and Phillip is beginning to tire."

Gabien threw his cup aside and stalked back out to meet the group. "Okay," he cried out, "come on!"

I stood and watched restlessly as Phillip and Gabien knocked the newcomers to the ground time and time again, and laughed all the while they did it. This was more play than work for them, and it was all a bit sad.

Eventually, I realised that the lanista, Simeon, was watching from his balcony. I glanced at him and he raised a hand to me. I nodded and went back to surveying the scene.

Eventually, the newcomers were too exhausted to go on. Only Samson remained on his feet, and seemed ready for more.

Gabien encouraged him to charge, looking weary himself now. I looked away to speak with Phillip and when I looked back, Samson had Gabien on his ass in the dirt.

Phillip laughed out loud and I noticed the lanista leaning forward from his perch.

It was obvious that Gabien was embarrassed and angry at being bested. "I didn't give the signal," he growled, trying to cover up his error in judgement as he scrambled to his feet.

I saw the master out of the corner of my eye. He was still in the same place, and looked to be keenly interested in what was going on in the courtyard with Gabien and Samson.

Samson and Gabien continued to struggle now in the dirt, both remaining on their feet, pushing back and forth.

Phillip nudged me. "What do you make of that?"

"I'm not sure," I replied. "Go on and help Gabien."

Phillip went running over. He grabbed Samson from behind while Gabien tried to kick his legs out from under him. Gabien received a kick to the groin for it, and Samson forced Phillip back against the wall. Gabien again tried to take Samson down.

Samson was strong, and determined. He let out a yell like a triumphant warrior when he smashed his fist into Gabien's jaw and skirted away from him.

I decided that the time had come to put an end to it. "Enough," I shouted, as I came forward. I couldn't let a common slave get the best of two of my gladiators to that extent. I gave Phillip and Gabien a look of disdain, and they went back inside, heads lowered. "Take the prisoners back to their cells," I barked to the guards.

The guards prodded them all back inside, some of them limping and bleeding badly.

Samson gave me a triumphant smile and folded into the line with the rest of them.

"Gold," the master called out to me from the balcony. "Come. I want to speak to you."

"That was interesting," the lanista said when I got to the house, "the spectacle between that newcomer and Gabien."

"Yes, but I am not surprised," I told Simeon, when he commented on Samson's performance. Simeon ordered a servant to pour me a glass of wine. That always meant that he was pleased about something.

"Sit," he ordered, which was a rare invitation. He lounged on one of the sofas in his sitting room, and I perched on another. He sipped his wine, and a half naked slave girl waved a fan over him. "He is quite incredible, this ah...?" the master paused.

"Samson."

"Yes, Samson. Who was he before?"

"The slave trader told me that he was a high ranking officer in the Spartan army, but the sellers sometimes try to deceive you to make you pay more. I believe however that he is from a prominent family. He is educated."

"Hence the haughty attitude. I expect you to deal with that, transform it into something we can use."

I nodded. "I will do my best." I waited to drink until he drank.

"You always do," he smiled. "He has great potential, this Samson. It will be interesting to see him tomorrow, what he will do. I'm putting Thad in the arena but then you already knew that."

I nodded. "I suspected."

"You are a wonder. How is it you always know what I intend to do?"

"I didn't know for sure," I lied. I couldn't make him think I was too smart, although he knew I myself was also educated.

"I trust you in these things, Gold. What are your predictions for tomorrow?" He smiled brilliantly as he drained his glass and held it out for more.

The slave quickly refilled his glass.

"Thad will kill them all," I replied, "except maybe for this Samson. I suspect Samson will do some damage to Thad, and try to protect the others. But in the end Thad will kill him, unless the crowd takes mercy."

"Does he know them, the others?"

"I don't think so. They are from various armies, not all Spartans."

"Curious that you believe he would try and protect total strangers when he is fighting for his own life."

"It is only a suspicion."

The master laughed.

"Master, if I may propose something?"

"Go ahead," he waved.

"I think that we should give the prisoner leniency if he is the last one standing. It would be a shame to waste that much potential on the whims of the crowd."

"Hmm," he seemed to consider that. "There is also the question of Thad. We don't want to lose Thad on a fluke. I will have the referee stop the fight if Thad's life ever appears to be in jeopardy, or if he seems to be losing the battle…to avoid any embarrassment. And let's hope this Spartan can win the favour of the crowd and they don't shout for the kill at the end."

I watched him drink down his second glass of wine. My plea for him to stop the killing of Samson, if it came to that end, had apparently fallen on deaf ears. I tried again. "It often depends on the heat." I proceeded carefully. "And it will be hot tomorrow. In your wise opinion, master, do you think this Spartan's life should be left to the crowd? Unlike you, the citizens are yet oblivious to his potential."

He laughed. "Not leave it to the crowd?"

"He is their enemy. They will most likely vote for the kill. I just don't want you to suffer undo loss."

He seemed to consider that. "When you first came and we threw you in against my champion, may he rest in peace, you had no weapons. Do you remember what happened?"

I nodded.

"The crowd recognised you for a champion and chose to spare your life. If he is worthy, this Samson, as you say, they will do the same. Stand," he demanded suddenly.

I put down my glass and rose to my feet.

"You will bathe with me. You are dusty. I will summon the slaves to wash us. Would you like that, Gold?"

"If it pleases you, master," I lowered my head. My likes or dislikes were of no importance to him, nor, at times, was my opinion.

"It does," he replied. "It pleases me immensely. My wife has retired to her quarters early this evening. She insists that the most beautiful women in Rome will be present tomorrow night and she needs to get her beauty sleep." He chuckled. "Personally, I don't believe if she slept for a century, it would do her much good."

I didn't comment on that. I wasn't expected to.

Their marriage had been an arranged one like many of the day. There had never been a great deal of affection between them.

"My son, Claudius, will be home from the boarding school soon," he said as he walked down the corridor. "He was the top of his class in military strategy, you know."

"You must be very proud of him." I followed him to the bath. I couldn't say that I was looking forward to seeing Claudius again. He had been fourteen when he left, a snotty little know-it-all who thought he was a general. He loved to come into the gladiators' quarters and torment us. He fancied himself one of us at one time and had a particular fascination with me. Now he was a grown man, almost twenty, and I had my doubts that the years would have changed him much.

I removed my coverings and set them aside, moving down into the water. The lanista did the same, motioning to me to move closer.

He leant over and studied me, running his hand over my jaw, tracing the scars on my massive chest. "Your beauty is astounding and each scar makes your body even more appealing." He was still tracing the scar on my chest when he asked, "Was this one from Stadoes?"

Stadoes was at one time the champion of Simeon's arch rival, Phineas. Three times we had clashed in the arena, and three times we'd almost killed each other but the crowd had always opted to end the contest before the decision was rendered. "Yes," I said.

"I remember the day you killed him. Did you have any remorse?"

"No." I said. I remembered his eyes. They were filled with surprise as I cut his throat.

"I knew you were going to kill him that day. The gods had predicted it. It was raining. You were both covered in mud. I had never seen such a glorious sight, so sexual. I had hoped to buy him."

"Yes, I remember."

"I would have loved to have seen you take him, on his knees. Ah, the glory, the possession, the ultimate victory of it, delicious. He would have bowed to you. One is always half in love with their enemy." His eyes looked quite dreamy. "Do you think he was in love with you, Gold?"

I doubted that. "If it pleases you to think so," I said.

He chuckled.

If Simeon could have, he would have been a gladiator himself. He'd romanticised it to the point of nonsense. But they all did. They had to because if they really saw it for what it was, it would be the end of them all.

"What would you do if I put you into the arena with Thad?" He asked suddenly.

My eyes widened. My heart beat quickened.

"I didn't say I would," he put up a hand before I could speak. "I couldn't bear to lose you." He touched my hair. He let his hand drop into the water and settle on my thigh. His fingertips moved over the head of my penis. "I asked you only what you would do if I arranged the contest that the Senate is dying for."

"I would meet him with honour."

"You would kill him."

I was surprised that he would say that, after claiming that the gods had predicted that I would die the next time I stepped into the ring. Had he lied to me? But I was in no position to remind him of that.

"He is a shadow compared to you, my beauty," he whispered. "And everyone knows it. The people know it, and so does he. That's why he longs to kill you."

"And yet you took me out of the contest." I met his gaze, something I rarely did, unable to hold back. "People think I hide behind you," I muttered. "They take me for a coward."

He removed his hand. "It is of no consequence what people think. Anyone who knows you knows that there is no cowardice in you. And I had my reasons for removing you from the arena. You know better than to question me, Gold," he warned. "Don't overstep your place. Slaves!" He shouted. "Get in here and wash us."

I leant my head back and closed my eyes as gentle female hands washed my body, as well as the master's.

When we rose from the bath, soft towels wiped us dry and I followed the master to his bed. He bid me to lie down and stood there looking at me for the longest time before he crawled onto the bed and began to move his hands over my flesh. "My beautiful gladiator," he whispered, "my champion. I should have asked the slave to oil your body. You look so beautiful with the oil. Take me. Possess me like you would one you have defeated in the arena."

I gently rolled him onto his side and did as I always had, upon command. I impaled him with my cock, and moved slowly but firmly inside of him. I was not to touch him anywhere else or kiss him, only this, only penetration. When it was over, I was always to leave his bed promptly without looking at him. It was a humiliation really for him to allow a lowly slave to penetrate him in that way. That's why he wouldn't allow me to look at him, but yet he craved it.

When he had ejaculated, I picked up my coverings and went back to the slave quarters, relieved that it was over, and anxious to wash off the sticky residue.

Chapter Two

Samson

As I sat huddled under the scaffolding with the roar of the crowd all around me, I was glad to not have wife and child at home like the others. We had been here for what seemed like forever and the waiting seemed endless. Two lazy guards kept one eye on us, and one eye on the spectacle, blocking our view of the makeshift ring.

Our hands and feet were shackled, and it made movement difficult and the heat seem even more acute.

This morning, two fully decked out gladiators had been led into the circle by a horn blowing and drum beating parade. They fought off two ferocious lions and left them wounded and bleeding in the middle of the arena. Finally they took mercy on the poor suffering beasts and killed them. The kill had not been that impressive. The lions had been chained and placed on a pedestal above them. There had been little danger to the gladiators. The lions were easy prey — just like we would be.

The crowd lapped it up however.

I recognised one of those gladiators as Gabien. I'd kicked his ass last night, and I had hoped he would be the one we'd be facing but I had my doubts.

At one point, a guard set down a bowl of water in front of each of us and some bread. It was a challenge to grasp the bowl. I spilled most it before it got to my mouth. The bread held little appeal.

I didn't know any of the men who would stand with me today in that arena. They were all strangers to me, but still I couldn't help feel pity for them. All of them were poor young peasants, who were forced to serve in various armies. All of them had children, and had spoken of them together in various dialects, somehow making themselves understood. The barriers which had existed between us were no more. We were all in the same boat and that boat was destined to sink.

I stayed quiet, and concentrated all of my energy on what was to come. I replayed the events that had brought me to this fate in my head.

We'd had an idiot as our commander, the son of a prominent figure who demanded his son be promoted into a high position, regardless of the fact that he had no ability to lead an army.

I was an officer myself, the leader of a group of men who had instructions to cut off the Roman army at Troy. We'd been capturing ground, and I hadn't lost one man until this commander decided he wanted to engage in combat.

His strategy made little sense to me, and I knew that he was going to get us all killed. I couldn't stand by and let my men get slaughtered, as would happen later this evening here in this fabricated arena.

I defied him. I defied him in front of what was left of my men. He stripped me of my command and led my men off to their deaths.

He left me in the middle of what was fated to be a field attacked by the enemy. I didn't stand a chance against a Roman army. And after running and hiding from the Romans for two days, they finally caught up to me. I pleaded for death but instead they took me with them back to Rome. During the trip, I was beaten and violated, and when I finally thought they were going to take my life, some Roman commander told me that I was going to be sold as a slave.

"Just kill me," I told him, my spirit almost nonexistent.

He shook his head, his words actually sounding compassionate. "You're strong, stronger than you think. You have survived these many days in captivity. You will take your chances on the block."

Naked and humiliated, I had stood on that block, being poked and prodded, jeered at by the crowd. I hated everyone in sight. Then I saw him. He walked through the crowd like a god. The people parted to give him room, whispering about him. He had a presence that demanded he be acknowledged—tall, muscled, dark-haired, classically handsome. He was dressed like a Roman, short toga draped over his shoulder, tied around the waist, falling just above his knees with those high laced boots on his feet. The brand on his shoulder, however, told me that he was no Roman. He was a slave.

He raised his gaze to me and began to bid.

I gasped. I recognised him. I knew that face. I'd seen him in the arena, wielding a sword overhead which would have weighed many a man down. He was the still-undisputed champion of Simeon, owned by a wealthy Roman land owner who looked for favour with the Senate.

He was a fellow Spartan like me, and from a prominent family. It had long been rumoured that he was too afraid of losing his long held title to step back into the arena, and had pleaded to his master to keep him out.

I wasn't sure that was true. I hadn't seen Gold at all today. Perhaps he didn't wish to be there to watch us die. The very sight of him angered me. He was a traitor to himself and to Sparta. Slave or not, he seemed to enjoy his work well enough, and all the brutality that went along with it.

Two clownish people wandered into the ring now and there was laughter. Even the guards laughed, watching the show. I looked over to see the discouragement and misery on the other men's faces, and I wondered at whose hand we would die.

I leant back against the wall with a sigh. I thought of my parents, at how they would be in disgrace because of my defiance. I'd never have the chance now to tell them the real story, tell them that I didn't desert my command.

I offered the piece of bread to the man beside me who indicated that he wanted it. I had no stomach for it. Every second, every burst of applause from the crowd brought us one step closer to our deaths, and I felt the pain of my companions. It was inhumane to make us stay here all day, waiting, in the heat, knowing our fate, but Romans had no mercy. They had no heart. And I wasn't sure that Spartans were any better.

When the sun dipped lower in the sky, the cool breeze created a much appreciated reprieve. The others had been dozing, their heads lolling against the wall. And while the others slept, I planned my first move in that ring.

When Gold stepped into the small alcove under the stands, his shadow closed out the sun. He ducked his head and went down on his haunches before us. In spite of everything, my heart sped up, and I cursed myself that he should have that affect on me. Frankly, I was shocked to see him there. I'd thought he wouldn't come at all.

His expression was unreadable. His chest was bare and he wore a mere slip of material wrapped around his hips. My gaze zeroed in on the scars across his chest for a moment then I looked directly into his haunting dark eyes. "Come to gloat, Roman?"

"I am no more Roman than you, and you know that. I came to see if you had any questions or if I could…"

"If you could what, go into that ring in my place?" I scoffed. "What is it you think you can do for these poor dupes now?"

"Them, not you?" He raised an eyebrow.

"Me? Don't worry for me, Roman. I plan on walking out of that ring tonight." I didn't really realise that I meant it until I said it aloud, but I did.

"Good luck then," he looked at the others then glanced at the guard. "Give them more water." He rose, still keeping his dark head ducked. "I think I should tell you," he added, "you'll be facing Thaddeus."

My jaw opened a little. I'd expected to face gladiators but Thaddeus was the champion. "Fabulous," I said between my teeth. "Your master has a strange sense of humour. Only him, why not you as well? Oh, I forgot, you're too much of a coward to go into the ring."

"Would you like that… to face both of us? Is Thad not enough of a challenge for you?" He gave me what could only be considered a grimace. "Apollo be with you," he murmured hastily, and left.

It was strange that he bothered to come and say goodbye, and even stranger that he blessed me with Apollo. Apollo was the god of healing and prophecy, and the only god we Spartans shared with the Romans.

We heard announcements again, and the crowd was back in force. It was early evening and it was time. We were unshackled, and the guards stayed close in case we bolted.

When I saw a man dressed as Charon, and another dressed as Mercury, it drove it home to me. The men standing with me were all going to die. And if I survived, it would be some kind of a miracle.

We were given our helmets and shields. The helmet was quite ridiculous and heavy, but we were told not to take it off. It reminded me of when I was sent away to military school at a young age and I was handed a sword. It was so heavy that it dragged me to the ground. How I'd hated the training but it was a boy's entire life. No time for anything else but training. I just hoped it paid off now.

Thaddeus, our challenger, walked out into the arena. I could see him clearly now dressed up in his sober Roman military uniform, his sword poised over his head as he flexed his muscles for the crowd.

"Gold, Gold, Gold," the crowd chanted. The announcer tried to shout them down, "Thaddeus from the House of Simeon, Champion of the Brotherhood. You will show respect!"

The chant eventually changed over to "Thad, Thad, Thad," as the announcer screamed, "Prepare for the enemy, the evil Samnites who have killed many innocent Roman country men, raped and pillaged and struck down our soldiers in their prime. Welcome the challengers!"

The guards pushed us out of our haven under the seats and into the arena. One of the others actually stumbled and fell to his knees. I raced forward and yanked him to his feet, pulling him back. "Not time to die yet, man," I hissed.

"Let the contest begin!" the announcer sang and Thad, who seemed like a giant to me, suddenly lifted that sword over his head and swung.

The champion was smiling but then why shouldn't he be? This was the easiest contest the barbarian would ever fight. And he could only enhance his reputation. One against six, five with little fighting experience; and all of us with nothing but a shield and helmet, which was more hindrance than anything else. There was no question that he would win.

I sincerely did what I could to help the others, fighting Thad off with my shield, distracting him best I could. I think he saw me more as an annoyance than anything else, as he cut me here and there, but nothing deep enough to slow me down. He wanted to make it last, give the crowd a show. I watched each man fall, one after another and when the fifth man finally lay bleeding and broken in the dirt, Thad made one serious error.

The crowd was roaring, cheering, chanting his name and Thad struck me down in the dirt. I saw my own death as the wind knocked out of me for a moment. There was blood running down my head and into my eyes, but instead of finishing me off, he went preening around the ring, victory assured. He was relaxed. He was too relaxed. I had time to feel the air rush back into my lungs while he flexed his muscles again in front of his admirers. I scrambled up and rushed him. My feet sunk in the blood soaked dirt as I gritted my teeth and forged on, two shields in my hands. I smashed the two metal shields on both sides of his head before he even knew what had happened.

He was a little stunned, not to mention enraged. He shook himself, and I didn't give him time to recover. I went right for his pleated metal tunic skirt and kicked him hard between the legs.

The pain in his eyes was intense and he cried out something and swiped his sword through the air, not really aiming at anything. In spite of that, it ended up missing me by a hair's breadth. I danced out of his way as he swung again and again. He was all around me. "You're dead, Spartan," he grimaced, the sword swiping low this time. I had a flash of being cut in half. I had dropped the shields and I frantically scanned for another. I spotted one a few feet away, lying beside one of the other men's severed head. I grabbed it, rolled on the ground and brought it up to meet his sword just in time. My heart beat like a drum in my chest as I rolled this way and that way, unseeing eyes on that head staring at me, warning of my fate. Thad brought that sharp blade down time and time again, in the dirt, growling in frustration as I managed to narrowly escape the blows.

Suddenly, he reached down and got a hold of my arm. I was yanked to my feet as I kicked out. He just about tore my arm off. I reached up and grabbed that awkward helmet off my head and swung it with all my might, smashing him hard in the jaw. I saw him spit blood. I think I knocked out some of his teeth.

He was fighting mad. The crowd was sounding collective gasps as I ran from him and Thad stalked me across the arena. I paused to get my breath for a second, scanning the ring, desperately trying to think of what I could do some damage with. I think I realised that maybe I wasn't going to walk out of there after all, but I wasn't willing to accept it just yet.

Suddenly as he came forward, running hard at me, prepared to strike the fatal blow, I remembered that move that Gold had done on me the night before, the one that had really enraged me. I wondered if I had the strength. In back of me directly were the boards that had been put up as a barrier. It was there Thad would land if I could do it, right in front of the senators. Best case scenario, I'd knock him out, worst case…well…I didn't want to think about that.

I crouched low as he got within a few feet of me and when he was close enough, I leant forward and threaded my arms through the legs, lifting up and out. I didn't quite get him over my head but I unbalanced him enough so that he fell sideways. I put one foot on his sword and the other on his arm, and I heard the crunch of bone.

I was about to reach down and take his sword when the referee, someone I had forgotten was even in that ring with us, came over and dragged me off Thad. Two guards held me suddenly in their grasp. The crowd was on their feet.

There seemed to be some confusion and the referee was looking up to the stands, waiting.

A voice now spoke out from above. I squinted my eyes, and tried to see who it was. I was covered in blood but I didn't really know where the bleeding was coming from. Probably everywhere.

"Now people," the voice called out as the crowd quieted, "since we have a tie, it is up to you. Do we let this enemy live, or die?"

I'd forgotten that was how it was decided, and I wasn't really optimistic. I was supposed to represent the enemy, and I'd almost defeated their champion.

I heard some people call out, "Kill him, kill him," but it wasn't the dominant cry. Perhaps it was the sun going down or the cooler air which circulated around them, but whatever it was, the loudest voices screamed "Let him live, let him live, let him live."

I was hustled from the ring. Someone was dabbing at me with a cloth, cleaning the blood off of my face. I was led away from the centre of the square, two guards at my side, and a horse drawn carriage waiting.

When I was told to enter the carriage, I was surprised to see Gold sitting in the back. Across from him was another man, thin and middle-aged with grey hair. I recognised him as the man who had examined me that first day.

I was bleeding everywhere but neither man seemed to take notice, or care. The older one knocked on the roof of the carriage and we started to move.

I sat beside Gold because the older man waved at the empty space beside him. I was uneasy sitting that close to him.

"Samson, I believe," the older man said.

Gold looked out the window. He didn't say anything.

I nodded.

"My name is Simeon. I am your owner."

I stiffened, although I knew he was. It was difficult to talk. No man owned me. I held my tongue, bloodied enough for one day.

"You fought bravely. You have won your life."

"Have I won my freedom then?"

"I'm afraid not. However, I will set your sentence for five years. During that time Gold will train you to be a gladiator. If you survive, you will be set free."

"And if I refuse?" I glanced at Gold who had stopped looking out the window and was now paying attention to the conversation.

"There is no refusal," Gold told me.

"He's right," the older man nodded. "Unfortunately, Samson, you belong to me. You are mine to do with what I choose. And I choose to make you a part of a proud tradition. Consider yourself favoured by the gods."

The carriage came to a stop.

A servant opened the door and helped the man out of the carriage.

I followed, Gold at my back.

"I'll take him back," Gold said, clamping a hand on my shoulder.

"Send Thad to me," the master demanded without turning around.

"Yes, Lanista."

Gold kept his hand on my shoulder all the way through the courtyard as the guards watched carefully. "You did well. I guess you did learn something last night."

"I borrowed your move," I told him.

"Looks like it kept you alive."

I said nothing. I wasn't about to give him credit. "He's in trouble, isn't he?" I said, referring to Thad.

"Yes. And so are you. Watch yourself. Thad is the vengeful type."

"I'll deal with him. Why don't you challenge him? You could take him."

"That's not your concern. Go inside," he indicated the gladiators' quarters. "Someone will look at your wounds. Tomorrow you will be branded and will start your training in earnest."

"Branded," I breathed. "And then eventually die in the arena to entertain Romans?"

"Yes. You got it."

He walked away, and I wondered what made him tick really. He didn't seem to have any feelings under that thick skin of his.

As I entered the quarters, several men stared at me. A few nodded. I wondered how it was going to be, me and Thad both here together.

Suddenly a little man came to greet me. "I'm the doctor. Please come. I need to tend to your wounds."

Chapter Three

Gold: Son of the Lanista

Gold wasn't sure what to say to Thad as they stood in the atrium of the great house. Thad was angry but he had no cause. Samson had fought honourably.

"This is your fault," he accused under his breath. "Now Lanista is angry with me. He says I humiliated his house."

I regarded him for a moment. "He is right. You did. Samson almost bested you earlier, and if the contest hadn't been stopped, he might have won."

Thad's anger bubbled to the surface. "You stand there and dare say that I could have been defeated by a common—"

I put up my hand. Frankly, I was sick of his whining. "This is not based on what I say. It is based on what actually occurred in front of thousands of eyes."

He fell silent, hitting his fist against the wall a few times.

I was sure that his arm was broken the way it was hanging but I knew that Thad was so angry he wasn't even feeling the pain.

Music drifted through the house now as the guests wandered around, sipping wine and eating Roman delicacies. Naked slaves served the guests, jugglers stood off to the side navigating balls, slaves outfitted like Roman gods stood in place, only moving their heads in pantomime as guests strolled by.

"You need a doctor," I glanced at Thad again.

"I need nothing but that Spartan's head on a plate."

"He bested you fair, brother," I said. "Take it like a man, and put it behind you."

He gave me a look which told me that it would take a lot of time to swallow what had happened.

"You should have that arm looked at. It is probably broken."

"He told me stay," Thad muttered. "The rich folk want to see me. They want to touch the champion."

The master came walking towards us now. He looked at Thad, narrowing his eyes. "I shouldn't have to chase you. Stop sulking. Come. I'll have a servant clean up those wounds. You will see the doctor later after the guests have a look at you. What happened to you in there today?"

He hung his head.

"You brought no glory to my house."

I could feel his humiliation and even if I didn't really like the man, I felt some pity for him.

"I'm sorry, Lanista, for today and…"

The master ignored him. "And you," he pointed to me, "you will come as well."

Thad looked resentful. I knew he didn't want to have to share the attention with me. Actually, I was more than willing to let him have it all, but it was not to be.

I gave Thad a slight push ahead of me. "Go on," I told him. We walked behind our master, followed by a guard.

Gracie had one of the servants whisk Thaddeus off to get his wounds cleaned the moment she spotted him. She seemed disgusted by his bloodied appearance, clicking her tongue when she saw him. "We can't have you looking like that," she said. "Go on," she waved him away with the guard, and turned to me. I stiffened when she grabbed my arm, and hugged it to her, pulling me into the crowd of guests. "Do you realise," she asked softly, "that every single woman in this room, even the wives of these old rich men want to be fucked by you?"

"Is that so?" I played the innocent, not bothering to add, that some of those people she spoke of included the husbands as well, not to mention her own husband.

She proceeded to parade me around the room as if I was in the arena, enjoying the idea that she had had me in her bed, and they hadn't. She stopped at various times to speak to some of the ladies. She bragged about our supposed sexual interludes when the master was out of earshot. I listened mutely as she discussed the size of my cock, and how I'd fucked her in the garden for an impossible length of time. I could hardly contain my amusement. A man would truly have to be a god to sustain an erection for the length of time she proclaimed.

"My son is home," she whispered to me, running her hand over my biceps, as she calculated where she should drag me next. "He is anxious to see you, Gold."

"Me?" The feeling was far from mutual.

"Yes. You remember what a great admirer of yours he was. He greatly admired your skill in the ring."

I had tried hard to forget, but actually, if my memory serves, it wasn't only my skill he admired.

Gracia led me right into group of distinguished female guests now. "Here he is, our Golden one," she announced, still rubbing my biceps.

With the elegantly dressed guests all around me, I felt extremely exposed. I wore only a short toga skirt and a gold plated necklace around my neck, a gift from the master for being undefeated after ten contests.

Several of the ladies laid their hands on my forearms. They asked about the scars on my chest as they traced them with their finger, and whispered obscene things in my ear about my supposed sexual prowess. Hands discretely roamed my biceps, my groin and my buttocks, while the ladies giggled. I stood perfectly still like a statue until it was over, looking straight over their heads.

I was almost relieved to be taken away from the crowd, even when I found myself looking at Claudius, the master's son.

"Hello Gold," he said to me, making no secret of examining every inch of my exposed skin. He was a handsome young man for his age, his eyes still filled with lust, and a need to get his own way. He hadn't changed. "Miss me?"

"Honestly?"

"No. Lie to me."

"I've missed you."

He laughed out loud. "I was disappointed to see that loser in the ring today. It should have been you."

"I don't fight anymore."

"My father is afraid to lose you." He leant forward. "You must be good." He lowered his voice. "Are you good?"

I acted as if I didn't hear him, wondering where Thad was. Maybe some of this attention could be lavished on him. He enjoyed it so much more than I did.

"Come on, Gold, do you realise how long I've been waiting? And I am your master."

"Your father is my master," I told him stiffly.

"You know that right extents to all the members of this house. You might be grateful. I did rescue you from those ladies."

I said nothing, but he was right about him being my master. The entire family owned me.

"And tell me, beauty, what kinds of things does my father master you in?" Claudius was smirking at me, his hand discreetly reaching down and rubbing my cock.

I shifted my weight a little. "If your father hears you say that, you'll be punished. You don't want me to tell your father the things you used to make the gladiators do when you were only fourteen."

He grinned. "Tell him if you want. He won't believe you."

"Yes he will." I met his eyes. "And I'm sure there are some things you'd really prefer him not to know, perversities that you liked to perform in the—"

"Okay," he put up a hand and cut me off.

I'd made my point. I didn't for one moment think it was going to get him off my back, but at least it would slow him down some. Claudius certainly knew how to educate himself in the ways of the flesh back then, and he had no qualms about using the gladiators' bodies for his own pleasures. I had been saved from his childish games due to my champion status, although I did remember getting closely inspected by him a few times.

"You drive a hard bargain, Gold," he flicked one of my nipples back and forth. "You'll have me on my knees."

I cleared my throat, looking for an escape route.

"Do you know," he leant against the wall, looking at me, "I used to watch you fight in the arena and I would dream of you fucking me?"

I looked around again, hoping someone would call me away. "You told me often," I said.

He licked his lips, reached over and pulled at the piece of material at my waist. "You should be naked."

I gently pushed his hand back. "Your father didn't request it."

He smiled. "He missed a delicious opportunity." He sighed then straightened up. "I brought a good friend home with me from school. He finds you very interesting as well."

"And I suppose I'm to be midnight entertainment?"

"You catch on fast," he blew me a kiss. "I told him you have a big, beautiful cock. He's very excited. I've got to get back to the party. Enjoy."

"There you are," a voice called out suddenly as I found myself alone in the hallway. I looked up to see my master, a goblet in his hand. "Don't hide out there, have some food, some drink. I have been singing your praises. Everyone is very excited about Samson. What do you think we should call him?"

"Does he need a new name?" I sounded a little gruff. I was still unsettled by Claudius.

Simeon laughed. "Of course he does. Samson has no pizzazz, not like the name Gold. And he needs to start thinking of himself as a gladiator. You're going to make him into a star, aren't you?"

"Of course, if that's what you want."

"I want far more than that." He came closer, smoothing his hand over my chest. "But I fear I'll get nothing tonight, not with everyone around."

That was fine with me. I wanted to go back to my quarters.

As the evening wore on, the party grew more decadent, too much wine, and too much heat led to people having sex everywhere, many of them sodomising the slaves, both male and female.

Claudius and his friend — who I heard was the son of a senator, which explained why the lanista was bending over backwards to please him — were standing on tables and singing when I decided to make my escape. Luckily everyone was just a little too drunk to demand anything from me and at the first opportunity, I managed to slip out and go back to my quarters without anyone stopping me.

Thad was excused earlier due to the injuries he'd sustained, and he now occupied a bed beside Aden, who was being tended by the doctor when I walked in. "What's wrong?" I asked.

The doctor shook his head. "He won't last the night," he told me.

I sat beside Aden, and held his hand. He was conscious for a few minutes before he died. He said my name.

"We joined our bodies," he managed, "but you never felt anything, did you?"

I swallowed over the lump in my throat. "I've always had great affection for you, Aden. You always fought bravely. You will die a warrior's death."

"No, I will die the way I have dreamt of dying, looking into your eyes. Gold," he whispered. "I love you, brother."

I squeezed his hand in mine.

"You will defeat Thad in the ring one day," he gasped. "You will…" He made a sound in his throat then his eyes closed and he lay still.

"Is he dead?" Thad demanded.

"He is," I pushed something heavy down into my gut, suddenly annoyed at Thad's callousness.

There was silence for a few minutes. All gladiators deserved that moment of reverence. And even Thad didn't break it.

"This Samson," Thad asked when I turned to look at him after a few minutes, "is he someone I should worry about?"

He was asking me as his trainer, and as his trainer I had a responsibility to be honest with him.

"Yes," I said. "He is someone you should be worried about."

I informed the guards of Aden's demise and walked down the corridor, checking the cells. I paused in front of Samson who sat there silently in the dark. "If I didn't give you my congratulations before, they are in order," I told him.

"I'm alive, barely."

"Yes. Now the real work begins."

"I guess I should thank you as well."

"For?"

"That move that you used on me last night, remember?"

"Yes, but you didn't get low enough, not enough leverage. That's why you couldn't throw him. Thad is a big man."

He nodded. "So it seems."

I was ready to move on when he said, "I know your family."

I stiffened. "I have no family."

"You were not originally from Sparta. Your father was a blood relative to the king. You were educated by the finest tutors and were a star in the military school."

"Did you have the doctor tend your wounds?"

"Are you not even going to acknowledge my words?"

Swiftly I swung open the door to his cell. I reached down and grabbed the Spartan by the throat and pulled him to his feet. I held him close to me. I could feel his hot breath on my face. "You will speak when you are spoken to, answer me when I question you, and keep your folklore to yourself. Is that clear?" I shook him for emphasis.

"Very clear," he replied, his voice laced with resentment.

I dropped him on the floor, walked out and shut the door to his cell. I locked it behind me.

I wandered back outside, many thoughts bombarding me. I didn't want to be reminded of where I'd come from. I'd been here almost fifteen years now, being a young man of only seventeen when I was arrested. I'd been brutalised and beaten into submission. I survived the first contest, and much like Samson, I was put in the ring without any means of defending myself. I was the last man standing, bloodied and near death, and the crowd had opted to save my life.

After that, I decided there was nothing left to do but train, to be the best, and to harden my heart against all emotion. My entire life revolved around that arena. I hated everyone, especially my own family, who'd had the means to buy me back from my master, but had abandoned me. They'd considered me a disgrace, but given what I'd done, that was not a surprise. It was for that I accepted my gladiator name. I didn't want to be a part of them anymore. And I didn't need that cocky Spartan reminding me of the past.

I sat outside for the longest time that night, thinking of Aden and looking at the stars in the night sky. I tried to feel something for him. I'd taken him many times, possessed him, fucked him hard in the still of the night, felt his mouth on my sex, but I'd felt nothing at all except need, and relief. And now that he was gone, I still felt nothing.

The sounds of laughter and music had died now at the master's house, and the night guard had fallen asleep outside at his post near the tree.

I stripped off my clothes and waded into the water a little ways away. I lay back in the slow moving stream and closed my eyes. I almost fell asleep.

When I returned to the gladiators' quarters, it had already begun to feel hot again. The sun would be up soon and there was much work to do.

I went to my bed at the end of the row of cells and fell into restless sleep. I saw the house on top of the hill where I'd grown up as a boy, the strict military school I'd attended, and my friends, the other boys who I recited lines and lines of philosophy with, shaded by the scented trees.

Desire. I saw a set of blue eyes, a broad back with a blur of rounded buttocks then the whip, lashing, falling across my flesh as a man was cut in half in the coliseum. I tried to clear the blood out of my eyes as I lifted the head by the hair. The crowd screamed in my ears and I could hear nothing but my own heartbeat. Then someone touched me, gently pushing back my matted hair, soft lips kissed my mouth and I whimpered. Blue eyes smiled into mine. *"It's okay, Nicolaus," the voice whispered. "It's okay now."*

I gasped and sat up straight. The sun streamed into my eyes. I looked around me as if expecting to see those eyes, hear that voice. I shuddered, and rose from my resting place.

The men were already digging into their breakfast when I emerged. Oatmeal and dried fruit was a typical breakfast, thought to provide us with energy and stamina.

Thad was at the breakfast table as well seeming to have recovered well from his wounds, although his arm had been immobilised.

Samson sat by himself at the table in the corner.

I extended my hand to the cook and was given a ration of oatmeal and apricots which I in turn put down beside Samson. "Eat. You're going to need your energy."

"He will, when I get done with him," Thad growled.

"You will keep your distance unless I tell you otherwise," I warned him. "I am the trainer, unless you wish to challenge me for the job?" I folded my arms across my chest and waited for his answer.

He quietly went back to his breakfast.

I went outside into the dusty courtyard and shielded my eyes from the punishing sun. We would work until noon then take a break and wait until it was cooler to continue.

When I gave the call, the gladiators came outside. I motioned to Samson. "Gladiator training includes increasing your strength and your stamina. That means that each morning you will run thirty times around this courtyard. After that you will do one hundred sit-ups, and lift those weighted pieces of iron over there. The others will lead the way. I will teach you how to use various weapons like the war chain, the net, the trident, the dagger, and the lasso. Also, we will perfect your training with the sword. If at any time you suddenly feel as if you want to use these weapons on me, I will cut you in half. Do you understand?"

He nodded.

"Good." I looked around to see the five others now running around the courtyard. "Go ahead. Run now and then follow them in the routine."

"And you," he asked, running his gaze over me, "who do you train with?"

"I train alone." I cracked the whip on the ground. "Move!"

He cast me one last look and began to run. He had long muscular legs and he ran well, catching up with Thad for at least ten times around then falling behind. He would soon be able to outlast and outrun Thad by the looks of it, but that would take a few weeks.

As they ran, I studied the men for any abnormality or development but was happy to see that for the most part, they were fit.

The heat intensified and I directed them to drink from the large bowl of water often to replenish the moisture they lost.

I put them into pairs after awhile, and had them toss heavy stones back and forth with alternative hands.

Samson was not used to this and he complained that his arms were screaming in pain after ten tosses. I told him to stand down, and gave him a few minute's rest.

He was doubled over, sweating hard, a look on his face that spoke of agony. I walked over to him and slapped a hand on his shoulder. "Gladiators accept pain without whimpering like a baby."

He glared up at me. "I am not whimpering like a baby!"

"That's enough rest, back to it. Thad," I called out, "come. Let us have a contest with the lasso." I knew that Thad was the best when it came to using it and it would amuse me to see Samson try and outsmart him. It also would give Thad an outlet for all the pent up anger he had for the newcomer.

Thad had Samson bound and tied within minutes of course, even with using his left hand instead of his right. Everyone was laughing as Samson sputtered and kicked and tried to free himself from the lasso. I was happy to see that the laughter was not malicious. Rather, it was more camaraderie than anything, and when Samson finally did get free, two of the gladiators went over to help him up. Thad seemed satisfied now as well and even went over and slapped Samson on the back once.

Just before noon as I was demonstrating some very precise sword manoeuvres to the men, Claudius walked out into the courtyard with another young man at his heels. They stood back, whispering in the shadows, as they watched the gladiators.

They knew better than to interrupt the training however and didn't interfere. Claudius was aware that the sun was high and that I soon would take the men inside. He bided his time.

I lowered the wood sword, keeping the men out a little longer than I usually did. "Later when the sun is low, we will pair and practice these moves. Now, your lunch will soon be ready. Go inside."

Samson was the last to go in. He stood and observed the master's son and his companion curiously then slowly disappeared into the building.

Claudius walked over to me, a coquettish look on his face. His parents had coddled him and he had more the demeanour of a lovesick schoolgirl than a grown man. That didn't make him any less dangerous however. He had a lot of power, and he enjoyed using it.

"Gold," he breathed as he moved into my personal space. "You left the party last night without asking. I came looking for you."

I didn't say anything. I just waited for whatever he chose to say next.

"This is my friend from school. He is very curious about gladiators. I told him you were the champ."

"Thaddeus is the champion," I replied.

"Are you contradicting me, Gold?"

"No," I said.

"No what?" he insisted.

"No, master."

"My friend wants to see your scars, and hear the stories of how you got them." He reached out and lifted my chin.

I said nothing, careful not to meet his eyes.

The other man moved closer, smiling.

"Is he not sensational?" Claudius breathed, moving his hand down between my legs and grasping my cock. I didn't move as he fondled it roughly.

The other one walked around to my back and scraped his nails down my flesh. "Is it true that the blood of a gladiator makes your erection last longer?" he asked, his breath in my ear. His voice was light and fine, another castrated rich boy.

"It is but a rumour," I said.

He ground his groin into my buttocks. "We shall see later."

"This scar is extremely interesting," Claudius said now as he traced the one on my side. "Where does it end?" he asked, his finger pausing at the top of my breeches.

When I didn't answer, he asked me again. "Where does it end, Gold?"

"It ends at my groin."

"Master!"

"Master," I added dutifully.

"His opponent almost took off his balls," Claudius laughed. "It would have been a shame."

"Yes," the other one said, as he moved a hand over one of my biceps. "My gods, but what a specimen of manhood he is. So muscular, so male."

Claudius smiled. "Want him?"

"Oh yes," he replied, licking my throat.

"I have the power to give him to you. Tonight," Claudius said. "Come now, our gladiator has work to do. Later," he said, winking at me.

I was swearing as I walked inside. Samson stood at the door eating barley soup. He glanced at me but didn't say anything. I went to get some soup myself from the cook and sat down in the corner.

A few minutes later he came over and sat across from me. I looked up but then went back to eating, trying to drown out the boisterous conversation of the others. "He is the master's son?"

I kept on eating. I had no intention of having this conversation with him.

"You are a champion, a trainer and yet he can treat you so callously."

"I am a slave. He is the son of the master. He can treat me anyway he pleases."

"He is an effeminate, snotty nosed, rich boy with an over-stretched anus and an over-active libido."

I raised an eyebrow then I did something that I rarely did, I laughed out loud.

Samson lowered his head, spooning up his soup and actually smiled faintly. "How are you going to deal with it?"

"I'm not going to deal with it at all," I got to my feet. "I will do as I'm told."

He stood as well, following me as I went to scrape my dish into the slop bin. "You would engage in an intimate act with those who have no respect for you, no respect for your body?"

I looked at him as if he was quite mad. "Intimate act? There is no intimacy involved. It is merely a service, to satisfy the lust of my masters."

"And what about pleasure?" He met my gaze.

Those eyes seemed far too intense suddenly. "Lower your eyes," I snapped, "when you speak to me."

"Gold," he placed a hand on my forearm, "Have you never experienced pleasure in coupling?"

I jerked my arm away as if he'd burned me. "Don't be ridiculous. There is no such thing as pleasure here. Lose your foolish illusions, Spartan, else they will be the death of you."

I walked away from him and went to rest.

I worked hard with them for the remainder of the day, not wanting to think about the master's spoiled son and his lustful friend.

When the sun went down, a guard came for me and I was led to Claudius' chambers and told to wait. I stood perfectly still. No one could reach inside of me and touch my heart. They could ravish my body, but never my heart. That was mine, and I'd encased it in stone.

It wasn't really a big stretch to imagine yourself as an object. In the arena, that's exactly what I was. When you entered, all eyes were upon you, waiting to see what your next move would be. In the chambers of those who totally owned you, body and soul, there wasn't much difference.

Claudius and his friend lacked imagination which was a blessing, and in terms of sexual prowess, they were quite disappointing.

When I was asked to disrobe, the two young men followed suit, thankfully spilling their seed before they got anywhere near attempting to defile me.

There was a lot of touching and examining, a lot of talk of my muscles and the size of my sexual organ. My scars were examined thoroughly and mostly it was Claudius who told the stories of each one, stunning me really. I had no idea that Claudius had followed my contests that closely.

After some embarrassing ejaculatory activity on the part of his friend, and some talk of wanting to drink my blood, a request Claudius refused to honour, his friend went off to his private quarters.

Claudius then ordered me to lie on the bed beside him.

He curled up beside me, stroking my chest and looking directly into my eyes. I was quite surprised at how sentimental he seemed. "I have missed you," he said.

I raised an eyebrow.

"You do not remember how in love I was with you before Father sent me to school. I cried and begged to stay here just so I could be close to you."

"I see." I wasn't sure what to say.

"You say you see," he laughed, "but you don't see. You don't care. You are a beautiful yet deadly killer sculpted from marble. I would keep you here in my bed always if I could."

"Your father would disapprove," I told him.

He sighed. "I wanted you so tonight, but I was too excited to complete the act. The sight of you is... " He kissed my jaw line. "With all the handling, you didn't get hard," he said, his hand moving over the length of my sex. "If I demanded it, you would, wouldn't you? You'd get hard for me."

"I'd have to obey."

"I'd rather you did it naturally because you desired me. But you don't desire me, do you?"

"I will desire you if it pleases you," I said. I knew his temper. I didn't relish a whipping.

He ran his hand over my bicep, my chest, along my belly. "Did you ever desire any man, or woman?"

"I can't remember," I said honestly. "Is desire the same as lust?"

"No, I don't think so. And you don't want to remember, do you?"

"Perhaps," I replied. I found his conversation unsettling. I wondered when he would tire of me and let me leave.

He grabbed my face suddenly and kissed me hard on the mouth. It wasn't a very good kiss, but it sent a message. "You're mine. Remember that."

I nodded.

Suddenly the curtains flew back and Claudius' father stood there. I saw fury on his face. I didn't dare move a muscle. "What's going on here?" he demanded of his son.

"I invited Gold to share my bed, Father," Claudius announced, lifting his chin defiantly.

I winced as the master came over to the bed and hit his son hard across the face. "I don't want you wasting your seed on the male sex until after you have taken a wife, and fathered your first son. Gold," he didn't look at me, "get out!"

I got off the bed quickly, reached down to take my breeches and walked out of the room, my head bowed. I could hear Simeon screaming at his son, and Gracia's voice wailing in protest. Everyone had their cross to bear. The guard laying wait in the hall followed me as I walked quickly through the house on my way back to the gladiators' quarters.

Chapter Four

Samson: Branded

The scent of flesh burning nauseated me. It has to be one of the most horrible smells, and when that flesh is your own, it's accompanied by excruciating pain.

The doctor tried to soothe the pain by spreading some kind of obnoxious smelling cream on it but it only made it worst.

Gold didn't go easier on me either. He expected me to run and train the same as on any other day. I don't know what hurt most, the physical pain or the psychic pain of knowing that you are no longer a free man, that you are owned by someone else.

When the sun became too intense, Gold finally took mercy on us and let us go inside, and I could hardly lift my arm anymore. The pain was blinding me, but I knew better than to say anything.

I stripped off my clothes and slid into the bath, lowering my arm all the way into the water to try and get some relief.

Phillip came to soak beside me. He gave me a sympathetic look. "The pain will pass in a few days," he said. "Just don't let Gold hear you complain."

"Wouldn't dream of it," I said, searching out the subject of our conversation. He stood against the wall, drinking water, and talking casually to Gabien. "He is exceptional," I said, not wanting to think about what this brand on my arm really meant.

He glanced at me. "Why, Samson, do we have a fixation on the trainer?" He laughed out loud.

I think I blushed. I punched him. "Shut up, you. I just mean...he's...he's a mystery."

"Don't go and get too enamoured with him. He doesn't have feelings like other men. You might get him to fuck you, but to Gold, that's all it will ever be, a release of tension."

"Have you," I asked slyly as I looked at him, "have you been with him?"

"No, not that I would have refused had he suggested it. Gold would break my heart if I let him get too close, and he knows that. That's why he keeps his distance. Aden and I were kindred that way."

"Aden, the gladiator who died last week?"

He nodded. "Aden was in love with Gold, gave himself to him any time Gold was willing. Gold knew how Aden felt and when Aden lost his discretion on the matter — told him he loved him — Gold cut him off."

"You mean Gold stopped fucking him?"

"Yes, and to make sure Aden got the message, he took another right in front of him."

"Which one?" I asked curiously.

"He is dead now, died in the arena almost a year ago."

"That was cruel."

Phillip placed a hand on my shoulder. "Gold is direct, that's all. He wants to be understood. If words don't work, then he communicates with action."

"And no one will ever have his heart," I said, almost to myself, as I glanced over at him.

"You've said a mouthful, brother," he answered. "Friendly advice, steer clear. Take your pleasure with others when the need grips you. Try to resist the temptation of Gold." He got up out of the water.

I leant back and closed my eyes. Take my pleasure with others, he'd said. Although I wasn't fully aware of it yet, the only one I would ever want to take my pleasure with was Gold. And eventually I would want to surrender to him, and in the heat of the moment, sentiment would have little to do with it.

I fell asleep in the water. And when the sun went down, I was rousted and robustly prodded out of the water.

I was rubbing my eyes when I was pushed outside by the guard and the first thing I saw was Gold and Thad fighting with wooden sticks.

The heavy wood clacked together like thunder as each man's baton connected blow after blow. Thad was sweating hard, his face contorted. He desperately wanted the upper hand. Gold, on the other hand was perfectly calm, and in terms of effort, everything seemed in slow motion for Gold.

Finally, Thad let out a yell and raised his bat high. Instead of meeting it this time, Gold whipped his own bat through the air, eliminating the distance between him and Thad's lower leg with a speed which was faster than the eye could follow. He evaded Thad's bat and hit Thad directly below the knee. Thad let out a yelp and went down in the dirt. One of Gold's feet clamped down on Thad's windpipe and he raised the wood over his head. "You're dead," he announced and stepped back.

Thad sat up quickly, rubbing his throat.

There was applause and some relieved laughter. The air had been tense when Gold had placed his foot on Thad's throat, as if he might have really followed through and finished him off this time.

Thad stumbled when he went to get up, and clutched the place where Gold had hit his leg.

Gold glanced around. "Proceed," he commanded. "Grab an opponent and imitate what you just witnessed. I'm here to guide you if you should run amok."

I stood there for a moment and watched him as he poured some water down his throat. The liquid ran down his chin and onto his chest. He was still the champion of the house of Simeon, and I didn't understand why he just didn't put Thad in his place once and for all. The rumours of his cowardice to all appearances rang false. So, what was it that kept him from the ring?

I brought up the question as I practiced the moves with Phillip.

He lowered his voice discreetly when he spoke. "It's the lanista. He doesn't want Gold to fight. He's afraid to lose him. He's too valuable."

"Then it is not Gold who requested to be kept from the ring?"

Phillip laughed. "Quite the contrary. Gold would do much to go back in the ring."

I mulled this over as we continued our contest. Phillip got the best of me twice. He whacked me a good one both times. Finally, Gold came over to observe us. I lost my concentration and Phillip whacked me again. This seemed to amuse Gold, and he laughed out loud.

"Are you making fun of me?" I gave him a dirty look.

"Frankly, yes, I am. I've seen children fight better than that. There are only so many times one can take a hit in the same place. You will be black and blue tomorrow."

"Then what am I doing wrong?"

"It's the way you hold your weapon," he offered. "It is again a matter of leverage. Here," he said, coming to stand behind me. His thigh brushed my buttock. I sucked in some breath at his closeness. I couldn't think anymore, couldn't even hear the words he was saying. He placed the stick in my hand, and reached around me. His hand covered mine. "Now," he urged, making the motion with me, "like that. Do as I have showed you. Try it again."

Phillip laughed when Gold walked away from us. "You didn't hear a word he said, did you?" he accused. I ignored him. We tried it again with the same outcome.

"Did you?" he insisted.

"I couldn't even breathe," I confessed, discouraged. I smiled now a little. How could I not? I felt somewhat giddy.

"Thought I told you it would be better to keep your distance."

"My head says one thing but other parts of my body are not in agreement."

Phillip shook his head, and grinned. "I hear you, brother. All right, try to get those parts to cooperate and I'll show you so that you can impress him."

"Or better, so he doesn't kill me," I muttered which set us both to laughing.

By the time we were told that we could stop for the day, I had mastered the move, maybe not perfectly but it meant Phillip was no longer getting the best of me. Gold watched us every once in awhile however he didn't even comment on the progress that I'd made. This ticked me off some. I wanted to please him. I wanted him to pay attention to what I was doing and give me praise.

I was dreaming.

That night when the guards came to lock me in the cell, I paced like a caged tiger. My body ached, and I felt lower than I'd ever felt in my life. The pain was a nagging reminder that I was owned by someone, that I was no longer free to come and go as I pleased, no longer free to own property or choose my profession, or to love. My life now revolved around the arena and soon I would be called on to perform in that arena, put on a show for the Romans. The best thing I could do was sharpen my skills and survive, and hope that I'd make it long enough to gain my freedom.

Finally, fatigue settled over me and I took to my bed. I had just started to dose off when I heard someone call out. "Gold!" I thought maybe I was dreaming but as I raised my head off the straw bed, I heard it again. This time the name wasn't being screamed out, it was being groaned. "Oh gods...Gold...yes."

Then I heard a loud bang then bang, bang, bang...consistently, over and over again, mounting in intensity. Someone grunted, "Uh, uh, uh, uh. Yessssss!"

I sat up straight. It hadn't been that long that I couldn't recognise the sounds of someone getting fucked when I heard it. Obviously the person doing the fucking was Gold.

I got up off my bed. I hardly dared breathe as I listened more acutely, straining my ears to hear. The banging slowed then stopped all together, and a few minutes again, it started again, faster, louder. It sounded like the place was going to fall down about my head. "Gold, Gold, Gold! Yeah. Yeah!"

I heard the others stir in their cells. They were awake now too. There were some whispers. I closed my eyes. I knew who the screamer was. At first I thought it was a woman, but then I realised the voice was male. It was Claudius, the master's son. It had to be. None of the gladiators had a voice that fine. I couldn't believe he had come here to the slave's quarters to make Gold fuck him.

I was trying to figure out my feelings as the sounds illuminated around me. I knew that I was obsessed with wanting to hear every sound, and that my fists were clenched at my side. I was angry I guess, angry that Gold was inside Claudius and not me. I couldn't help but wonder if Gold was enjoying slamming Claudius into the wall.

"That boy's tender flesh will be black and blue tomorrow," one of the gladiators called out, and everyone laughed.

"Yeah, but he'll be smiling," someone hollered back.

Suddenly a guard walked by, and banged his sword along the bars. "Shut up! Go to sleep. Mind your business."

There was dead silence suddenly. No more banging or groaning. Maybe Claudius realised that he had an audience and had became self conscious, or maybe found himself a muzzle. I settled down and tried to sleep. But the image I had of Gold pumping his cock into Claudius wouldn't leave me. I could imagine his skin gleaming with sweat, his face contorted from the effort, his lusty grunts and groans as he came. Or maybe Gold wouldn't utter a sound.

I woke up exhausted and my cock was hard. I tried to discreetly take care of it before the guard threw my cage open but I didn't have time.

I went to the bath with an erection, and did my best to disguise it as I slipped off my breeches.

Philip was sniggering at me and I knew he'd seen it.

"Shut up," I told him.

"No shame," he said, "many of us wake up that way. I suppose last night's performance didn't help any."

I slid into the water. He came to sit beside me.

"Claudius?"

"Sounded like him."

"I'm shocked he would come here to the slaves' quarters."

"When you want it, you want it," Phillip replied. I felt his hand slide over onto my thigh. "I can take care of that for you." He met my eyes.

"Here?" I croaked. It was tempting.

He met my gaze as he moved his hand onto my erection. "No one will see."

Gold suddenly walked into the room. His short breeches showed off his muscular thighs and his chest was bare as usual. His hard muscles gleamed with perspiration. He looked as though he could use a bath himself.

I kept my eyes on Gold as Phillip massaged my cock under the water, oblivious to the others around us.

I tried not to make a sound or show it in my face but it wasn't easy. Then the worst thing that could happen, happened. Gold removed his breeches right in front of my eyes and walked down into the bath.

He had the most magnificent cock, but one could expect nothing less with a body like his. The minute I saw his cock swinging between his thighs with the most perfect shaped balls below it, I ejaculated into the water.

It surprised Phillip I guess because he moved his hand away like he had suddenly touched fire. My entire body went into spasm and I let my head go back, and stifled a moan.

When I lifted my head again, Phillip had distanced himself from me. Gold was looking directly at me from where he sat nearby in the water. "You look tired today," he commented.

I blinked and pursed my lips together. I hung on to that feeling of pure and utter bliss for a few more minutes. "Ah, yes," I licked my lips, and dipped my hand in the water. I squeezed my cock gently. "It wasn't exactly quiet last night."

Phillip was staring at me as if I'd suddenly gone mad. I realised that I'd made a mistake.

"You had best," Gold stood, "mind your own business, and not listen to things that don't concern you." His voice was hard and severe.

"I'm a...sorry," I stuttered.

He got up out of the bath and swished some of his long dark hair back from his face. "And from now on," he glanced at me, "save the cock handling for your cell. It doesn't serve well as general entertainment."

There was laughter. I tightened my lips. "Bastard," I hissed under my breath.

If he heard me, he didn't pay attention. Instead he walked naked out into the sunshine to dry off.

Two of the other gladiators instantly started blabbering at me. "Are you crazy, brother? You are never to mention things like that. What the masters choose to do is not to be spoken of. You could be whipped for that."

"You could be killed for that," Phillip corrected. "If the master finds out that their indiscretion is the stuff of gossip, he will not take kindly to it."

"I hear," Gabien leant closer, "that Claudius has been forbidden to use Gold for sexual purposes until he marries and has a son."

"Not to mention the rivalry between father and son," Phillip scoffed.

"Father and son?" I blinked. I wanted to know more.

Phillip stood in the water. "Yes. It's not only Claudius who likes to be skewered by Gold's champion prick."

Thad scowled. "As if he can wield that any better than anyone else can."

"Apparently Gracia thought so," Phillip sniggered, "for Gold was always her choice even after you became champion, wasn't he?"

Thad made a grab for Phillip. Phillip pulled him out of the water and began to punch him.

Gold came rushing inside. "Stop! Now!" He ordered. "What is this?"

I got out of the bath myself and watched carefully.

"Nothing," Thad said suddenly, and ruffled Phillip's golden hair. "All in fun, right brother?"

Phillip glared at Thad. "Right," he muttered between clenched teeth.

"Fine," Gold glowered at them. "Get dressed, Phillip. It's time for practice. There will be a contest in two days in the arena."

"Who? Who?" came the chorus of voices.

Gold looked around at the excited gladiators and over at me. "We have yet to decide," he said. I had the feeling there was a message in there for me.

That day Gold paid me a lot more attention than I would have liked. He seemed to be especially vigilant with my training and for me that was an indication that he was preparing me for the arena.

Phillip sat close to me at lunch and whispered next to my ear. "I think it's you."

"No kidding," I sneered, eating my soup. "But with who?"

Phillip shrugged but his gaze strayed to Thad.

"No," I shook my head, "must be another gladiator from another house. Not Thad."

Phillip ate quietly.

The thought so disturbed me that after the sun went down I approached Gold and asked him directly. "Is it me?"

"Is it you, what?" he asked. He was eating his supper outside in the courtyard. He didn't look at me.

"Am I to be put into the arena?"

"I don't know."

"You do know."

He turned his head and looked at me.

"Gold, you have some idea."

"Perhaps."

"It unsettles me."

He turned back to his food. "If I think you're not ready, I won't allow it."

"Can you prevent it if the master wants it?"

"He often listens to my advice."

"Because you fuck him." The words came out before I intended them to.

"Where did you hear that?" he demanded, his expression dark.

"I spoke out of turn."

"Yes," he said between clenched teeth. "You do that often. It will bring you much trouble."

I ignored that. "Can you really convince him not to put a gladiator in the contest if his heart is set?" I persisted.

"I have no control over what he does. I only have some influence. He seeks my counsel then does what he pleases." He shrugged.

"If I go into the arena, will it be with Thad?"

"Absolutely not," he grunted, glancing at me. "That would be madness."

I breathed a sigh of relief.

"You are not ready for Thad."

I stiffened. Even though I knew that to be true, my pride took a hit. "Will it be with one of the gladiators here?"

"No. It is a contest with a gladiator from the House of Phineas, a contest to honour the death of a prominent senator who has just died."

"Can I win?"

"That depends who Phineas chooses to fight you. If it is one with far more training than you, then no, you can't win."

"That doesn't put my mind at ease."

"That's because it's not meant to. There is no such thing as an easy mind in this world." He went over to scrape his plate. "Samson," he said suddenly. He moved close to me and actually looked down into my eyes, something he rarely did. My pulse raced and my cock reacted most noticeably. "You'd be wise not to gossip about what goes on between the masters and the gladiators. It will not win you favour. They expect slaves to be seen but not heard. We are not to pay attention to their goings-on."

"Has it always been that way?" I asked him gently.

"Which way?"

"You...subjected to their every whim, sexual and..."

"I am property," he replied stiffly, and pointed at me, "and so are you. If you catch the eye of the master, his wife, his son, or any of the guests they have visiting their home, you will be called upon to perform some duty or

another. It could be in bed, or out. These people, they…"
He trailed off for a second.

"They what?" I urged.

"They're not like everyone else," he said softly, still close
to me. I had to fight everything in me not to reach out and
touch his face. "They have everything…too much, really.
They own land and they own people. And when they're
bored, when they need to reaffirm their power because
inside they feel small, they may call on us to do the most
ridiculous of tasks."

"Why?"

"Just because they can," he replied. When he went to
move away, I touched his forearm. He gave me a curious
look but he didn't move away.

"Would it offend you if I told you that I am drawn to
you?"

"No," he said. "It wouldn't offend me."

"If I asked you to…"

He shook his head and moved away now. "I am waiting
for a guard to come and get me to take me to the house. I
have a meeting with Simeon."

"In his bed I presume," I snarled.

He lifted an eyebrow and actually smirked at me. "Just
as good a place for a meeting as anywhere else."

I watched him walk off and anger took hold of me with a
grip I hadn't expected. I knew Gold had said that
deliberately just because he knew it would piss me off.

I sputtered as I went back inside. Thad was sitting in the
corner staring at me. When I looked at him, he grinned.
"Getting nowhere?"

I narrowed my eyes. "What do you know about it?"

He laughed out loud. "I see the way you look at him.
Might as well forget it. He's not interested."

"How would you know?"

He shrugged. "I know that if he did get the itch, it would take more than a little snotty nosed boy like you to scratch it."

I went mad. I lunged at him like a mad tiger and we rolled on the floor, punching and kicking, finally rolling around in the dirt outside.

Thad kept laughing at me which made me all the angrier. The other men came outside now, cheering and laughing from the sidelines.

Then suddenly just as I got on top of Thad and began to batter his smug face, the laughter died abruptly.

A hand reached down and yanked me up off of Thad. "What are you doing?" Gold demanded, his dark eyes fuming.

Thad laughed and stood up, brushing himself off. "We were just having a workout," he said.

I jerked away from Gold. "He pissed me off."

"Yeah," Thad laughed, "I told him if your cock was in need, he wouldn't be first choice."

"You bastard!" I yelled and pulled away from Gold. I went at Thad again. This time I knocked him hard enough to stun him a little. He went down in the dirt, cursing my name.

Gold stared at me as if I'd lost my mind. I was embarrassed of course to think that he knew what I'd gone off about.

"You are confined to your cell," Gold barked at me.

"Fine," I told him. "Take his side." I stalked off inside, and tried to block out Thad's laughter.

I went directly to my cell and slammed shut the door. When Gold walked in, I was sitting on my bed, arms crossed in front of me.

"What do you want from me, Samson?" He looked down at me.

"Nothing. I want nothing."

"You might as well tell me now, get it out of the way. We can't let this interfere with your training."

"Fuck the training and fuck you."

"Listen, you," he muttered, and yanked me to my feet. My chest was crushed to his. Suddenly I wanted to feel his lips on mine so badly, I could taste him. "You are going to be respectful or…"

"Or what?" I challenged him. "You'll beat me, you'll whip me. Go ahead, anything is better than this."

"Than what?" He breathed.

"Don't you feel it? Can't you feel anything or have they driven all feeling from your heart? Gold," I said softly. I reached up with my free hand and touched his hair, "I—"

Suddenly a voice called out his name. "Gold! Your presence is requested at the house!"

The door to my cell opened. Gold released me but he was still staring at me. "Coming," he said, without breaking the eye contact.

"Gold," I pleaded, "I only want to…" I searched for the right word. Love wouldn't be a good choice. "I only want…"

"Don't," he whispered.

I closed my eyes as he walked away. I'd made an idiot out of myself. Worse, everyone knew it.

Chapter Five

Gold: Deep in the Night

The incident with Samson disturbed me far more than I wanted to admit. It weighed heavily on my mind as the guard escorted me to Claudius. I was not looking forward to another session with him and his friend.

I was surprised to find that he was alone. And as if to answer my unasked question, he said, "My friend has gone home. I decided I wanted you all to myself after all." He looked at the guard. "Go away!"

The guard nodded. He rounded the corner but he wouldn't be far.

Claudius lowered the curtains around his bed. He came up to me and wound his arms around my neck. "Gold," he whispered, his lips touching my cheek, "my parents are at the house of some rich man they hope to impress. We are alone, all night."

The slaves and guards didn't count. Even now a female slave stood in the corner of the room. They were, for the most part, not even considered human, only fixtures.

"I want you to fuck me the way you did in the cell when I came to you." He ran his hand over my chest.

I nodded.

He backed away from me. "Disrobe and let me look at you awhile. I want you to want me, Gold. Do you? And don't say it just to please me." He paced up and down. "I want it to be true. Do you want me?"

I had no choice but to say, "Yes," as I took down my breeches. I stood there naked except for the gold plated chain around my neck and told him what he longed to hear.

"Then prove it," he insisted, his gaze on my cock. "If it gets hard, I shall believe you." He removed his toga and stood there naked as well. "If it stays soft, I will know you have no desire for me and I will be very displeased."

I sucked in some breath. Actually, the sight of his pale, thin body did little to inspire my lust, but I knew I'd better give him the illusion. He was young and unpredictable and therefore far more dangerous than his father. I thought of Samson, his hard body, the shape of his mouth and I felt my desire grow, but I was annoyed that it should be so.

I told myself that Samson was on my mind only because of the childish scene he'd pulled tonight. I had a fear that he might become another Aden and that I didn't need. However, in spite of my annoyance with Samson, I conjured an image of him in my mind, the way he was looking at me tonight in that cell. *Desire.* That's what I'd seen in his eyes.

"Um, that's it," Claudius groaned as he came closer and wrapped my cock in his fingers. "Hard. You do want me, don't you, Gold?"

"Yes," I hissed. Right then, I needed something.

"Yes, what?" he fondled my cock a little more roughly.

"Yes, master," I murmured as he led me to the bed by the cock.

He lay down on the bed on his back and opened his legs to me. "Pleasure me with your mouth and your tongue and then do what you did the other night. Make me scream."

I leant down between his thighs and began to lick his shaft which was already half way there. He would probably spend his seed before I even got inside of him. But it didn't matter. I turned off my thoughts and went through the motions.

Claudius reared up and clutched my hair. He pulled hard. I winced as he wrapped his legs around my neck. "Take me," he demanded. "Take me now."

I roughly pulled his hips upward and spread his ass. I knew what he wanted. He wanted to be taken, to be rode, used, and I slammed into him as callously as I might any enemy of war.

He screamed and cried out, ejaculating on my belly and my chest. I pumped him harder until I felt my own cock release then waited for word from him to withdraw.

He pulled me down to the mattress as I was given the sign and I lay on my back beside him, trying to get my breath.

He crawled on top of me and began to kiss me, his mouth bruising mine. I can't say I liked it much. He moved his mouth away finally and kissed all of my chest and my abs. Then he put his head in the stickiness of my groin.

"Stroke my hair," he whispered.

I let my hand fall on his head.

"Gold?" he said suddenly.

"Um?"

"If you could have anything, what would it be?"

"I would wish to face Thad in the arena."

He raised his head, looked at me. "Not your freedom?"

"What would I do with freedom?" I asked him.

He stared at me for a few minutes before he asked, "And if you defeated him, what would you do then?"

I didn't answer. I didn't want to defeat him.

"I don't understand. Facing Thad could mean death."

"Yes, but death is freedom, isn't it?"

He laid his head back down. "Me also, I wish for freedom. You could come with me, away from here. I would give you your freedom if you'd stay with me."

I actually laughed. "That's not freedom if I had to stay with you."

He moved up and placed his head on my shoulder. "It would be for me. I don't want to marry and have children. I don't want to be a lanista."

"Perhaps you will be a senator instead."

"I don't want that either," he sat up, made a face. "All I want," he said, looking at me, "is you. I've always wanted you, to be beside me always. I love you, Gold."

"You are perhaps too young to know what that means."

"And you do?" he scoffed. "You know love?"

I shook my head. "No."

He settled down beside him again. "Stay here with me, Gold. I want to sleep close to you."

"As you wish," I replied but I really longed to get back. I still had a lot of work to do with Samson to prepare him for the contest.

"I wish," he replied sleepily.

A short while later, Claudius was asleep and I lay there, unable to close my eyes. I was concerned that Simeon would come home and find me here with his son. He'd be furious. On the other hand, I didn't dare leave without Claudius telling me to.

Fortunately, Claudius woke very early and told me to go back to my quarters. I was suffering from lack of sleep and in no mood for nonsense.

When I walked into the courtyard, the men were already training and I was grateful for that. When I walked by Samson, who was doing his push-ups on the ground, he stopped, got to his feet and glared at me.

I figured it was best to ignore him and I went inside and got some breakfast. I didn't expect a lecture.

"You have responsibilities."

I turned to see Samson standing in the doorway. "What?"

"You heard me. He had no right to keep you there, and what if his father had come home? He would have punished you."

"You should go back to your training before I decide to punish *you*."

"Go ahead," he cajoled. "But you know I speak the truth. That boy will get you into trouble with his father."

"I cannot disobey. What would you have me do?"

"Tell the lanista. Let him deal with it."

"What is this to you?" I threw my plate aside.

"I care about you."

"Worry about your own hide," I growled. "Now get back outside and go to work, or face the consequences." I picked up my whip and held it up in the air.

He laughed at me and marched back outside.

Whether it be the boost of confidence he'd received lately due to all the training, or if it was just in him to defy authority, Samson really thought I wouldn't use the whip on him. However, he was pushing me, and right now I was on the edge.

When I walked out into the bright sunshine, Thad pounced on me. He pressed up against my flank and said in my ear, "If it had been me who spoke to you like that, you would have laid whip to my back before now."

I was in no mood. "Get back to your training," I snapped, "or I shall lay whip to your back before long."

Thad grumbled and walked away.

I decided the best way to deal with Samson was not to deal with him at all. Therefore I forced myself not to look at him often. He, along with the hot sun, was playing on my last nerve.

When a guard came walking across the courtyard to inform me that the lanista was now home and wanted to see me, I damn near tore his head off. "Can't you see I'm busy here?"

"Would you like for me to tell him that?" the guard sneered.

"No," I replied.

"He bought a slew of new slaves at market," the guard said as I followed on his heels.

I sighed inwardly. "What does a slew mean?"

"It means a wagon full," he grinned sheepishly, "and a lot more work for you."

He laughed as he left me in the atrium. I waited patiently for Simeon wondering how many slaves he'd purchased and what his immediate plans for them were. Hopefully some were house slaves.

"Gold," Simeon said, as he walked into the room. "Have you heard the news?"

"Yes. You've made a big purchase."

"Phineas has at last count, fifty two gladiators. I have but five. I've allowed the stock to dwindle. I was given a tip by a source I have spying for me in town. It was a little out of the way auction. Incredible really."

That probably meant that the slaves being sold were stolen goods, illegal.

Claudius now came to stand beside his father but he didn't acknowledge him.

"Congratulations. How many did you purchase?" I inquired curiously.

"I bought some very nice house slaves, five female and two male, strong, fit and very beautiful. And I selected seven young men who may grow into fine gladiators. I would like you to take a look. I regretted not taking you with me, but I know you are preparing Samson."

"Then we are to put him in the arena?"

"Yes. I, of course, gave Senator Homis the choice of which gladiator he would like me to use to honour his father. Naturally he said you. I then offered him Thad after I explained you were not available. Then he suggested that we use the one who almost defeated Thad in the ring."

"Will Phineas use his champion?"

"I have no idea who he will choose. He will attempt to please the senator, I presume."

I felt panic set in. "I don't believe that it would be fair to put Samson in the arena with a champion his first time out."

"I have no control over that. Just ready him."

I nodded.

"I leave Claudius with you for the inspection. I would like you to teach him what to look for in a potential gladiator."

I inclined my head.

"I'm sure that Gold could teach me many things," Claudius commented.

I lifted my head and glanced at him but said nothing.

"I'll tell the guards to bring them in from the back, and Claudius will give me a report on your assessment later this evening."

As soon as the lanista left the room, his son moved closer to me. He ran his hand over one of my biceps most possessively and said softly, "When father came to speak to me today, I thought I was in trouble. I thought someone had told him that you were here with me last night. I was ready to whip one of slaves to within an inch of their lives." He traced the brand on my arm. "But, all he wanted was for me to watch you inspect a bunch of naked men. I shall enjoy that immensely."

I said nothing. I turned my gaze on the line of newly arrived slaves who trembled on bended knee. I suddenly noticed the one at the end had been watching the interaction between Claudius and I most intensely. I quickly put myself in front of him. "Eyes down!" I commanded.

He lowered his eyes but not before deliberately pausing at my groin. He knew I noticed. He wanted me to notice.

"What do they call you?" I demanded. "Keep your head down," I said before he could raise it again.

"Sullis," he replied.

"Where do you come from, Sullis?"

"Carthage," he replied, confirming my original theory that many of these enemy soldiers were stolen from their immediate captors. Carthage was a far distance.

"Stand," I told him.

He stood, and looked right at me. His eyes were extremely light. They seemed almost translucent. His hair was fair and slightly curly. I walked around him and studied the fine muscles across his back, felt his forearms, his biceps. He was strong in body, muscular yet fine boned, about five eleven in height. He'd do nicely.

When I came back around to the front, his lips curled into a leer. "Will I do?"

I reached over and grasped a handful of his hair in my hand. I pulled back his head with a jerk. He gasped as I looked down into his eyes. "You will not look me in the eye unless I give you permission. You will not speak unless I request it, and you will show respect in this house or I will beat you to within an inch of your worthless life. Is that understood?" I jerked his head back again for emphasis.

He nodded.

I released him.

Claudius moved close to my ear. "That was exciting," he whispered. "I want you to dominate me like that. Do you hear me?"

I nodded. "Whatever you desire," I told him in a voice only he could hear.

He smiled. I moved to the next candidate. The others were adequate enough, save for one that was more boy than man. I forced myself to speak a little more softly to him as I told him to rise.

He was young and trembling like a leaf. He looked as if he'd been crying. I lifted his chin, studied him. "What's your name, boy?"

"I...I..." he began.

"Speak!"

"Maris," he stuttered.

"Where do you come from, Maris?"

"I am an Iberian," he said as tears spilled down his cheeks.

I sighed. This again confirmed my suspicions that some of these slaves were caught illegally for profit by traders. "How old are you, boy?"

"I am thirteen, sir," he swallowed.

I dropped his chin and glanced over at Claudius, who busied himself with the task of inspecting the genitals of the most generously endowed among them.

I walked over to him and waited patiently for the inspection to end. He noticed me suddenly and dropped the man's testicles. He'd stood there enduring the handling without a sound. "Yes?"

"May we speak in private?"

"Of course," he said, and led me down the hallway. "What is it?" he asked when we were a fair distance from the slaves.

"That boy, he is Iberian, and only thirteen years of age. He doesn't belong here."

Claudius glanced over at the boy then at me. "If he's here, it's because he belongs, Gold."

"He's Iberian."

"So?"

"Iberia is the ally of Rome. And he's yet too young to be a soldier anyway. Obviously he was taken by traders illegally."

"Thirteen is old enough. Aren't the young men of Sparta sent to military school at a younger age than that?"

"Yes, but--."

"Then he will learn to be a man, won't he?"

At that moment, I hated him.

"Now, get back to it. Finish your inspection and give me your report so I may take it back to my father. Then get them out of here. They need to bathe. They smell."

I nodded.

He paused. "Perhaps we should throw these ones into the arena for a pre-show before the big contest."

"You speak of the contest planned against one of Phineas' gladiators. I have yet to have final confirmation."

"Yes," he smiled, "we wanted it to be a surprise. I suppose father won't mind if I tell you now. He was planning on telling you tonight. The Destroyer is to be put against that smug, good looking one. What's his name again, the Spartan? Samuel?"

"You speak of Samson," I tried not to let my disapproval show. "Samson is not ready for the Destroyer."

"It was the senator who decided, Gold. And as for Samson's readiness, it is your job to make sure that he is ready."

I bristled. "Can you tell your father I would like to speak to him?"

"He's busy now but I will pass on the message. Now, what is your assessment of the new arrivals? I must give father the impression that you have taught me something."

"I will finish," I walked back down the hallway past the alabaster status of Jupiter and Mercury.

I examined the other five men then returned to find Claudius lounging on a sofa in the next room.

"Well?" he demanded, drinking from a silver goblet.

"They all seem adequate except for my concerns about the young one. He is not fit for the arena."

"I wouldn't trouble my father with that, if I were you," he said, as he munched on some grapes from a plate a servant boy held out to him. "He won't like knowing that he made an error in judgement. He handpicked them himself this time, you know. Anyway," he waved his hand, "go now, Gold. I will send for you when I want you.

Have the guards take the new slaves to the gladiators'
quarters, and see to them."

I bowed my head slightly and left.

As I walked across the dusty courtyard, a slight breeze
blew back my hair. The men had gone in for their supper.
Training was over for the day, except for Samson. I would
need to do some private training with him this evening if I
was to ready him for Phineas' champion.

The new arrivals were quickly led to their cells, and
there was much conversation among the others as I came
inside.

I, of course was immediately bombarded with questions,
all being thrown at me at the same time. I put up my hand
and called for silence.

"We hear that Thad is to be put into the ring with the
newcomers," Phillip was the first to make his voice heard,
peering at me curiously.

I glanced at Samson who sat in the corner quietly then
returned my attention to Phillip. "That is untrue."

"Who then?" Thad insisted. "Are we are to put the child
against the Destroyer?" He laughed. The others joined
him.

"The boy is here erroneously and not to be touched," I
let my gaze move around the room, "in any way! Is that
understood?"

I saw Thaddeus raise an eyebrow. He knew what a risk I
took saying that aloud.

"Ah, but such tender flesh," someone murmured.
"Untouched, smooth virgin..."

"Enough!" I snapped. "The boy is under my personal
protection. Touch him, and deal with me."

"Then it will be you teaching him how to be a man,
Gold?"

I looked around sharply to look at Samson. "What I do with the boy is not your concern."

There was a chorus of "Oooooooooo."

"The new ones will come to wash. Stick to yourselves and leave them be, or I will have you sent to your cells. They will be given some training tomorrow. I would appreciate your support."

Phillip nodded at me.

"More meat for the slaughter," Gabien muttered.

What could I say? He was right. "Guard," I said to the soldier who stood in the corner, "open the cells and bring the slaves to the bath."

The guard went to get the men.

"Samson," I said, not bothering to glance at him as I walked past, "outside with me, now."

Samson followed me out. He looked at me curiously. "What is it?"

I ran a hand through my hair. "You are to face Phineas' champion in the arena."

Samson didn't react at first. Maybe he wasn't able to grasp the ramifications of that straightaway.

"When is it to be?" he responded finally.

"Soon. Although I haven't had final word as of yet. I shall know this evening."

"I can't win this, can I?"

I looked at him. "You must enter the ring believing that you can win."

He looked away.

"Samson, I know the Destroyer. I faced him in the ring a few years ago before he rose to such heights. I defeated him."

"Yet, he still lives."

"He is a crowd favourite and they voted to save him."

"Lucky for me," he half laughed.

I smiled faintly. "You have an advantage. I know how he fights. To defeat a contender in the arena is as much a battle of intellect then it is of brawn. The Destroyer has been overly blessed of brawn, but I'm afraid he was solely neglected when it came to intelligence."

Samson laughed aloud now.

The sounds of our laughter mingled together and drifted across the courtyard. It floated away on the night breeze. We both sobered. I swallowed as Samson looked at me. Something in his eyes made me feel quite warm in spite of the breeze. I cleared my throat. "Tonight, we will train, and I will tell you all I remember about the Destroyer." I slapped his shoulder and moved away. "Keep the faith, brother."

Suddenly just as Samson was about to reply, I heard someone screaming. I ran inside to see a guard cuffing the boy called Maris across the head. "Stop your blubbering," he cursed at him. "Stop acting like a little girl!"

I marched over to the guard and grabbed the boy out of his hands. "Leave him alone," I told the guard.

"I'm in charge of guarding these slaves," the guard told me arrogantly. "You can't tell me how to do my job. This has nothing to do with training, slave. Mind your own business."

I held the boy close to me. He was still crying. "This one is my business. He has been sent here to me. I'll deal with him."

The guard gave me a cold look and turned away. I took the boy outside. I held him by the shoulders and looked down into his terrified eyes. My instinct was to speak softly to him but I knew that wouldn't be wise. I had to toughen him up or the others would eat him alive, boy or not. "Stop it," I told him. "Stop crying!"

He tried to regain control but he was struggling.

"I know you're scared but I won't let anyone hurt you. But you will need to do as I say. You need to act strong and tough even when you're terrified. You must never let them see the hurt, the pain or the sadness. You understand me?"

He nodded.

"That's the only way to get respect. And if you have their respect, they won't try and hurt you."

He nodded again. Then suddenly, he went into my arms, wrapping them around my waist. I didn't expect that. I stood there, my arms at my side, not quite knowing what to do. I waited but he didn't release me so I placed a hand on his hair for a second then patted his back. "Okay, boy," I said and moved him away from me. "You'll stay in my cell tonight with me, okay?"

"Thank you."

"Now, go inside and eat. The cook will give you something. Tell him I said so."

He turned and left me.

When Samson spoke to me, I turned around, surprised. I'd forgotten he was still out here. "That was kind of you."

I shrugged. "Let's get to work."

I worked with Samson for some time. In the moonlight, our silhouettes cast menacing shadows across the yard as I showed him technique. And as much as I instructed him in technical matters, I told him what I remembered from that battle. I gave him a profile of the gladiator he would face. As I recalled the details of the Destroyer's style of fighting, I relived it.

It was one of the last times I had fought in the arena. I was cocky then, under the belief that I was immortal.

The Destroyer, nicknamed so by his fondness for crushing his opponents face under his foot, had been just biding his time for a chance to face me in the arena. There was currently no champion at the House of Phineas. I'd just killed Stadoes, the last one, and he was now the favourite to succeed him. If he could defeat me, his fame was assured. I knew his determination alone would make him difficult, if not impossible, to best.

I was not as prepared for this one as I thought. He was a giant of a man with bushy black hair and terrifying eyes. If ever there was an image of a true barbarian, he was it.

The contest was held to celebrate a Roman military victory, and therefore a huge event which lasted three days. Over sixty gladiators fought to the death in that arena, and my battle with the barbarian was to serve as the grand finale. It was the one everyone was waiting for.

The weapons were strewn across the arena, and we were free to choose whatever we could get our hands on—a lasso was in the centre and several swords were scattered about, still stained with the blood of those who'd only just been felled by them. As I walked into the ring, my eyes immediately made a mental picture of where the weapons were.

The crowd was wild, and the sun was already low in the sky. Too much celebrating and too much wine—the spectators were giddy on blood.

I grabbed the first sword I came to and wielded it over my head. This gained a roar from the crowd. To them it was a signal that I was ready.

The Destroyer took his time. He lumbered over to the side and picked up the lasso. It wasn't really protocol. First man to pick up the weapon determined which one would start, but this barbarian didn't care about the rules.

There was some collective booing. He swung the lasso and tried to catch me up. He didn't want to clash swords with me because at that time, I was rumoured to be unbeatable with the sword. I realised that he would try and best me with something else first.

He tried several times to trip me up with the lasso. I swung at him with the sword and hit him from the back. I was faster but he was a huge bugger and I knew that if he got hold of me with his hands, my chances of survival were low.

I dealt him several blows with the sword but it was if his skin was made of armour. I cut him and he hardly seemed to feel it. Finally, his swinging of that lasso paid off and he hooked me around the ankles. He dragged me towards him through the sand as I struggled to free myself. I slashed at the rope with my sword but I was moving too fast.

When I was under him, I wiggled from side to side to avoid his foot and struggled to free myself again. He kept me at arm's length so I couldn't reach my feet and I couldn't do any harm to him with my sword. I screamed out something in frustration and he laughed at me. I swirled to the side, sprang up onto my knees, and dragged him forward. The motion caused him to stumble. He fell in the dirt. The crowd went crazy.

I cut the rope and tried to undo the knot round my ankles as he got to his feet and wrapped his fist round the handle of a sword. He brought it down on my shoulder blade. For a moment, I thought he'd cut me in half. He must have hit the bone because although it was bleeding, it wasn't as bad as I imagined. It hurt like hell though.

I pulled the rope off my feet and scrambled to get away from him. My sword was still clutched in my hand. He came at me and for a long time, our swords clashed like thunder in that arena.

I cut him a few times across the chest and missed his gut by inches. He sliced me a good one across the top of the head and I cursed, the thick blood dripping into my eyes, blinding me.

The contest went on. His sword flew out of his hand at one time which sent him running across the arena. I chased him, and took him down by planting my sword in his back.

He was on his knees again. I came around to the front of him and he looked up at me as I held the sword at his neck. He raised his finger, indicating that he had it. He was ready.

The crowd, however, had other ideas and rather than slice off his head with my sword, I put it down in the dirt with the crowd chanting they wanted to save him.

The referee, who'd actually hid off to the side at one time from fear, came over and held up my arm. The crowd seemed happy with the outcome as they carried the Destroyer out of the arena.

Samson nodded at me as I put down the makeshift sword and stopped talking. I'd told him all of it that I remembered. "So I must strike fast and hard with the sword and not let him get to the lasso."

"Exactly."

He moved closer and placed one hand on my bicep. He slid his palm over it for a second. "I want you," he said suddenly. "I may die in that arena. Please, let me have you before I fight. If I'm to go to…"

I swallowed, suddenly gripped by sentiment. I touched his cheek with my finger. "You will defeat him."

"So your answer is no?"

Desire. It was there again, in my mouth and this time further down. My cock. It was hard. Samson seemed to know it because he reached between my thighs and wrapped his fist around it. I sucked in some breath as Samson led me around the building and placed a hand inside my coverings. I closed my eyes as he fondled my cock and moved even closer, and licked a trial down my throat and my chest with his tongue.

"Um," he murmured. "You're beautiful," he whispered. He pulled my coverings down and lowered his mouth to my hungry cock.

I pressed his face to my groin. He sucked along my shaft with his lips.

When he took the head of my cock into his mouth, I muffled a cry of pleasure by placing my forearm against my mouth.

Samson continued to suckle and lick my cock. He massaged my balls at the same time. When my hips moved involuntarily forward, his mouth came off my cock with a smack and he stood up, shucking down his own breeches. He pressed his chest to the wall of the building and glanced at me. "Take me," he urged. "I want you inside me. Go. Now."

I moistened my fingers best I could and began to prod his asshole with the tips.

"Um," he rutted against me. "Deeper."

I pushed my fingers into him, three of them and he grunted from the impact then moaned softly as I began to thrust them in and out.

"Like that?" I breathed.

"Oh yeah," he whispered. "Oh, um…yeah."

I withdrew my fingers and spread his legs wide with my hand. "Want to be my whore?"

"Yes," he hissed. "I want you. Go on. Impale me."

I flirted the head of my cock against his opening then spread his thighs even wider. I pulled him away from the wall and bent him forward then plunged my cock into him and began to thrust hard.

He moaned and I moved my hand around to his mouth and covered it. At one point, he bit into my hand. I wrapped my hand around his waist, turned him around and tipped him over the water barrel. I slapped his ass a few times, pulled out then went into him again.

We were both breathing hard, oblivious to everything around us and it took me a few minutes to realise that the guard was calling my name.

I wanted more of his ass and he wanted more of my cock but it wasn't to be. "Zeus's cock," I muttered. I located my coverings and began to put them on. Again I slapped Samson's ass and he laughed as he stood up. He wrapped his arms around my neck and pulled me in for a kiss.

I wasn't used to kissing but this one held me sway. He was the one who pulled away, not I. "You have a great cock and you know what to do with it. I look forward to the next time."

I grinned at him. "Arrogant, aren't you? How do you know I'll have you again?"

He laughed. "I know."

I walked around to the yard and signalled the guard. "What is it?"

"Master wants you, now. What were you doing around back?"

"Pissing, you mind?"

He shook his head and I followed him to the house. I glanced back once to see Samson go inside then continued on my way.

"I have good news for you, Gold," the lanista told me as soon as I was brought into the house.

I waited.

"We have decided on something special for the pre-show tomorrow. I will put you, Thad and Phillip in the ring against the new slaves. And I will arm everyone. Actually weapons everywhere. What do you think?"

The thing I wanted most of course was to be put in the arena again, but not against those who had no idea how to defend themselves. It would be a massacre. And, what about the boy? I couldn't kill that child, or stand by and watch another of us do it.

He was waiting for me to express my appreciation. "Thank you, but master, there is no glory in that."

"It's for the fun," he laughed, biting into an apple and throwing me one. "All in fun."

Chapter Six

Samson: Taste of love and death

I was high. I would probably face certain death in the arena within a few days but I was happier than I'd ever been in my entire twenty-two years. I'd touched ambrosia, had ambrosia inside of me, and no matter what happened now, I'd been as blessed as any god.

I waited quietly in my cell, and hoped that Gold would come back soon. I didn't want to think of him at the master's house, his body being used by Claudius or his parents.

I fought sleep but it soon overcame me and when I opened my eyes, my cell door was open which meant it was morning. As I walked through the tomb-like row of cells, I could hear noises ahead of me, a lot more than before because now there were fourteen men in this ludi.

I wondered if the new ones were to be put into the arena for sport as I had been when I arrived, and what was to be done with the boy.

I searched the room for Gold when I walked past the cook. He handed me a bowl of oatmeal and fruit. I thanked him.

Neither Gold, nor the boy were anywhere around. I was concerned. I sat down beside Phillip, whose eyes were on one of the new arrivals, who sat devouring his oatmeal at the next table.

"Hey," I said to Phillip. "Where is Gold?"

He never took his eyes off the other man as he replied, "He went outside earlier with the kid."

"Ah. Any news?"

"About what?"

"Phillip? What so takes your attention?"

"That new man, Sullis is his name. He's something else."

"Handsome enough," I said, but he didn't interest me.

"That's not what I mean." He looked at me finally, and put down his bowl. "The way he acted this morning. He's randy as hell. He doesn't seem to understand his situation."

"Randy?" I laughed.

"Oh yes, and he's got his sights set on Gold. Wants him badly." He nudged me with his elbow.

I stiffened. "He got randy with Gold?"

"Yes."

"Gold put him in his place I hope?"

"He didn't seem to pay much attention. He seemed distracted this morning." He lowered his voice. "He didn't get back here until dawn."

"Zeus's cock," I swore.

He laughed aloud. "You should get over this little crush you have, brother."

"It's not a crush!" I protested and stood.

103

"Calm your temper," he laughed. "Only having some fun. Did you hear that Thad, Gold and I are to be put in the arena against the fodder?"

"Oh no," I said.

He shrugged. "What? It's a show."

I left my half-eaten oatmeal behind and walked outside looking for Gold.

Gold stood off a ways in the distance, the boy by his side. He had a hand on his shoulder. I thought twice about interrupting them. They seemed deep in conversation. I could only imagine what Gold would feel if he was forced to kill the boy in the arena. Would he leave it to one of the others?

I waited until Gold turned and headed towards me, the boy at his heels. He looked at me questioningly when he saw me. "You need something?"

I wanted to say, *Yes, you, I need you*, but I wouldn't of course. "I just wanted to know if you learned any more about—"

He put up a hand. "Go inside, Maris," he told the boy.

When the boy had disappeared, Gold looked at me. "You already know everything you need to know. And I am to be put in the ring with the fodder, along with Thad and Phillip. Claudius told me."

"What else did Claudius tell you?"

His expression didn't change.

"Were you with him last night?"

"No."

"You didn't come home until dawn."

"I was not permitted to leave."

"Were you with Claudius?" I insisted.

"No."

"Then, his father…his mother? Who?" There was anger in my voice that I couldn't disguise.

"Discretion forbids me to speak. Was there something else?" he asked stiffly, obviously not used to being questioned in this way.

"The newcomers, they are to be..." I trailed off, and glanced at the building. "The boy, what are you planning to..." I trailed off. "He will die."

A shadow crossed his face, "Not if I can help it." His teeth were clenched.

We stood in silence for a moment. It was sprinkling rain and it felt good on my skin. I wanted to prolong the contact, the two of us together, alone. I wanted to touch him so badly I ached all over. "Can you?" I asked finally. "Help it?"

He pursed his lips, but didn't answer.

"I hear the new one named Sullis is a handful." I tried to sound casual as we headed indoors.

He paused and glanced at me. The smug bastard actually grinned. "Ah, news spreads fast in this place. Jealous, are we?"

I muttered something under my breath and walked off in the other direction. And he actually laughed aloud.

In spite of the fact that I was annoyed with him, it was good to hear him laugh. It was deep and male, and filled the structure, causing the others to pause just to hear it. There was not a lot of laughter here.

"You tickled him," Gabien commented on his way past me.

"Yeah," I grunted. "He's laughing at me, believe me."

Gabien chuckled. "Come on outside, brother, and let's joust. I'll laugh at you too."

"Oh yeah," I gave him a playful shove. "I'm game. And we'll see who ends up laughing at whom."

We went outside wrestling a little with the makeshift swords as we went then began to practice in earnest.

We were all sweaty and hurting when Gold brought the others out into the courtyard. We paused in the shade to give them a sympathetic look. Even Thad came over and stood beside us, and looked as if he felt some pity for them.

Phillip joined us soon after, acting like he'd paused to drink some water. "See the haughty one," he pointed out discreetly, "look how he preens. Is he dense? Doesn't he know he'll be dead soon?"

"Might just be the bravado he needs to see him through this," Thad shrugged his massive shoulders. "Samson here survived it, maybe he will too."

I watched as this Sullis moved closer to Gold. He appeared to hang on his every word. He was the first to volunteer to help Gold demonstrate how to use the sword and the shield. He touched Gold's hand as he took the makeshift sword from him. He made direct eye contact with him. I fumed.

Later we went inside for supper and I sat alone and played with my food. I tried not to sulk but I was having a hard time. It was made worse when Gold came in with Sullis at his side. They were deep in conversation.

When Sullis walked off to get his supper, I got up from the table and approached Gold. "How did they do?"

"Sullis might have a real chance, the others..." he shrugged.

I glossed over his reference to Sullis. "Will they have swords and shields?"

"Yes. Somehow the lanista heard me this time and he's agreed. But they will go up against three gladiators, rather than one."

I nodded. "The boy? How did he do out there?"

"He's not in training. He's not going into that ring," Gold said, his gaze settling on Maris in the corner. I noticed that Sullis sat beside him, and talked to him softly.

"Is Sullis his keeper now?"

"For now, yes. When I can't, he offered to look out for him."

"I would have done that."

"You have enough to worry about right now." He turned around and in a loud voice, he announced, "There is a party tonight at the house to celebrate the upcoming contest. Some of us will be summoned."

"Some of us?" I echoed.

"Yes," he glanced at me, "You, Phillip, Thaddeus and I. They will call us to be readied. Stay alert."

"Wait," I grabbed his forearm. "What does that mean, readied?"

"It means," Thaddeus growled in my ear, "we are to be oiled and decorated so that we can be the big shiny toys the lanista's guests play with."

Gold was ready to move off when I said, "When is the contest then?"

He took his arm away. "Tomorrow," he replied.

I sucked in some breath. "Why didn't you tell me earlier? You knew last night."

"There was no point in having you carry that burden before its time."

He was gone. He'd left the room and I knew that he now weaved his way down the corridors back to his cell.

Tomorrow. Tomorrow, I would face the Destroyer. It might be my final day on this earth, I thought. If it was, tonight I was determined to have my way with Gold again.

The guards came for us a little while later. We were told to strip off our clothes and get into the bath. The others

107

were all sent to their cells and locked in for the night. After we'd washed, they took the four of us to the big house and into the kitchen area.

I stood there with my hands in front of my genitals feeling self-conscious. Phillip stood beside me and Thad was on the other side with Gold.

A slave girl pulled me out into the middle of the floor and began to cover me with an oily substance that made my skin gleam. Another slave moved up beside me and fastened a harness around my hips with a leather strap. When she lifted my cock into the strap, I gasped.

She looked like she wanted to giggle.

After that she brushed out my hair and pushed me to the side.

The slave girls repeated the same procedure with the other three men, and when they got to Gold, they seemed giddy.

He actually lifted his cock and placed it in the holder himself, brushing the girls' hands aside.

He looked scrumptious all oiled like that, his muscles bulging and defined.

I was hard just looking at him. And at that moment, I wanted to grab him and roll around on the floor with him, letting our slippery bodies rub all over each other.

Music from a sitar sounded and I realised that the party had already begun. Naked slave girls rushed in and out of the kitchen carrying food and wine.

A guard appeared. He tried not to look at us. "Gladiators are to be out in the main room. Move!"

We were hustled off to a designated place, lined up and put on display like a row of statues. Gold and Thaddeus were first in line and Phillip got to stand on the other side of Thad. I was on the end, the last one, far away from Gold.

I peered around at the toga-wearing guests who stood around drinking wine and eating morsels off trays. They reached out to fondle the slaves and marvelled at the entertainers who were dancing and juggling, and playing sad music.

The guests began noticing our appearance and the lanista clapped his hands to draw their attention. He walked in front of us, his hand out in the air. "For your pleasure, tonight, ladies and gentleman, I give you four of my finest gladiators. Gold, the champion, and Thad, the acting champion. Phillip, with wins of over ninety percent, and Samson, the slave who survived the ring when all five of the others with him perished. Tomorrow, Samson will take on the Destroyer!"

There was applause.

"Inspect and handle them as you will. They are at your service."

I wrinkled my nose. I didn't like the idea of being at anyone's service, and I didn't think of myself as one of the finest of anything.

They were all crowded around Gold and Thad now, which relieved me somewhat.

Phillip grinned at me. "They'll get to us. Don't worry."

"I'm not worried," I muttered. I glanced down at my cock, held upright with that ridiculous piece of leather and tried not to think about how humiliated I was.

The lanista's son, Claudius, came to me first. He ran his gaze over me and actually swirled his finger around the head of my cock. I stiffened.

"Relax," he laughed. He spilled some wine down the front of his toga, leaving a large purple stain. "They'll do a lot more to you before the night is done. You are nice," he smacked his lips. He smoothed his hand over one of my biceps.

At the same time two older women walked over to gawk at me. "Beautiful muscle definition," one said but her gaze settled on my cock.

"I find the entire gladiator thing quite barbaric," the other woman shuddered, as she studied my chest.

"Um," Claudius told her softly, "barbarians they are, but if your husband could fuck like one, you'd be a happy woman."

The woman feigned a look of shock but she put her hand on my chest anyway.

"Why don't you taste him?" Claudius asked with his mouth close to her ear. "I'm sure my father would loan him out."

"But my husband," she gasped, but she still moved her fingers over my chest while I tried not to move.

"He doesn't have to know," Claudius smiled.

She removed her hand, sighed and walked off.

I felt like a common whore in the market place and I resented that little bastard for making me feel like one. And of course I resented him for far more. But I was property and he wanted to make sure I knew it.

"Shocked?" Claudius asked me a few minutes later as the lanista and two other men stood close by inspecting Phillip.

"No, master."

"You lie. You hate me, don't you? And it's not only because I tried to give you to that old woman as a plaything. You know exactly what I'm saying, don't you, Samson?"

I swallowed hard.

"Just remember who he really belongs to," he sniggered and walked away.

It wasn't easy standing there for hours, enduring the handling and comments of strangers. I was forced to bite my tongue more than once. I heard several of the guests actually offer money in exchange for our sexual favours, and was relieved to hear the lanista turn them down. "These are fighting men. They are not whores. If you wish sexual favours, the house slaves, male or female, are available for your pleasure free of charge."

And the guests took full advantage, often in plain view, savagely raping the house boys or house girls.

Although the lanista seemed opposed to pimping us, I knew he wouldn't hesitate to make us sexually service someone if they were important enough to him. I'd heard the others talk of it, and hoped for this night to pass.

The only advantage to this ridiculous posing was that as I was standing there, I was privy to a lot of conversation that was going on between the guests.

I discovered who was bedding who, and who wanted to bed who, and also what the guests really thought of their hosts.

Roman society was like the Spartan one when it came to a hierarchy of class. You were either born into the right class or weren't. Our owner might be a rich man, but he would never be considered equal to some of the guests in attendance, who considered him to be beneath them.

They enjoyed the hospitality and the pleasures offered but that's where it ended. I heard one Senator say that Simeon would never enter the Senate, 'no matter how many of those moronic barbarians he amassed.'

Suddenly the music died and the lanista clapped his hands together for silence. "Ladies and gentleman," he said, "I hope you are enjoying the festivities this evening. We are all anticipating the entertainment tomorrow and ask the gods for good weather. There has been much talk this evening about the fact the House of Simeon has two great gladiators in this room, and that the question of who is the better has never been settled."

I stiffened. I looked down at Gold and Thad. They both moved around a little restlessly.

"And tonight, exclusively for my very special guests, I will allow Gold and Thad to do a mock demonstration for you!"

The guests grew noisy, loud applause and shouts rang out all around us.

"This is not to the death. This is a simple demonstration and not official in any way. The winner will be winner for the evening. And tomorrow you may see both my champions in the ring fighting the new arrivals, before the main contest."

"Yes, Simeon," a distinguished gentleman in the front said loudly, "but for Gold and Thad, defeating these new slaves will be like squashing mice."

Everyone laughed.

Simeon smiled. "Come over to the other side of the room where my slaves have prepared a mock ring. Gold, Thad," he called, "come."

I craned my neck to see where they were going. "Are we not going to be allowed to see?" I asked Phillip.

"Leave it be," he said. "You don't want to see it."

"Gold will be all right, won't he?"

Phillip lifted an eyebrow. "Gold will squash Thad like the mice that old man was speaking of. But the aftermath will not be pretty."

I was confused, not sure what he was talking about. "May we see, mistress?" I asked the lanista's wife as she walked past, careful to keep my eyes down.

She stopped, smiled at me. "And what will be my reward?"

"As you please, mistress."

She laughed. "Come then." She looked at Phillip. "You too."

We crowded around in the back, and craned our necks as Gold and Thad were given mock swords and shields. I was relieved to see they were wooden swords.

"Begin," the lanista called out.

There was much noise and shouting as wood hit wood, echoing in the great room. I couldn't see anything. I nudged Phillip, who was taller and asked him if he could tell me what was going on. "It won't be long now," was all he would say.

A shout rang out. "Gold, Gold, Gold!" Then applause filled the room.

"Gold!" the lanista called out. "He is still the undefeated."

I looked at Phillip. He stared back at me. "What does this mean?" We moved against the wall as the guests headed off in different directions.

"It was better with the question still in the air. Now, Thad's resentment will grow, his need to challenge Gold greater than ever."

"Then it would have been better if Thad would have won?"

He nodded.

We were told to go back to our places. We were standing in that line when Thad walked by. I could feel the anger radiating from him.

Gold was still among the crowd, being fawned over by the guests. I was beginning to understand what Phillip meant.

Chapter Seven

Gold: Alliances

I wished I had deliberately lost the competition with Thad, and I think it was my intention to do just that. But once the contest started, the gladiator spirit had me in its wake, and I couldn't stop until I had him on his knees, with the fake sword at his throat.

Thad had been humiliated, and even though the master announced that this little competition meant nothing officially, I could see that in the eyes of the crowd, it was a confirmation that I was still the champion of the House of Simeon. There would be trouble in the future between Thad and me, of that, I was certain.

After the competition was over, I was anxious to get back to the gladiator quarters. I needed to be at my cell to carry out the plan I had worked out with Regina, Gracia's personal slave.

I'd hoped that the lanista would dismiss us all back to our quarters. He didn't. The guests were all around me, talking in excitement. The lanista was revelling in it. He wasn't about to cut short the pleasure.

Regina had already given me several signs from across the room that she was ready, but I was helpless to do anything.

I pulled a guard off of Regina once who was just about to rape her. The master had punished the guard for trying to touch his property and beaten me for attacking the guard.

After, in gratitude, she offered to do something for me in return. Up until now, I hadn't called on that favour.

Regina was Gracia's favourite and allowed to go to town on her own, which gave her an advantage I didn't have. Also, she had taken one of the guards as a lover which gave her access to his set of keys whenever they were required. She could take the keys from him when he slept and get them back to him without him even knowing they were gone.

Regina had agreed to smuggle Maris out of the gladiator quarters, especially when she saw how young he was. She intended to do it before sunrise but I needed to be there in the gladiators' quarters, to distract the guard while she ran off with the boy.

Finally, I noticed that the lanista appeared bored with all the attention being lavished on me. He led me off to where the other gladiators stood.

Thaddeus glared at me, and Phillip looked dead on his feet. Samson was being examined by a young man who seemed to have taken a great interest in him.

I wasn't sure how I felt about that. I didn't have the right to feel anything. It was just that I'd shared an intimate embrace with Samson, and it felt very fresh, as if it had just happened, and I wasn't exactly comfortable with the way that man ran his hands all over him.

"I'm very proud of you," Simeon told me, "and if it wasn't for the contest tomorrow, I'd ask you to spend the night here with Gracia, and myself."

He was feeling generous. It was rare he shared me with his wife. Gracia must have done something which pleased him immensely.

He seemed to hesitate. "Go now, all of you," he glanced at the others.

"Thank you, master," I told him.

A guard led the way. Phillip and Thad followed but Samson was detained by the guest. I didn't look back. Instead I nodded at the slave girl and she smiled at me.

Thad said nothing. He kept his head down and just went directly to his cell, as did Phillip. I kept a look out the front and saw Regina hurry past, and head around back. She held up the keys as she did.

The guard that detested me the most walked in, the one I'd attacked in Regina's name. I sighed inwardly. Just my luck, it had to be him on duty. He still bore the scar on his face.

"What are you doing up?" he demanded. "Why aren't you in your cell, slave?"

I knew he would escort me to my cell. Once I was locked in, he would patrol outside, and around the back. Regina would be caught. I had to delay him. "I have just returned from the master's party," I announced. "The master seemed uncertain about wanting me to stay at the house tonight. I was told to stay here and wait. In fact, I thought you had come to get me."

"I've had no such word from the master. Now, get into your cell before I put you in your place where you belong," he sneered, coming closer, "on your knees with my cock up your ass, you arrogant bastard."

Where in hell was she? Had she gotten him out already? I hoped he wasn't fighting her. The boy had grown attached to me in a very short time. He'd told me he hated his father and he didn't want to go home.

The guard was trying to shove me towards my cell now. I tried my best to slow the process but it was no use. I had no choice but to physically restrain him. I knew I'd pay for it later but it was better than the alternative. As many people as I had killed, I knew that I couldn't slaughter a young, defenceless boy.

I sprang on him, and hit him several times. I took his sword and threw it aside. He struggled with me but not for long. In a few minutes, he was on the floor, moaning, blood running down his face from his head.

I raced to the cell. It was open. Maris was gone. I ran around to the front and outside. I couldn't see anything. They must have gotten away. I sure hoped so.

Guards raced towards me now. One of them was the guard I'd hit. He held onto his head, angry as hell. I took a step back as one of the men reached out for me.

The one I'd attacked held the tip of his sword at my throat. "You're going to pay," he growled. He hit me hard in the face.

"Seize him," he barked to the other two, "take him to the lanista. He tried to kill me."

Another guard came running now. "A slave is missing. It's the boy."

I sighed inwardly.

The guard glowered at me. "You did this. That's why you didn't want to go to your cell. You helped that prisoner escape." He actually smiled. "You've done it this time."

The party was still going on as I was dragged into the main hallway. The lanista barrelled down the corridor. He looked angry. He was accompanied by the guard I attacked. He was still wiping the blood off his forehead. It was a wonder he didn't pass out.

I braced myself for the worst.

"Gold," the master demanded, "what is the meaning of this? Why did you attack the guard? Where in Hades is my property?"

He was trying not to yell but I could see the struggle on his face which caused him to grind his teeth. There were still guests in the other rooms and he was trying to exercise discretion.

I didn't reply. I had no reply actually. What could I say? I looked down at the floor.

"Did you beat this guard to hasten the boys' escape?" He was close to me now. I could feel his breath.

"He did," the guard interrupted. "He--"

"Shut up!" the lanista told him. He asked me the same question a second time, this time his voice boomed in the great corridor.

I lifted my head, looked at him. "He was only a child. I will not murder a child."

There were several guests now staring down the corridor at them.

I knew if there hadn't been witnesses, he would have struck me. He took a step back instead. "You know you will have to be punished for this, and the price of that slave will come out of any earnings you make."

"You are going to do more than just whip him, make an example of him," the bleeding guard insisted anxiously. "Punishment for helping a slave escape is death!"

"Silence," the lanista turned to the guard. "You want me to destroy my most valuable possession? I will put *you* on a cross before Gold!"

The guard fell silent.

He sighed. "I will not punish him until after the contest. He needs to be in good shape tomorrow. After," he paused, pointing to me "you will be taken to the centre of the courtyard, given five lashes and hung there for two days as an example. Thad will take your place as trainer for that time."

I figured I'd gotten off lightly.

"Take him to his cell," the lanista ordered one of the other guards, "and you," he said to my victim, "stop bleeding all over my floor, and see the doctor now."

He nodded, bowed his head and turned to leave, not at all happy about my punishment.

I was shoved forward.

"Wait," the lanista motioned to the guard. "Leave us a moment."

The guard nodded and left.

The lanista faced me. He looked at me a long time and came close, pressed his forehead to mine. "Why did you do this?" He moaned then stepped back. "I don't want to punish you. You have given me no choice."

"I understand. I bear you no ill will. I knew the consequences when I made the decision."

"And your accomplice? If you tell me, I'll decrease the number of lashes."

"You will have to beat me more, master. I will never reveal it."

He stepped away. "So I figured. Very well. Let it go then. We'll say you acted alone. Ten lashes."

I lowered my head. "Yes, master."

"Guard," he shouted, "take Gold back now and Samson, as well. They both have a big day tomorrow."

I didn't sleep all night. I was wound like a coil. I thought more about Samson than myself and suddenly I wanted to be with him.

When the keys rattled in my cell at dawn, I sat up on the bed. It was Regina.

I quickly shortened the distance between us. "The boy?" I whispered.

"Safe. I gave him the money you had given me. He should be all right. He fought me."

"I knew he would."

"And you?"

"I am to be punished, but it will be nothing like the punishment of killing that child."

She nodded. "I have to get back. Do they know about me?"

I shook my head. "And they won't."

She smiled. "I will feel your pain. When is it to be?"

"After tomorrow. Don't burden yourself with it."

She was about to leave.

I put out my hand. "Regina. Leave it open."

She nodded and hurried out.

Usually, my cell was left unlocked at night, and I could use the keys to unlock the other cells if I had the need. This was in my capacity as trainer. But of course, I was to be punished, and so last night, the guard had locked me in. The morning guard wouldn't know until this evening, even if they communicated among themselves. Most times they didn't.

The job the guards performed here required very little effort, and most of them were profoundly lazy and incompetent, which was to my advantage.

I walked down the row of cells to the end where Samson slept soundly. I inserted the key into the lock, and he woke. He looked at me curiously. I placed a finger to my lips and motioned to him.

He got up off his bed and followed me silently.

The guard on duty was out front. I could see him walking back and forth, probably to stay awake as he waited for his replacement.

"Where we going?" Samson asked me.

I took his hand and pulled him along behind me. "A place I know. We'll take a swim in the river."

He smiled at me. He knew we'd do much more than swim.

I led him to the path through the trees to where the water flowed. The sun hadn't yet risen in the sky. It was grey. We stripped off our clothes and waded into the water. It felt cool and refreshing. I felt Samson's hard body move against my back and I closed my eyes. He reached his arms around me and stroked my cock. I swallowed, leant back against his chest and felt his lips at my throat.

"Gods," he moaned, "how I've been longing to touch you like this."

I allowed his hands to roam over my chest then concentrate their efforts underwater, fondling my cock and handling my balls. His stiff cock prodded my ass and suddenly I wanted him there, inside me. I wanted to feel the vulnerability of it, the surrender. "Yes," I urged.

He groaned, "Great gods," and pulled me up out of the water. There on the bank we went down together. I kissed his wet skin all over, took his cock and his testicles in my mouth, tasting the tangy muskiness of him. I moved my lips off his genitals and licked his nipples then captured his mouth with mine, before lowering my cock into it.

He sucked my cock like a young baby might suckle their mother, hungrily and with determination. When I felt close to the edge, I pushed away. "Put your cock inside my ass," I invited as I met his gaze. The grass was high and in the early dawn, everything looked hazy, uncertain.

I moved onto my knees. "Come on," I told him. "You want to, don't you?"

He nodded but looked hesitant.

"What is it then?" I stroked my own cock for a moment. This was no time for talk.

"Are you giving yourself to me because you think I will die today?"

The question fell between us, heavy and ominous.

"Is that what you think?"

He didn't answer, just looked at me, fear in his eyes.

"Samson," I said gently, "if I offered my ass to every gladiator I thought would die in the ring, my ass would be as wide as the sea."

He began to laugh. "I suppose," he managed.

"Now," I lowered my voice, "are you going to take me, or not?"

He reached out, grabbed my face between his hands, and kissed me hotly. I didn't mind his kisses so much. In fact, I kind of liked them.

He swung around behind suddenly and like a solider might mount his horse, he mounted me.

His cock stabbed deep within me and I welcomed the pain. It was pain I could cling to when I felt the lash on my flesh. It was pain that, unlike the whip, would eventually fill me with pleasure.

Samson moved inside of me and I started to move with him. I matched him, thrust for thrust. We moved with swift and smooth motions which wrung cries of pleasure from both of us.

I didn't worry about the sound carrying to the slave quarters. I didn't really care. And for those moments when Samson was inside of me, I didn't feel like a slave, or even like a gladiator. I was just a man, lost in feeling, feelings that had been long since buried.

Samson worked my cock as he worked my ass and when he emptied his passion inside of me, I pumped out mine in his hand and onto the grass.

I lay flat on the ground with Samson on top of me. He turned my face and pressed his lips to mine. It didn't matter if we got caught. It had been worth it. And I'd do it again in a heartbeat.

We managed to get back just as the sun rose. Our fingertips lingered a few seconds in the darkened corridor as we went our separate ways back to our cells. No matter what happened today in that arena, we had that. And no one could take it away.

I didn't tell Samson about what had happened with Maris, or that I was to be punished for his escape. He'd find out soon enough. I didn't want to ruin it for him. He'd looked so happy as we walked back from the river. I still marvelled that it had been me who had the power to put that smile on his face, given what he was to face today.

The preparations had been made for the competitions. The crowd would be treated to a variety of contests during the three days, sponsored by Simeon and his arch rival, Phineas. Phineas was considered to be the richer of the two but both men were playing to the Senators. Both hoped to be a candidate for elections. Each lanista would use their gladiators today to best the other.

Right after breakfast, the troupe, which consisted of Samson and myself, along with Phillip and Thad, were taken by prison cart to the arena.

Those who would face us had been taken to the arena separately before dawn.

When the forum came into view, I heard Samson gasp as he saw the newcomers in cages at the side of the road. The citizens walked past and hurled things at them through the bars.

Samson sidled over to me, stumbling a little as the cart hit a rut in the cobble stone road. "Why are the Romans so cruel?"

"It's not cruelty," I told him. "It's order."

"Order?" He looked at me in disbelief.

"Good and evil, the message that wrongdoers will face punishment, and that valour deserves reward."

"You're a philosopher now?"

"Perhaps."

"There is no valour in slaughtering innocents."

"You are correct. But to the people, they are not innocent. They are criminals, enemies."

"But some of them are not."

"It really doesn't matter who plays the role as long as the roles are represented."

"You must have been a good student," he said.

"No, I was a rebellious student actually."

"Is this your punishment?"

"It could be," I replied.

When the cart began to enter the thong of people headed to the forum on foot, the driver shouted and cracked his whip to get the people to make way.

Some people recognised us and shouted out our names. Children ran alongside the cart.

When we finally got through and the driver pulled to a stop at the side of the arena, we were told to get off the cart. The guards led us through to the back entrance where we climbed the steps to the stands.

The lanista was there with Gracia and his son.

Present were also several prominent Roman citizens, mainly land owners and Senators. On the other side was Phineas and his family — his wife and his teenage daughter.

The lanista stood up as we filed in. "Ah, here they are, my fine gladiators," he announced to Phineas. "The best of them."

Phineas stood. He was a handsome man, much younger than his rival. He smiled and sat back down. His daughter ogled us boldly and said something to her personal slave, who giggled in return.

Phineas' wife whispered to Gracia. She pointed to me and said something which caused Phineas' wife to look quite scandalised.

The Destroyer was nowhere in sight.

The four of us stood quietly in back of the master, next to the favourite slaves, one of them Regina. The crowd had begun to fill the stadium and were already boisterous.

"If the Destroyer wins today," Phineas suddenly called over to Simeon, "would you allow me to purchase one of your gladiators?"

"He won't win," Simeon called back.

"I said, if he does. If you are that sure, why not wager?"

"What would I get in return?" Simeon demanded.

"What do you want?"

"Ten of your finest."

"Agreed," he said.

This caused Simeon to look aghast. "Agreed, surely you jest?"

"I will give you ten of my best in exchange for..." he paused, looked at me, "Gold."

Simeon laughed aloud. "Now, I know you jest."

"You don't use him in the arena. He is wasted in your house. I will give you twenty, and I'll throw in two of my prettiest house slaves."

I sucked in some breath. *Damn. Was I being sold, traded? Did I want to be?*

Samson looked concerned. He met my eyes. I looked away.

Suddenly all talk came to a halt. Simeon stood and welcomed everyone. "Let us begin," he called out, "with some comedy to lighten the mood." The sounds of flutes and horns sounded. The lanista cracked a whip by his side. "Begin!" he shouted and fell back into his seat, laughing.

Several comedic figures dressed like women ran out into the ring with what looked like wooden spoons. They began hitting one another in a haphazardly fashion humorously imitating some of the gladiator moves.

The crowd loved it.

Phineas proudly announced that these slaves, which belonged to him, often amused his guests for hours.

"I wouldn't know," Simeon mocked, "I've never been invited to one of your parties."

After this, several of Phineas' gladiators fought. They wore the customs of the enemy and incited the crowd to call for blood.

The contests were for fun and, although blood was spilled and the crowd decided on the winner, none of these contests were to the death.

Several hours after the high sun, the lanista stood and announced, "The contest you've all been waiting for is here. Gold is back in the arena, with Thad and Phillip. They will take on the enemy, the dreaded Semnites, and conquer them for you! A fight to the death!"

The crowd went wild.

The guard waited for us to follow him down the stairs to the entrance of the arena.

Samson, who stood at my side, discreetly clutched my hand in his for a second then released it. Thad led the way in. He put up his hands as his name was announced, then

Phillip and I did the same. We walked around the arena several times and some people threw flowers at us. Finally, we stopped in front of the stands where the lanista sat.

"Enter the enemies of Rome!"

A chorus of booing was heard as the five prisoners came in. They already looked defeated, except for one. I looked over at Sullis. He actually winked at me. I looked away. He was one crazy son of a bitch, maybe just crazy enough to live through this.

"Begin!" the lanista cried out.

Swords and shields were strewn everywhere and I watched as our opponents scrambled to pick up anything they could.

I leant down and picked up a shield. I saw that Thad had taken the two remaining swords. I swore under my breath. We were a troupe. He was not supposed to be limiting my chances by taking an extra sword he didn't need. What in hell was he doing?

Phillip had already been attacked by one man in the far corner. Phillip had put him on his knees. A cheer went up as Phillip quickly cut off his head.

Sullis cracked swords with Thad now. I marvelled at his skill. There was something not quite right. He wasn't what he seemed. He fought like one of us.

Phillip was playing with another man, biding his time to prolong the show before he finished him off. My attention was suddenly taken up by two men who attacked me from both sides.

I held up the shield to ward off one blow and tried to wrestle the sword away from the other. I had to do some pretty fancy work, as I used my body and the strength of one arm to finally subdue the one on the right so that I could defend myself from the one on my left.

When I felt the blow from behind me, the pain ripped through my shoulder. It made it hard to breath. I heard the crowd go completely silent. I knew who was on either side. There couldn't possibly be one at my back, unless it was Sullis. I turned, the pain excruciating. My eyes widened as I saw Thad with his sword raised high, ready to strike again. The sword was dripping in blood. My blood.

Thad let out a crazed yell and thundered after me. The referee tried to stop the fight but Thad hit him so hard, he flew in the air. The crowd was on their feet. Thad stomped across the ring, still advancing as I kept backing up. I had nothing but a shield.

I stopped in my tracks. I was almost against the boards. I had nowhere else to go. I went to the left, the pain in my shoulder now radiating down my chest. *Stay on your feet.* I searched the ground for anything, wondering if I could bend over at all. Everything was a blur. I managed to dodge blow after blow, but I could no longer hear the crowd. Soldiers raced into the ring but Thad threw them off, one after the other. I went to my knee. Thad brought his sword down again. I thought it was over. Then a sword swung up in front of me, and pushed Thad back. "Gold! Take it!" It was Sullis. He pushed the sword into my hand.

I wrapped my fist around it, and struggled to my feet. I saw red. Somehow my rage took over. I went after Thad with a vengeance. How dare he turn on me in the ring? It was unforgivable.

It was the match everyone had wanted to see and as our swords clashed, blow on blow, each impact caused the pain in my shoulder to move into my jaw. There wasn't a sound in the arena.

We stumbled over the dead and stared into each other's eyes and the battle went on. Every cut he gave me, I gave him one in return. He slashed me across the ribs and I cut his forearm almost to the bone. He jabbed me in the gut but not deep enough to do any real damage, and I reached out with my free hand and punched him so hard in the mouth, teeth flew in the air. I could smell death. And at one time, I thought I saw the ferry man walk out into the ring and motion to me. Either way, one of us would not be walking out of this forum today.

When I finally had him, I knew it. He knew it too. It was in his eyes. I could taste the victory. I swung my sword in the air, and hit him right in the jaw. He went down hard. Blood poured from his lower face, and bathed his chest. He dropped in the sand. His eyes looked clouded, and for a moment, I almost felt pity for him. I looked down at him, and the pain in my body reached an intolerable level.

He held up his finger in surrender. If the crowd would have shown mercy, I would have spared him.

The crowd chanted. "Iugual! Iugual!" It was over. They wanted me to finish it. I nodded at him and swung again, this time, taking off his head at the neck. The throat gaped open, his head tipped back then rolled onto the ground. Blood covered my chest and my face. My hands were coated red. The referee ran out and held up my good arm.

I bent over, picked up Thad's bleeding head by the hair and held it up in air. I looked up at the stands and the lanista was on his feet, a strange expression on his face.

A variety of flowers flew into the ring. I heard the crowd roar again, chanting my name. I looked for Samson but I couldn't see him. My chest heaved, and the pain was incredible but I felt alive again. I was back! I was back!

Chapter Eight

Samson: Fate Worse than Death

There was a sense of relief which flooded through me when I saw Thad go to his knees, relief that was mixed with horror. I shuddered when the guard led me down the stairs to the arena. The crowd still chanted his name, and some slaves were gathering the roses which littered the ground.

He'd enjoyed it. The look on Gold's face when he lifted that bleeding mass that was once Thad was one of pure ecstasy, more profound than when he'd come inside me.

The people in the crowd were like animals, screaming for blood, the pleasure seemed to increase as each man fell. I wondered what it would feel like to be on the ground and know at that moment that thousands of people were crying for your death. I didn't want to find out.

I looked around me as I waited by the entrance to the arena. Slaves fitted me with armour, a helmet, a shield. I was the one they would root for. Phineas' gladiator was in the role of the enemy. That surely gave me an edge if I ended up on my knees. At least I hoped.

I wondered if Gold was all right. He looked to be in bad shape when he finally left the arena, and I wasn't sure what had really happened.

One minute, Thad was chopping off the heads of his opponents, and the next, he was hacking into Gold's shoulder.

When Thad prevented Gold from having a sword, the lanista jumped to his feet and cried out, "Stop the contest, stop it! What in hell is he doing? I'll crucify him for that!"

But his words were drowned out by the crowd, who were booing Thad, and urging Gold to go after him.

I was sure Gold was dead at one point but he hung on, managing to escape Thad's sword at every turn. Then I closed my eyes, sure that it was the end, only opening them when I heard the crowd utter a gasp in unison.

Sullis had saved him. He'd warded off Thad's blow and given his sword to Gold.

Yes, I was bothered with the why. I was bothered by the exchange of alliances that had occurred in that ring, and the motive for it.

I knew Thad's. Gold's defeat of him, even in the mock contest at the lanista's house, was too much for him to bear. He needed to prove himself, to prove himself the true champion once and for all.

But even if he had defeated Gold, chances were the master would have put him to death. There would be no glory in it in the end.

I leant against the wall and closed my eyes for a second, feeling the sword in my hand. *Stay focused. Go in there with one goal, to kill.* Those had been Gold's words to me, and I played them over and over in my head.

Suddenly, I heard some commotion and Gold appeared, an anxious doctor trying to hold onto him.

"Gold," I said, moving to him. "Are you all right?"

"No, he isn't all right," the doctor muttered. "If he dies, the lanista will have my head."

"Please," Gold told the doctor, leaning on the wall, "give us a moment, and then I promise, you can poke and prod me all you want."

The doctor nodded and walked away.

Gold glanced at the guard. The guard nodded at him and turned his back.

"Ha," Gold smiled weakly, "even the guards are giving me my due today." He winced a little.

"Gold, you're hurt. You should…" I reached out and touched his arm.

"It's okay, I will. I had to see you. Be careful, and remember what I told you. He's big, but that means he doesn't move so fast. Wear him out, make him chase you around. Make him vulnerable then go for the groin."

I made a face.

"It's either you or him."

I nodded. "I know. Why did Sullis save you?"

"I don't know."

"What will happen to him?"

"I'm sure the master will reward him by saving his life. He'll be trained."

I nodded quietly. "I still don't understand."

"It's a mystery. But I'm grateful to him. He saved my life."

That made my stomach knot. "Don't be too grateful," I murmured. I wanted to be the one to save him. Damn that Sullis.

Gold tried to laugh. He did that when he thought I was jealous. He didn't quite manage it. He put his hand to his side. I could see the blood when he took it away.

"Go," I urged. "You need attention."

"I wanted to be here to watch the competition but..." He went to his knees and lost consciousness.

"Guard!" I called out.

Two guards came, and took him away. The frantic doctor ran along behind him and they disappeared from my view.

I was worried, not only about myself but about Gold. I wondered what I'd do if anything happened to him. I loved him.

There was the sound of music now, horns blowing and people again started to shout for the competition to begin.

They quieted as the lanista began to speak. "Citizens of Rome, and distinguished guests, it is the competition you've been waiting for, a match to the death. Two men enter, only one will leave. You remember him as the one who got away, who faced the sword and lives to speak about it, the only survivor, who you chose to spare. Is he worthy? You decide, welcome...Samson!"

I walked out into the ring and the referee came and paraded me around, my arm up in the air. The crowd cheered, some booed. The Destroyer also had his following.

Once in the middle of the ring, I looked up to see Phineas rise from his seat. "Please welcome," he shouted, "from the House of Phineas, the champion, you know him, you fear him, The Destro...or...yer!"

When the doors opened on the other side and the gladiator walked out into the ring, my eyes widened. He was more Cyclops than gladiator. Gold wasn't kidding. He was a bloody giant.

Most of the crowd snarled and swore at him. One woman near the front threw a purple flower at him and cried. "Get him, Destroyer, then crawl between my silky thighs!"

There was laughter.

We were made to face each other. He looked like a snorting bull as he glared at me from behind a burnished mask. All I could see were his fierce dark eyes.

"Fight!" a voice rang out.

The Destroyer let out one cry and brought his sword down hard on the ground. It had begun.

Chapter Nine

Gold and Samson: Mixed Reactions

When I opened my eyes, the doctor's face loomed in front of them. He looked relieved. I knew why. If anything happened to me, he'd probably be severely punished, even put to death. "Thank the gods," he whispered. "I almost lost you." His forehead was beaded with sweat. "How are you feeling?"

"Weak," I grunted. "Don't fuss. I'll be all right."

"You have lost a lot of blood. You need to sleep."

"Is it over?" I tried to sit up.

He pushed me back down. "Stay still, Gold."

Phillip walked in suddenly.

"Phillip," I pushed the doctor's hand away and sat up anyway. "Samson, does he live?"

"He does," Phillip nodded with a smile.

"He killed the Destroyer then?"

"Not exactly," Phillip chuckled. "'Twas not the most glorious of battles, brother. The Destroyer dropped not because of Samson but due to his own efforts. Samson just wore him out."

The doctor shook his head and left us.

"No glory for Samson, or the house, but at least he is in one piece," I muttered. "Where is he?"

"At the master's house. We are all supposed to be there for the celebrations. The master is entertaining Phineas and his company. Since there was not really any clear winner, they seem civil. The master permitted me to come and see you. He wants a report back."

"Tell him I'm fine." I lay back down.

"I'm glad. I..." he trailed off and looked around in surprise as Sullis appeared in our midst.

I was surprised to see him walking around freely, but then maybe the lanista had rewarded him for helping me in the arena.

"Leave us, if you please," Sullis told Phillip. "I would have a word alone with Gold."

I nodded at Phillip. "Thank you, brother, for your concern." I waited for him to leave, curious as to what Sullis had to say. I still didn't understand why he did what he did.

"I owe you a debt," I told him, trying to sit up again as he came closer.

"You owe me nothing." He ran his gaze over me. "Lay back, rest."

The pain gripped my side as I lowered my body. "You fight like a gladiator."

"I am a gladiator," he met my gaze.

I was speechless.

"I belong to the house of Phineas. I was at one time his champion."

I narrowed my eyes. "Then how did you end up being bought by Simeon on the block?"

"It was arranged."

"Arranged?" I was totally perplexed.

"Phineas wants you. He's been obsessed with you from the first time he saw you fight in the arena. I didn't understand why before." He placed a hand on my chest, and caressed it for a second. "But I do now."

"Simeon would never sell me to Phineas."

He removed his hand. "But things have changed. Over the years, Phineas has offered ten of his fittest gladiators in your place, along with higher and higher amounts of gold. The answer has always been negative. You are the one source of his esteem, without you, he has nothing. And, you are fucking him."

I said nothing.

"I understand discretion. We are alike, you and I."

"We are not alike," I snapped. "You are a liar. You have deceived me, deceived everyone."

"I am sorry for that. I had no choice. But we are alike," he stressed. "Like you, I am a slave but I'm a privileged member of the lanista's household. I am only one step removed from being a free man."

"But you are not a free man," I bit back. "You still must obey."

He smiled faintly. "Yes. I must obey."

"What does your lanista want with me?"

"He wants to restore you to your former glory, put you back in the arena where you belong. He knows you are the best there is."

I met his gaze. My heart pounded in my chest at the prospect.

"Gold," Sullis said softly, "your life will be much better with us. You will not sleep in these filthy slave quarters. The lanista has a special room in his own house for those who bring him glory, and the ludi, it is a real training school with excellent trainers and—"

I calmed myself. "I will simply be exchanging one prison for another. Surrounding oneself by luxury does not freedom bring. Total obedience in one place is the same as another."

"It is true he asks for total obedience but still there is pleasure. And you will fight again, Gold." He moved closer still, his breath on my face. "I know it is what you want most. I saw you today, the look on your face as you held up Thad's bloody head. You were born for this," he leant down and moved his lips next to my cheek. "And you were born to fuck," he moaned gruffly. His hand moved down my chest and settled on my cock where he fondled me for a second.

I brushed his hand away.

He stood straight again. "The boy is safe," he announced suddenly. "I thought you'd like to know."

"The boy?" I sat up fast, the pain gripping me hard. "He was part of your plan as well? You son of..."

"We didn't know you would plan his escape. He was supposed to be here when Phineas arrived." He frowned. "You came close to ruining our plan. But it doesn't matter. Tonight Phineas will tell Simeon that he's knows how he illegally bought the son of a very prominent ally, a free individual, and if he doesn't agree to let you go at our very generous terms, we will inform the boy's family, along with the authorities. He will be finished."

"The boy is where?" I demanded angrily.

"Safe, with us now."

"He should be home with his family."

"You know yourself that the boy doesn't wish to go home. He hates his life. And if we let him go, then our plan won't work."

"Your master is no better than Simeon," I accused.

"You'll think differently in the end. And I'm sorry that you will be separated from Samson. One day, you might even have to meet him in the arena." He walked a few feet away. "I'm sure you won't find it as easy when you hold his head up in victory."

I sucked in some breath. That thought settled over me like a shroud.

"Sleep now," he raised a hand. "You'll feel better soon."

"You're lucky to be alive, Samson," Phillip told me as we stood quietly off to the side, and watched the small group of people help themselves to the wine and plates of food going around.

I wanted to ask about Gold but then Claudius stopped in front of us. He'd overheard the conversation.

"Yes," Claudius said. He flicked one of my nipples with his finger. "Lucky the big clod fell on his ugly face. However, didn't make for much of a main event. My father was disappointed."

Simeon didn't look that disappointed to me. In fact, he looked pretty cheerful considering he'd lost one of his prized gladiators. Thad's demise seemed of no consequence to him as he continued to brag about Gold and his victory in the arena.

I, however, still had a hard time digesting what I'd seen today—the look on Gold's face as he held up Thad's head. There was a gleam in his eyes I'd never seen before. It was unnerving.

I looked up and noticed that Phillip had drawn the attention of two young men now. I watched as one of them drew off the loin cloth that hung around Phillip's waist.

The other man wrapped his fingers around Phillip's cock and began jerking it from left to right.

Phillip tried not to move but I knew it was a challenge for him. It was probably painful, never mind irritating.

"Nice and large," one laughed. He tipped back his glass and emptied it, letting it fall onto the floor. "Ever been fucked by one of these?" he asked his companion loudly.

His companion was busy examining Phillips hard, muscled chest. "Um," he circled one nipple with his finger tip, "no, but I'd love it. Wonder if we could. Uncle Phineas never lets us play with them at home. He plays with them, though, and often."

Claudius stood nearby and watched the scene closely. He seemed to be enjoying the show.

When one of the young men moved around to the back of Phillip, Claudius intervened, "Boys, you can't violate the gladiators now, and especially not in public. Only I can do that."

"How much?" the one who stood behind Phillip asked. "How much gold would it take to let me fuck him?" He was clutching Phillip's buttocks in his hands.

Claudius sobered. "No price. The house slaves are for fucking, not the gladiators."

"I'd love to fuck Gold." One of them licked Phillip's shoulder. "Have you ever fucked him, gladiator?"

Phillip remained mute.

"Phillip, and especially Gold," Claudius snapped, suddenly pulling Phillip away from them, "are off limits. Now, crawl back to your mothers and leave my gladiators alone."

They walked off, muttering about how rude Claudius was.

I resented the possessiveness in his voice. I wanted to scream at him, tell him that Gold didn't belong to him but there was no use in doing that. When it came down to it, he owned Gold. He owned me. We were his to do with as he pleased.

Claudius pulled Phillip and me close to him. "You're mine, both of you." He let his gaze move over us. I could smell the alcohol on his breath.

He motioned to both of us to follow him.

Phillip looked at me, and I at him. We both knew what was to come.

He took us behind the curtains of his private chambers, away from the party guests. Claudius lay back on the lounge chair, and ordered Phillip to pull the curtain around us. He looked at me. "Take it off," he indicated the covering around my waist.

I slowly removed the loin cloth and let it fell to the floor, feeling very uncomfortable.

"Um, very, very nice, both of you. Now," he spread his legs and began to rub his own cock, "take each other's cock in hand and make them hard. Go on," he breathed, "do it."

Phillip reached out and began to fondle my cock and I stroked his as well. And after a few minutes, we were both breathing hard. Our cocks were standing straight out and brushing against each other sensuously.

"Stand there, don't move," Claudius directed. He got up off the bed with his own cock protruding out between the folds of his robe. He ran his hands over both our chests, pulled and pinched our nipples until we were both moaning softly. "Don't touch your body," he commanded. He slapped our cocks hard until tears stung our eyes, handled our balls roughly, and rolled them in his hands. At one time, I thought I was going to collapse. Our cocks were both slick with come and ready to spill over and still he made us wait. "If you come, I'll beat you," he whispered.

He walked around in back of us. I felt a finger invade my ass. I closed my eyes, moaned, my hips thrusting in and out. I thought of Gold, his hard cock in my ass. I bit my lip. Claudius did the same to Phillip. He began finger fucking both our asses at the same pace, twisting in and out from side to side.

Suddenly he stopped, pulled out of us, and came around front again. He pushed me onto my knees and placed his cock against my lips. "Suck," he grunted.

I took it into my mouth and began to suck his cock. He turned sideways and glanced back at Phillip. "On your knees, down. Spread my ass and insert your tongue inside of me."

Within minutes, Claudius was moaning and coming in my mouth as I swallowed obediently and Phillip continued to play in his ass.

Phillip reached between his thighs as he rimmed him and stroked my cock. I did the same to him. Claudius didn't seem to notice or care.

When Claudius had come in my mouth, and I finished licking him clean as he instructed, he ordered both of us to lie on the floor on our backs. "Play with each other's cocks. Make them stand up," he demanded. He was rubbing himself again, his tongue playing around his lips as he watched us with lust-filled eyes. At one point, he took a whip off the wall and held it in his hand. I couldn't help wonder what he planned to do with it.

After we were hard again, Claudius got on his knees in between our bodies and played with both our cocks. He fondled our balls again, and pinched our nipples. The exploration of his hands made it clear that we were truly his property to play with as he pleased. Suddenly, he stood and snaked the whip down the length of my body. I held my breath. He lightly whipped my chest, my nipples, and my cock. I dared not cry out. Then he turned and did the same to Phillp, who turned his face away.

The whip caused the blood to rise in my cock, and in spite of the pain, which was mild, I was feeling extremely needy. If he hadn't been my master, I would have grabbed him and pumped into his ass like a mad man.

Claudius threw the whip aside suddenly. He straddled me, leant over and sucked both my sore nipples then guided my cock into his ass. He bounced on it, used it, and made it slice into his ass at various angles. I winced from the sheer brutality of it but eventually I came, and my entire body vibrated with the pleasure.

He crawled off of me and switched to Phillip. He glanced at me. "Make his nipples stiff as I take his cock."

I rolled on my side. Phillip's nipples were already hard from the whipping and a delight to play with. I slid my fingers over each hard nub then pinched and pulled on them. Phillip licked his lips as Claudius took hold of his erection. He moaned out loud as I continued the nipple play, actually enjoying it. Claudius had already swallowed Phillip's cock with his ass. He used him as brutally as he had me, and Phillip pumped up into him, thrashing in a frenzy of heat and need.

Claudius crawled off of Phillip's hips and lay back on the floor. His chest heaved. He wiped the come off his cock and licked his fingers. "Very nice, boys," he said. "Now, go back to the party before you're missed. And always remember, you are mine to do with as I please. And let's keep this between ourselves, shall we?"

We wrapped the loin cloths around our hips and left quietly. Neither one of us said anything. I glanced at the red marks on my chest and guessed they'd fade soon enough.

As we walked now back to the main room, we noticed that it seemed quiet. The guests seemed to have gone. Then suddenly, we both paused as we heard two men arguing.

"I invite you into my home, give you my hospitality and this is how I am thanked?"

"Simeon," Phillip said softly.

I nodded. I hoped the guard at the end of the hall wouldn't suddenly see us and take us back to the slave quarters.

Phineas' voice retorted. "You are the one who broke the law. You've been careless. I've offered you my protection."

"Yes, in exchange for my most valuable possession!"

I reached out and clutched Phillip's arm. "Gold?"

Phillip put a finger to his lips and we hunkered against the wall.

"At a very generous price."

"My answer is no."

"Then I will have no choice but to report your activities. The family is well connected. Your chance to enter politics will end. You will always be what you are now, Simeon, a useless lanista with a second rate ludi. Put this behind you, rebuild. I offer you ten of my finest, and a trainer. I will give you a trainer as a bonus."

There was silence.

"No," I whispered to Phillip. "He can't...he can't sell him."

The guard had spotted us now and he came walking down the corridor. "What are you two doing?"

"Nothing. Waiting," Phillip said.

"It's all right," Claudius said as he came towards them, waving at the guard. "You may take them back to their quarters."

"Come on," the guard barked.

I went as slowly as I could, hoping to hear more. As we got to the main door, I saw Sullis. He looked right at me and bowed his head then gave me the biggest smile.

On the way back to the slave quarters, Phillip looked at me. "What was that all about?"

"I have no idea. I need to see Gold."

"Not tonight," the guard replied, overhearing. "Wait here."

A few minutes later, another guard appeared. He motioned to me, Phillip and Gabien. "Come on," he grunted.

"Where are we going?" I asked Phillip.

Phillip shrugged.

Gabien leant closer to me as we walked. "I don't know but it has something to do with Gold. He was dragged out of here a few minutes ago by two guards. I think they're going to whip him."

"Whip him?" I echoed. "He's been hurt. He can't be whipped. And why? Why would they…?"

"Did you not notice the absence of the boy today?" Gabien mentioned.

In all the excitement I hadn't paid it any mind. I gasped. "Yes. Maris wasn't in the arena." Then I knew. Gold had helped him escape. "Oh no," I gasped.

"Punishable by death," Phillip muttered.

As we rounded the ludi, and entered the main courtyard, my entire body stiffened. Gold was there, his wrists tied up over his head to two separate poles and his ankles likewise. He was completely naked, and one of the guards stood poised with a whip in his hand. "Let this be a warning to you," the guard called out. "Disobedience, aiding a slave to escape, or violence against the guards will not be tolerated. Ten lashes, and if it was my decision, more."

Ten lashes. I strained against my constraints and wished he'd just get on with it. I glanced up at one point and saw the slave girl who'd been my accomplice. There was terror on her young face, but she needn't be scared.

"Your conspirator in this crime," the guard yelled at me. "Tell me who, and I'll show mercy with the whip."

I murmured something.

"I can't hear you." He moved closer.

I murmured again.

"Speak up, what is the name?"

When he was close enough, I raised my head. "This is what you seek," I cried out and spat directly in his face.

He wiped his face with his hand and stepped back. "You're going to wish you hadn't done that, barbarian." He moved around behind me and let the whip fly. It came down on my back like a razor, wracking pain throughout my body. I gasped and bit my lip. *Embrace the pain. Embrace it. Don't let it break you.*

It came down on me a second time, then a third, and a forth. It made a whizzing sound as it curled in the air. I moaned softly each time, fighting not to lose consciousness. I didn't cry out.

Then I heard a voice in the distance. "Stop! Stop! Stop this immediately."

Though the pain, I heard someone say my name. A hand picked up my chin and looked into my eyes.

"Take him down," the voice told the soldiers, "and bring him into the house." Someone stroked my hair, and said words I couldn't hear.

"Wait!" a voice replied. "Only the owner of this slave can do that. I have been ordered to—"

146

"I am the owner of this slave," the man's voice replied. "Do it now!"

I hadn't had any sleep. I lay awake all night thinking of Gold, thinking of everything that had happened and trying to make sense of it all. The sound of that whip, the way it had cut into Gold's broad back, blood and sweat flying in the air, and Gold's stubborn refusal to cry out for mercy. I'd felt it as if it was happening to me, so had Phillip and Gabien.

I had a hard time accepting that Phineas had bought Gold. How had that happened? Why would Simeon let him go? We were all dumbstruck at the way Phineas had touched Gold, speaking to him so softly, his outrage at what had been done to him.

None of it made sense.

The next morning, Gold was brought back to the slave quarters. I went right to him. He was sleeping on his stomach when I walked in. I watched him, forfeiting my breakfast before training. I hesitated to wake him, knowing that sleep at least brought relief from the pain. His back was a mess.

Finally, I stood at his side, looking at his face. I wasn't sure how I would endure his leaving. I supposed we'd never see one another again.

Gold's eyes opened. He smiled at me. I was never so happy to see that smile in my life. "Are you better? Are you in much pain?"

"I'll survive."

"Gold," I squeezed his hand, "why did you do it, why did you...you know the penalty for helping a slave escape. It could have meant your death."

He didn't answer, only squeezed my hand back.

"Phineas is now your owner?"

"Yes."

"How?"

"It's complicated. Sullis told me."

"Sullis?" I stiffened. "And what does he know?"

"He belongs to Phineas. He was once one of us."

"That cock of Zeus. He..." I wanted to kill him.

"He had no choice. He is as much slave as we are. He was only following orders."

I began to tremble. "You will leave here, leave me? We will never see each other again."

"That is regretful, but Samson, I will fight again." He lifted his head.

I saw the hope in his eyes, and I resented it. "You would rather risk your life in the arena than stay here with me. I love you, Gold. Doesn't that mean anything to you?"

"I told you, don't love me."

"I don't give a damn what you told me. I do. I can't..." I trailed off, swallowing hard.

"I am powerless to do anything," he told me.

"You want to be their puppet. You want to kill and die in the arena to entertain the Romans. You want that more than me." Tears filled my eyes and I turned away.

He grabbed my arm and pulled me back. "It's who I am. It's all I know."

"That's not true. You were a free man once. You were educated and noble. You had pride and..."

"I'm a criminal," he said softly and turned on his side.

I narrowed my eyes. He had never told me how he'd come to be here. "Criminal? I thought you were a soldier, captured like me."

"I killed my own father."

I blinked. That was a heinous crime. "You killed your own father? Why?" I looked down at his face.

"It's better left in the past. And I'd do it again in a heartbeat. Oh, Samson, can't you see? It's my fate, my destiny, to fight and die in that arena, to regain the honour I lost when I disgraced my family's name. There is no room in my heart for love."

That hurt much more than any sword could. I nodded. "Very well then. And Sullis, what of him? If you go with him, will there be room in your heart for him, or will you also tell him not to talk of love?"

"You talk nonsense. There is no sentiment between Sullis and myself."

"He saved your life in that arena yesterday and I see the way he looks at you, that hot, young gladiator with the smouldering eyes. I wonder if finally he will be the one to melt that hard heart of yours." I shook my head.

"Stop it, Samson," he muttered.

"I'll never forget you, Nicolaus. I will remember you, and love you until I take my last breath."

I watched Samson as he turned and walked away from me. I closed my eyes for a second. I could still taste him on my tongue, and feel my cock inside of his body. I was grateful to him for restoring desire in my heart. And I knew that deep inside, I loved him as much, maybe even more than he loved me. But he could never know that.

I was unsure of my destiny. I wanted only one thing, and that hadn't changed, to die in the arena with honour. It didn't really matter whose house I did it under, or whose hand took my life.

I fell into a restless sleep, many thoughts speaking to me. *Love.* It was a strange word, complicated, nothing like desire which was simple and pure. I loved my mother and my sister, but that love was uncomplicated by physical need. Even so, that love had led me here to this place of pain and misery.

When I had slit my father's throat, I'd felt such a deep sense of satisfaction, the likes of which I'd never known before. There was this feeling of finality. *You'll never hurt them again.*

He'd been a hard and unfeeling man, my father, blessed due to his connection to the king, a man prone to the drink, prone to brutality. People pretended to love him, but only because he had power and money. His patronage was worth everything to some and with that, he made people into his personal whores. He could make and break lives, and he did so without care.

When he drank, he was a monster. He beat my mother black and blue, and began to repeatedly violate my sister at the age of ten. I came home from military school on visits with a mix of apprehension and urgency. I worried about my mother and sister constantly.

As a boy, there was little I could do. My father never struck me, only the females, but he never hugged me either. I was told to be a man before I even knew what that was, and to my father that meant drink hard, fuck hard and fight to win.

The military training moulded me into exactly the kind of man my father wanted me to be—unsentimental, hyper masculine, and brutal.

One summer, I returned to find my sister gone. My mother had told me in confidence that she was with child and my father had sent her away to be punished. The paternity was blamed on a soldier in my father's employment and he had been condemned to death. I knew the child belonged to my father. I insisted on knowing where he'd sent my sister. He refused to tell me. So, I killed him.

When I think back, I realise I was filled with rage at that moment—that all the times I couldn't act were complied into this one time when I could. I was a man now, without sentiment. And my father had reaped the direct reward of what he'd sowed.

As it turned out, my mother didn't protect me from the authorities when she found me standing over my father with blood on my hands. She actually spit on me as I was taken away by the guards. And shortly after, while I languished in a prison cell, I found out that my sister had died in childbirth. My uncle, a magistrate, who knew the character of my father, could have saved me, but he did nothing. Due to the fact I came from a prominent family, I was sold on the block rather than put on the cross. Now I know that dying on the cross would have been more humane.

So, love terrified me. Love brought pain and, for the most part, had always been unrequited. No one had ever loved me, except maybe for my sister, but she was dead, a victim of a senseless world which had little use for women. But it was the only world I had. If I was put back into the arena, there I would finally have a taste of freedom, freedom to choose where and when I would die.

With Samson, even if I gave into what I felt for him, we could never be together, especially now that I had been sold. The undeniable realisation that now Samson and I would be forever separated was overwhelming. Finally I had accepted the inevitability of love, only to have it ripped away.

Samson watched quietly the day they took me away. I saw the pain in his eyes. I lifted a hand, gave him a faint smile.

He didn't smile back. Before I was completely out of earshot, I heard him call out to me. "Nicolaus, we'll be together again. I promise!"

HOUSE OF PHINEAS

Dedication

For those who fall in love with the story.

Chapter One

New Beginnings
Gold...House of Phineas

I opened my eyes and looked around. Gone were the rustic brick walls and the musty dampness. My head rested on a pillow and I was lying prone on a comfortable day bed, a sheet of satin under me.

I had no idea how long I'd been here or how I got to this place. The breeze blew back a haze of white curtains in the distance and suddenly a man walked through them. He wore a toga and had a short cropped beard. "So, how are you, Gold?"

I glanced down at my wounds and noticed they had begun to heal. "I...where am I?"

"You are at the House of Phineas. We've been watching you closely. You will soon be fit again." He brought me some liquid in a silver flask. "Drink," he urged.

I lifted my head, drank and sputtered a little. I wiped my mouth on the back of my hand.

"You can sit up. Move around a little. It will be a good thing."

"How long have I been here?"

"More than a fortnight. You had a fever. You slipped in and out of it."

I wiped a hand over the stubble on my face.

"Today you will take a bath and the slaves will shave you. I will have food brought."

I threw my legs over the side of the day bed. I was still wearing the raggedy loin cloth I'd had on in the arena. I wasn't shackled. Dizziness seized me for a moment but I fought it.

The doctor watched me. I stood on my own and walked a few steps, stumbled, placed a hand on the wall and continued.

"You may wander around. Explore a little," the man told me. "You are free to go where you please."

I looked up in surprise.

Suddenly a naked slave girl walked in with a tray of food. There was cheese, meats, and grapes. I reached over and grabbed some of the grapes in my hand and ate hungrily.

"Easy," the doctor told me. "You need to go slow."

I nodded, and began to actually chew the food.

The slave girl smiled shyly at me as she waited patiently for me to devour what was left on the platter.

I walked through the curtains after I'd finished. A soldier stood guard in the hallway. He glanced at me then away as I continued down the corridor. The house was enormous, far larger than Simeon's, the walls hung with elaborate tapestries. I arrived at the front and looked out the door. My eyes grew large. In the distance, there stood an enormous structure, off in the field. Even from this far, I could hear the shouting, the cracking of the whips, the clacking of the swords. I breathed in the fragrant breeze. It called to me, magnolias and apple blossoms.

"You like it?" a voice asked.

I turned suddenly to see Phineas standing there.

I lowered my head. "Yes, master."

He laughed slightly. "I love the sound of that, you calling me master." He reached out and touched my biceps. "I've waited a long time for you, Gold."

"Yes, master," I said. I wasn't sure what else to say.

"You are anxious, aren't you?"

"I am."

He smiled. His hand continued its exploration, moving across my chest, and touching the scars. "I'm anxious too, to see you fight, to..." he pressed his lips to my chest, "have you in my bed."

He stepped away as if it was a chore. He licked his lips. "You may make use of the house as you like," he said. "You are my guest."

Guest? "Guests get to leave."

He looked at me sharply. "I'm sure you regret that."

I didn't reply.

"I will give you a lot of freedom. I will pamper you like none other," he said. "But I will not tolerate disrespect or disobedience. Is that clear?"

I nodded.

"You want to fight again, something that Simeon kept you from. I will give you that. What I ask in return is your complete submission to me, in all things. Take off that dirty loin cloth." He clapped his hands. "My personal slave will take you to the bath and shave you. I'm sure you will find him pleasing."

A young man appeared now, his body naked and oiled.

I couldn't help but gawk at him. He was mesmerising.

"You like?" the master asked me.

"He is beautiful," I said, respectfully.

He smiled. "After your bath and your shave, perhaps I will let you take him."

"As you please, master," I replied respectfully but the thought excited me.

The young man walked across the terrazzo floor, and I followed. The master walked at my shoulder. He placed a hand on my neck and bent my head forward.

I was aware of many slaves standing around watching the procession.

The master sat on a lounge near the bath and clapped his hands again. We went down into the warm water and I sat. The water felt good and I actually uttered a little moan of pleasure.

The beautiful slave began to wash me, limb by limb, and by the time he got to my penis, I was filled with lust. It was the way he stroked me, so sensuous and seductive.

"Out of the water," the master demanded.

I stood up, water running down my body, my cock hard and ready.

The master stood and walked over to where we were.

The slave boy dried me carefully then began to rub scented oil into my skin.

Phineas' hand reached out, palm side up and the boy poured scented oil into it. He grasped my cock and began sliding his fingers up and down. I let my head go back, licked my lips.

The master's robe fell on the floor. "Leave us," he barked to the slave boy, who hurried off. He moved around the back of me and wrapped his arms around me. His slippery hand moved over my chest, across my nipples as the other continued to stroke my aching cock.

He pulled me back in his arms, and forced my head onto his shoulder. Taking my mouth hungrily with his, he

158

groaned and stroked my cock faster, his own erection pressing against my ass.

He pinched and played with my nipples then moved his hand to the back where he impaled my ass with three of his fingers. He began fucking me with those fingers, stroking my cock, only slowing when he thought I might spill my seed.

I moaned again, and moved my body against him and he nibbled my ear. He was skilled with his hands and he had me completely in his power. It had nothing to do with my status. Slave or free man, it would have made no difference.

"Ah, my young stud," he whispered. "I knew we would find such pleasure together. Your body is exquisite. I could spend eternity touching it, playing with it. I want to inhale you, swallow you whole. I want to fuck your ass, your face. I want to make you mine. Say it, say, yes master, I am your whore."

"Yes, master," I swallowed, my hips working, "Oh...yes, I'm your whore."

He stopped stroking my cock. He cuffed it instead, squeezed it then reached under me to fondle my balls. Another finger went up inside of me. I moaned deeply, my anus stretched further than I thought possible.

He pushed deeply. I let out a cry.

"To dominate you like this," the master groaned, "is immensely pleasing." He pinched my nipples hard again and slapped my cock. Then suddenly, he pushed me to my knees.

He stood in front of me now, his cock touching my lips. "Take it, take it and suck it."

I brought him quickly to orgasm. He stumbled back and gasped as I stayed on my knees, my cock aching for release.

After he'd recovered, he came close again. He played slowly with each nipple until I thought I'd die. He reached down and handled my cock but didn't bring it release. Then he ordered me to stand. "Beautiful," he whispered. "You want me, don't you? You want to fuck me, or fuck anything, don't you, whore?"

I nodded. "Yes, master." At this state of heightened excitability, I'd be inclined to fuck almost anyone.

"Not yet," he whispered with a smile. "I want you hard. Stay that way," he insisted.

"Yes, master," I muttered, narrowing my brow. *For how long?*

He picked up his robe and called for the slave. The young man hurried in.

"Shave him, and make sure he stays hard."

"Yes, master," the slave nodded. "It will be my pleasure." He indicated that I should lay back down on the day bed as he began to prepare the razor.

Phineas waited while I had lowered myself again on the bed. He reached out and pushed my thighs apart. "I will let you have the slave eventually for my pleasure," Phineas smiled at me, "but tonight, you're all mine. I've waited too long to share you."

The slave began to lather my lower face with some creamy soap. He leaned over me and brushed his fingers over my chest, moved them down to my sex and gripped my shaft in his hand. He smiled and squeezed my cock a few times.

I swallowed.

"I wish I could take care of your problem," he said, removing his hand and tipping back my head. He ran the sharp knife over my jaw and rinsed it in a bowl of water nearby. "If I did, I would be punished." He licked his lips. "Might be worth it. Would it be worth it, Golden one?"

I stifled a moan. My cock pulsed with a life of its own, the slave's handling of it a few seconds ago didn't help its strife.

"Why do they call you Gold?" he asked, a hand balancing on my chest while the other hand skilfully rubbed the knife again over my bristled jaw. "Your hair is dark, not golden."

"It hasn't to do with the colour of my hair. It has to do with the amount of gold I won for my lanista."

"Ah." He rinsed his knife. "I have heard that."

"What is your name?" I breathed, looking into blue eyes, eyes that reminded me of Samson.

"My name is Jemin."

"Where do you come from, Jemin?" He had the look of the exotic, Egyptian maybe.

"I don't know," he said as he wiped at my face. "I've always been here. I believe I was born here in this house."

"And your mother, who was she?"

"A house slave. She died giving birth to me."

"And your father?"

"I have no idea who he was. It is rumoured that he was a soldier. He might have been another slave in this house. When I was a boy, my master was Phineas the first, the father of my present master."

I nodded, thinking that he may have been fathered by Phineas' father. It happened all the time. Illegitimate children born by slaves were never acknowledged. He did bear some resemblance to Phineas. "Was he kind to you, the father of Phineas?"

"He ignored me for the most part but I always obeyed. His wife mothered me at times and Phineas, who is ten years older, used to play with me when I was young."

"He is kind to you then?" The knife began to scrape the other side of my face.

"He is a..." He lowered his voice to my ear, "a benevolent master, as long as you are obedient but if you defy him..." He trailed off as his gaze strayed over my body. "Oh no," he said suddenly. "You are..." He pointed, "no longer stimulated."

I glanced down at myself. This talk had distracted my cock somehow and I was fading.

"The master will not be pleased." He put down the knife and began to touch me. His touch was quite delicate as if he was afraid to hurt me. He lifted my cock and stroked it a few times. We both watched as it revived. I licked my lips, lifted my hips. I wanted him to take it in his mouth. I closed my eyes. "Gods, suck me."

"I can't," he shook his head as he backed away. "I want to. I can't."

I nodded. "How old are you, Jemin?"

"I believe that I am nineteen," he replied, attending to my face again. This time his hand trembled.

"Stop," I told him, laughing. "You hand is unstable and I'd like to keep my face."

He smiled. "And such a nice face it is."

I licked my lips again. My gaze moved over his smooth naked chest and I noticed that his sex was also wanting. "I'd love to be inside of you right now."

He turned away, rinsed his knife. "The master will allow you to have me soon enough. I am anxious," he told me as he met my gaze again and swiped the knife over my cheeks. "You are large. Many of the men the master has gifted me to have been small and...quite unsatisfying. Did you have a lover where you were before?"

Something felt painful suddenly but I pushed it away, the love I had for Samson rising to the surface. "I did," I answered. "But I must put him behind me now." My words rang false on my tongue. I don't believe that I could ever do that.

"Was he beautiful?" He wiped my face again.

I nodded. "Yes."

Jemin put the knife aside. "You are finished." His hand settled on my chest and moved down to my stomach. He handled my cock again, massaged my testicle. My chest heaved. I reached out and covered his hand with mine, pressed it to my cock. "Please?" I pleaded. "Release me and then you can revive me again. Please?"

He swallowed. "I cannot." He kept his hand there though, as his gaze penetrated mine.

"Hello Gold," a voice announced. "Am I interrupting something?"

Jemin jerked his hand away quickly and turned to the bowl, busying himself with something.

I found myself looking at Sullis. "Not at all," I said.

His gaze darted to Jemin. "What were you doing?" he demanded.

Jemin turned around, the bowl of murky water in his hands. "The master told me to keep him hard. He was fading."

Sullis nodded. "You looked as if you found it a most enjoyable task."

He lowered his head.

"Leave us," he told him as he moved closer to where I lay.

Jemin bobbed his head and hurried away.

I went to sit up but he placed a hand on my chest and pushed me gently back down. "Don't. I'm enjoying the view."

I didn't comment but at that moment, I felt my nakedness most acutely.

"I wanted to say welcome," he said softly, his tongue tasting his own lips as he let his gaze wander over me. "How are you feeling? You wounds seem to be healing nicely." He reached out and touched my shoulder. "What about your back?"

I shrugged. "I don't think about it."

He laughed. "No. You wouldn't. If you're feeling up to it, I have been given permission to take you to the ludi, show you around. I want you to meet the trainers."

"Very well," I said but I looked down at my erection doubtfully. "Am I to go to the ludi in this condition?"

He laughed. "No. The master has given me permission to…" he trailed off as he lowered his hand onto my cock, "take care of it for you."

I closed my eyes. "Thank the gods," I whispered.

He chuckled softly. "Is it painful?" he whispered. He stroked my hair back as he wrapped his fist around my sex.

"Uncomfortable."

He lowered his head and ran his tongue around the head of my cock. He met my eyes at the same time.

I sucked in some breath. "Do you plan to tease me?"

He shook his head. "Oh no," he shook his head. "I plan to please you." He licked around the head of my cock again and moved his fingers down my shaft. His other hand reached under and cupped my balls and he opened his mouth and took my cock. He swirled his tongue around the shaft, and sucked with his lips up and down as he reached further under me and stroked my anus.

As I bucked into his mouth, I felt my arms being pulled up over my head. My body was yanked up, and my head lowered over the end of the day bed. I glanced up to see Phineas standing behind me. He gripped my wrists, pressed his hand on my forehead so that he could widen my jaw and lowered his own cock deep into my throat.

I tasted his cum on my lips, in my throat and with his urging, I closed my lips around his cock and sucked and licked him. He placed his hands on my shoulders and began to thrust wildly in and out of my mouth.

Sullis was driving me wild with his finger in my ass as he bobbed his head up and down my cock.

The vibrations from the hard ruts of my master made me feel as if my head was about to come away from shoulders. My body jerked of its own volition as the master ejaculated down my throat. He lifted my head some so I wouldn't choke, and at the same time, my cock pumped into Sullis's experienced mouth.

"My fine slut," Phineas hissed as he reached down my chest and pinched both my nipples.

Sullis wiped his mouth on his hand and stepped back. The master moved around to the front and crawled on top of me. He covered me with his body then lifted my legs up over his shoulders. "I want to fuck you now, Gold. Your ass, your cock, it's mine."

My head went back as he plunged his cock inside of me. I was amazed that he was erect again so fast. He rode me hard but his cock was of average size and after I adjusted to it, it wasn't at all painful.

He came quickly. His body trembled as he grabbed my thighs and lowered his head, his chest rising and falling quickly. He crawled off of me and looked at Sullis. "Fuck him," he urged. "You want to."

"Oh yes, thank you," Sullis said. "Thank you, master."

"Down on all fours," Phineas barked.

I slid off the day bed and went to my knees. With his foot, Phineas pushed me forward.

"Fuck him," he told Sullis again.

Sullis got down on his knees at my back. He took his time touching my nipples, my cock. "I want you to be ready," he whispered in my ear. He was stroking my cock as he invaded my ass. I bit down hard on my lip. Sullis was blessed by the gods with his large cock. It was thick and long and filled my ass to capacity—and it hurt. I gritted my teeth. A gladiator embraced pain and that's what I did. When he began to ride me, I moaned and the pain rapidly turned into searing pleasure.

* * * *

Samson…House of Simeon

Simeon was not in good spirits. He stayed cloistered in the big house, brooding. Even the arrival of the ten new gladiators to the ludi didn't seem to appease him. It was Claudius who took control and saw that all was in order as the new gladiators were assigned their cells.

I watched the parade of muscled contenders as the guards brought them inside and Claudius dictated they should be lined up along the wall. Phillip, Gabien and I stood on the sidelines quietly. We weren't quite sure what all these new arrivals would mean for us in the long run. However, we did know that we'd have to work much harder if one of us were to become the new champion of the house of Simeon. The gladiators before us were seasoned and experienced.

Claudius walked up and down now inspecting them, his arms behind his back. He didn't know the first thing about gladiators, but he liked to give the impression that he did. "Trainer," he bellowed, "step forward."

I did a quick head count. Eleven. One of these gladiators would become the new trainer. It only served to remind me that Gold was gone, lost to me forever.

Phillip seemed to sense my lament because he reached down beside me and took my hand a moment.

Ever since we'd come together for Claudius that night in his private chambers, Phillip had been quick to touch me. I found it both stimulating and unsettling. I knew he wanted me. In my own way, I wanted to surrender to that touch, but Gold had my heart. He always would. I don't know why. It made no sense. It's just the way it was.

Phillip let go of my hand as a man took two steps out of line and Claudius began to examine him. "What is your name, slave?"

"Julian," he replied, his eyes lowered.

"Julian, um," Claudius circled him and ran his hands over his well muscled biceps. "Strong. What brought you to this fate?"

"My family," he replied. "I refused to marry so my father volunteered me to the job for ten years."

"Nice father," Claudius chuckled. The guards sniggered as well. "Why did you refuse to marry I wonder? Do you prefer cock to cunt?"

"Yes, master," he said.

"I see." He looked down the line. "Strip. Prepare to be branded. You are now the property of the House of Simeon. You will fight for the honour and glory of this house. Fight well and you shall be rewarded. We are currently without a champion. The prize is there for the one who is worthy of it."

He stepped back. His gaze caressed the nakedness of the eleven men who stood in front of him. Outside one of the guards fired up the branding iron. I wrinkled up my nose.

"I suppose we'll be smelling burnt flesh until the gods stop feuding."

Gabien found that funny. "You got that, brother. What do you think of the specimens?"

I shrugged. "No one impressed me." But I'd lied. There was something very appealing about our new trainer. *Julian.* I had the distinct impression that he would be a strict taskmaster. I wondered when he'd fought in the arena. His story intrigued me. To give your own son into slavery was severe. Julian must have been adamant about his refusal to marry and produce offspring. I wonder who had trained him, what his story was. I imagined I would eventually find out.

We wandered outside as the eleven men lined up, naked in the sunlight, each waiting for the soldier to place the brand on his arm. I kept my eyes on Julian who headed up the line. He reminded me somewhat of Gold, which was probably why he appealed. Dark hair, dark eyes, tall and massively built, his admission that he preferred to be in the company of men excited me.

Gold had been gone now for over two weeks. I was in bad need of a distraction, something which would get me past the misery of losing him. Perhaps this big, rebellious Roman was all the medicine I needed.

* * * *

"It will be a big change for you," Sullis mentioned as we walked in the direction of the ludi. "Can you handle being dominated by another?"

I narrowed my eyes. "Is that a joke?" I asked him.

He smiled. "I mean, can you handle taking instruction from another? After all, you were the trainer at Simeon's.

Now, you will be under the guidance of a trainer, several in fact."

"One can always improve and learn. Perhaps these trainers can teach me something."

He met my gaze. "I doubt that."

The structure which served as the gladiator quarters was enormous and Sullis informed me that it housed seventy gladiators to date, which included five trainers. The cells were extremely small and hardly large enough to stand in. I noted that the accommodations for gladiators of Simeon were actually a little more spacious and less restrictive. Of course, it was easier to keep track of and control a small number, so increased restriction was most likely a result of the volume.

There was great activity in the yard as men trained vigorously with wooden swords, either challenging one another or attacking the posts which were set up for training.

I stood by with Sullis and watched the activity, noticing the curious glances I received. I recognised no one except the present champion, the Destroyer, whom Samson had tied in the arena.

He stared down at me as I walked past but quickly went back to his jousting.

Sullis pointed out the five trainers although it would have been unnecessary. They were easy enough to spot. He rattled off the names, and I quickly decided not to try and remember them all. I would meet them all individually soon enough.

The first trainer I met was a man named Horace. He was a Jew who'd survived the revolt. He wasn't a big man but he was quick, and not long on words. He nodded to me when Sullis told him who I was. He paused, studied me for a moment then said, "You are the greatest who ever walked among us." I acknowledged his comment with a polite nod and he quickly went back to his work. I marvelled at his speed as he drove his opponent back and put him down to the ground.

We walked on. "Your name commands great respect here."

"Hmm. And I'm sure it will command much jealousy as well. It would be best to put me here in the gladiator quarters." Although I didn't relish the idea, it was better not to hold me above them like this. "It is unheard of, for me to share the lanista's house."

"We have a private place in the back of the house. We are separate enough."

"We?" I lifted an eyebrow.

"Yes. You will share my space. Does it cause you grief?"

"No. It is better than sleeping here," I muttered.

He placed a hand on my back. "Don't concern yourself with the envy of your peers. You have earned some privilege. You were Simeon's champion, and soon you will also be the champion of this house. Come. We return to the house. The master will have a party to show you off to his guests. Tomorrow you will begin to train again."

Our quarters were two day beds separated by curtains. It was far more comfortable than I was used to. I was resting comfortably on one of the beds when I heard a young excited voice cry out, "Gold!"

A small boy was on top of me now, hugging me tightly. I sat up and gripped his face on both sides, pleased to see him. "Maris! Are you well, boy?"

"Yes, very well. I have missed you. I was so excited when Phineas told me you were coming."

"Maris," I said, looking into his eyes. "Don't you miss your family?"

"No. I want to stay here. I want to be a gladiator, like you."

I chuckled. "Look at me, boy, see the marks on my flesh. Are you sure you want to be like me?"

He nodded. "Yes. I love you,"

I was touched by the sentiment. I watched as one of the house slaves came to take him away. He was well dressed, looked fit and well. What could I say? I, too, had had an unhappy home. I was glad to see him safe.

* * * *

"Is he to be your new plaything?" Claudius sidled up beside me as I stood watching each man receive the brand.

I glanced at him. "I don't understand, master."

"Julian. He reminds you of Gold perhaps, masterful, masculine, keeping his emotions hidden. You like that kind of man."

I didn't answer. I wanted to tell him that if I remembered right, so did he, but he would have considered that insolent, and I would have been punished. I bit my tongue.

"I will summon you and Phillip tonight," he paused, smiled, "and maybe Julian."

For some reason, my pulse sped up.

He studied me for a moment and laughed. "Maybe," he glanced over his shoulder at me he walked away.

"What was that all about?" Phillip asked as I headed back inside.

"It's just Claudius, who enjoys his power immensely."

Phillip laughed and took off his coverings. He sunk into the bath. "Tell me some news, brother."

"Fine," I sighed as I undressed and slipped into the bath beside him. "Expect to be called on tonight."

"With you?" He lifted an eyebrow.

I smiled. "Yes."

"Then I shall await his summons with great anticipation." Phillip placed a hand on my thigh under the water.

A guard glared at us. "None of that," he growled.

Phillip removed his hand and placed it above water. "I lost something," he smirked. "Just trying to retrieve it."

"You'll lose some flesh from your hide if you try it again," he glared at Phillip.

We both had a hard time containing our amusement as he walked away.

The next few hours before bedtime were spent making conversation with the newcomers. I tried to get close enough to Julian to engage him in conversation but he was surrounded by the men who'd come with him. They all knew each other, of course, and we were actually the strangers.

Gabien managed to strike up a conversation with two men, both Spartans, named Adeci and Thomaso. Phillip and I eventually joined in. We discussed the pain of branding which was really bothering the one called Thomaso. And later the conversation switched to who we thought might be the next champion, a title that everyone in the room wanted. I tried to turn the conversation to Julian, thinking if I couldn't talk to him, I could at least talk about him, but the minute I tried, we were interrupted by another, who changed the topic of the conversation to food when he announced that he was hungry.

I almost gave up on talking to Julian until I noticed that he had slipped outside and was conversing with the guard. Quickly, I squeezed through the crowd of men and walked outside. The guard began to pace a little as I came out. Julian turned around and we came face to face. Oh yes, he was handsome. He took my breath away. I wondered if it just wasn't my feelings rebounding. His face, his body, everything seemed familiar. *Gold.*

"Hello," he said.

"Hello," I replied. "I'm Samson."

"I hear you may well be contender for champion."

"Is that so? Is that the rumour?"

"Pretty much." He shrugged.

A shiver went through me. Every move he made seemed sexual suddenly. I was losing my mind. I allowed my gaze to move over his broad naked chest, framed on each side by metal arm sleeves. A trail led down his stomach to the piece of material which covered his groin just to his muscular thighs.

His smile broadened a little. "Oh," he said.

I laughed, embarrassed, realising that he was aware of my scrutiny.

"Do you like what you see, Samson?"

I licked my lips and nodded.

He put his head back and laughed heartily.

I wasn't sure how to take that.

He clamped a hand on my shoulder. "Becoming champion will not be so easy now with ten new men to challenge. It would serve you better to keep your mind on more serious matters."

It started to rain just as he disappeared inside. I rolled my eyes then actually smiled a little. Why was I always attracted to such cantankerous men?

A short while later we were sent to our separate cells for the night. I was dreamily pondering the idea that maybe Julian was lying in a cell near to mine when my door opened and a guard ordered me to get up. "Come with me," he barked.

I followed the guard down the hallway.

The guard shoved me forward and I anticipated seeing Phillip, maybe even Julian. I was perplexed when we reached the back, and neither of them had been collected.

"Where are we going?" I asked the guard as he led me through the grass.

"We are taking the long way to the house," he replied. "The master asked for discretion."

Was I to serve Claudius alone tonight?

When we arrived around the side of the big house, it was not Claudius who awaited me. It was Simeon. He motioned for us to enter.

The guard was ordered to leave the room when we entered the atrium. Simeon paced up and down for a few minutes while I waited. He was disturbed about something, as evidenced by the way he threaded his fingers through his hair. I wondered if this was about Claudius.

"Samson," he looked directly at me, "you have the potential to be the next champion of the House of Simeon. In fact, you must be. We cannot allow one of Phineas' gladiators to rise to champion in my house."

I wanted to point out that they were now *his* gladiators but he apparently didn't see it that way and I was in no position to disagree.

"He cursed me. The bastard! He cursed me under the guise of giving me a fair exchange. He took the best I had, that cock of Zeus, my Gold. He took my Gold!" Simeon put his face in his hands, and moaned in agony.

I didn't know what to do. I stood very still.

After a few minutes, the lanista raised his head from his hands. He came close to me. I could smell the wine on his breath. "That bastard gave me ten slaves, ten of his best gladiators, anticipating that one of them would rise to be champion of this house. If that happens, I will be finished,

finished! My name will be nothing. Don't you see," he clutched my arm, sweat bathing his face, "I have no choice. You," he pointed at me, "you will train and train, and surpass them all. You will be my champion, and then," he clenched his fists at his side, "and then," he looked at the ceiling, "you will kill his champion. You will take Gold's head in the arena!"

Chapter Two

Strenuous Activities

I'd had no idea I would be assigned a private trainer until Phineas introduced me to him. Since I'd been here, I had trained with the rest of the troupe. The trainers were more than skilled, but as the weeks went by, I quickly realised that they had little to show me. And eventually, Phineas realised it as well.

Several times I was pitted against the Destroyer, and I bested him each time. Phineas and Sullis were delighted and applauded wildly when I put the Destroyer on his knees. There was no question that my title was secure.

Phineas and Sullis realised that if I was to excel further, I needed a personal trainer, someone exceptional. One morning when I got up, the slave named Jemin brought me some fruit as he was prone to do, and a message that Phineas wanted to see me immediately. I was perplexed that Phineas would request me so early in the morning. He had taken me to his bed two times in the last weeks, and allowed Sullis to have me once as well. Other than that, I'd not been touched. Maybe that's why the sight of Jemin seemed so inviting.

I stretched and yawned as my gaze settled on Jemin's naked limbs. He wore only a thin loin covering and it left little to the imagination. His chest was naked except for some jewelled nipple clamps and a gold collar round his slender throat. I wanted him quite badly. My cock ached to take him. I wasn't sure why. Maybe it was because he'd been promised to me, but never given. Perhaps it was the desire I saw in his eyes every time he looked at me. Phineas and Sullis had reignited a fire in my belly and I needed it satisfied. Right now, the fire was stoked, and it was accompanied by an almost sacred intensity. I knew Jemin felt it too. "I will come immediately," I told him.

He smiled at me, sweetly, and I suddenly felt extremely protective of him. If he was indeed the half brother of Phineas, it was a shame he'd been deprived of his birthright. But I couldn't change that.

I stood, placed the material between my legs and wrapped it around my hips. He stood and watched me, and moistened his lips with his tongue. I could image those lips clinging to my cock and it caused me to place a hand on it to calm its reaction.

"He waits in the atrium," Jemin said as his gaze assessed me, and remained on the obvious protrusion in my coverings.

"You see what happens to me when I'm idle," I laughed slightly, and tried to make light. It was true. At the other house, I'd been occupied all the time with training the men, and catering to Simeon. I'd had little time to think about desire...until Samson came. He made me pause. *Samson.* I missed him so much. I worried for his welfare, and wondered how he was. I pushed it away. I had to.

Thoughts of him created a longing that I couldn't dwell on.

Jemin moved closer to me, too close. The breeze blew the curtains around us. He touched my face. "I wish you idle always then. Gold," he said softly. "I shall die soon if I don't have you."

I looked down at him. "No, you won't die," I smiled. "Go now before you find yourself in trouble."

"It's the kind of trouble I crave," he said with a mischievous grin.

I ruffled his hair.

"Do you think he might ever let you have me?" His expression looked hopeful.

"Perhaps, when he craves that type of amusement, but I would guess we'd have an audience."

"I care not. I wouldn't care if you took me in the arena in view of a thousand and more. As long as you possessed me, and made me feel that fine cock of yours inside of me."

I reached out and yanked him even closer as his words stirred my desire again. I let my hand move down his flank and around to capture his ass cheek in my hand. I fondled it freely for a second, so hard and firm, delightfully round. "How many men have fucked you?" I asked him gruffly as my lips caressed his cheek.

He moaned softly as I gave his ass a quick sharp slap. "Um, I can't remember," he whispered. He turned his face so that our lips were aligned. They didn't quite connect but I inhaled his breath. "Good love of Zeus," he groaned. His hand slide between our bodies and he rubbed his knuckles over my hardness. "I will lose my mind if you don't fuck me soon," his lips moved up to my ear and he nibbled it a moment.

The sound of footsteps approaching caused me to thrust him away from me. It was Sullis. His gaze surveyed the situation for a second then he smiled. "Good morning, Gold."

Jemin picked up the fruit bowl and quickly fled the room.

"I was just about to go to Phineas," I said. I let my arms hang down in front of me, hoping to hide my erection.

He smirked at me. "Good. We have a personal trainer for you and we'd like you to get to know him."

"A personal trainer?" I lifted an eyebrow.

"Yes. The master intends to spare no expense where you are concerned. And you do need to keep your mind on your…ah…" his gaze moved to my groin, "training."

"Of course," I said.

He moved closer to me. "I would like nothing more than to take care of that for you but Phineas has advised a diet of abstinence for now. He doesn't want to drain your energy." He moved his hand over my chest, circling one nipple slowly then trailing his fingers down to my waist. "Keeping you tense, twisted into a knot of desire and raging need, will only fuel your fighting spirit."

I didn't like the sound of that.

"Come," he whispered, almost, but not quite brushing my erection.

I sucked in some breath and followed him. I couldn't help but wonder as I walked down the corridor, if Jemin wasn't after all just a pawn in the master's game. Keep me hard, keep me wanting. Perhaps the desire in Jemin's eyes was contrived, there only because the master demanded it. Suddenly I wasn't at all at ease with these games, and I had a feeling that they would only get worse.

* * * *

I was sure that Simeon was slipping into madness. And his madness affected everyone around him. Up at the crack of dawn, the gladiators were to train until the noon sun. We broke to eat and rest for a very short time then trained again until the sun went down.

Simeon would often come to watch us, snarling and hollering like some kind of uneducated moron.

Julian was an excellent trainer, far more severe however than Gold, but I had the feeling Simeon had coached him, insisted on this persona he wore. My attraction for him was still there, but I was too exhausted to think much about it. And his severity with the troupe didn't endear him to anyone.

I hadn't realised how conflicted Julian was about how he was driving us. Men were dropping from fatigue then hit with the whip if they didn't get to their feet and keep on training.

When Phillip stumbled, and fell one day outside the slave quarters, Julian rushed to see to him.

I noted the tender way he picked him up in his arms, calling for water. He tipped the cup to his lips and stroked his hair. "Phillip," he urged. "Phillip?" He looked up at us as we all stood around. "This slave is completely dehydrated and suffering from exhaustion. Guard, summon the doctor. The rest of you, back inside."

We stood around inside watching as Phillip was carried to the place where all the injured were taken. It was basically a small alcove equipped with stone slabs which served as beds. The doctor rushed in shortly after and we waited for news.

I was worried about Phillip. He hadn't looked well the last few days, and he was having difficulty keeping up with the others. Gabien sat beside me but no one spoke.

The lanista arrived shortly after, and he didn't look pleased seeing us all sitting around doing nothing. He waited until Julian appeared and demanded an explanation. "Why aren't these men training? There is a huge contest coming and we need these gladiators to be at the top of the game."

"These men will not even be in the game," Julian snapped, "if you insist on working them to this extent. Some of them can hardly stand up. And Phillip will not be able to fight if he doesn't get some rest."

No one uttered a sound. For Julian to speak to the master like that was unheard of. The master could have decided to put us all to death at that moment.

"How dare you! Guards," he shouted, "seize him. Bring him outside, along with the rest."

Made to follow the rest outside, my stomach was turned in knots. *Oh no.* I couldn't bear the thought of them whipping Julian. It brought back memories of how that guard had whipped my Gold.

Julian struggled and shouted obscenities as the guards ripped off his clothes and tied his hands above him.

Simeon stood in front of us. "Let this be a lesson to you. You are lucky to be alive. You owe me your gratitude and your obedience. Defy me and this is the result. Is that understood?"

There was a chorus of, "Yes, master."

He turned and walked over to Julian. He picked up his chin and stared into his eyes. "Don't ever think you know more about my property than I do." He stepped away, looked at the guard. "Five lashes!"

I winced each time the whip came down on Julian's back. The force of it pushed him forward and he would bend double then straighten his back again. His handsome face was contorted with pain but he was silent, sweat covering his skin, blood flying in the air as it flew off the whip.

When they untied him, he went to his knees.

I saw Claudius standing now in the corner. The expression on his face was unreadable. Didn't he see what was happening to his father? Didn't he see that the loss of Gold had driven him insane? Perhaps he did. But if he did, he said nothing, nothing at all.

We were given the rest of the day, and most of us spent it in the bath, trying to soothe our aches. Julian joined Phillip, and the doctor tended them both.

Later that evening, I went to see Phillip. He was awake and smiled when he saw me. "Samson?"

"Are you feeling better, brother?" I asked him.

"Yes."

I looked over to see that Julian lay on his side, his head turned away. I flinched as I looked at the marks on his flesh, a crisscrossing of thin lines coated with some kind of salve. "Is he all right?" I asked Phillip.

"He's a good man," Phillip replied, "a brave man. He reminds you of Gold, doesn't he?"

I nodded and looked away. I shivered suddenly and thought about what Simeon had told me, thinking about what I didn't want to think about.

"What is it?" Phillip asked me.

"Simeon wants me to..." I cleared my throat. I couldn't say it.

"Wants you to what, brother? Tell me?"

"He wants me to take his head in the arena." There. It was out.

"Pit you against Gold?"

I nodded.

Julian turned his head suddenly and looked at us. "He wants Gold dead," he said.

"Why?" Phillip whispered.

"He can't stand the thought that he doesn't own Gold anymore," Julian replied. "I believe the only way he will rest is if Gold is dead by the hands of one of you. That way, he proves that he doesn't need Gold to beat Phineas."

"I fear he's lost his mind," I added.

Julian nodded. "You could be right on that one, brother."

"What you did took courage," I told him.

He shook his head, grunted a bit with the effort. "We couldn't go on like this. I had to say something before you all fell. I tried in vain before to make him see that he will destroy his investment, that he must take care of his assets. He is not thinking at all."

"And Claudius, could we not get through to him?" I insisted.

"We'd have to get him alone. Simeon has been curtailing his son's activities as of late and encouraging him to court several young women in the territory. He is often absent."

That explained why I'd seen so little of him.

"But, you could be right about trying to get through to the son. Gracia is also an avenue. I believe I have some favour with her."

My eyes widened. "She has requested you service her?"

"If she had, I could not say," he replied.

"Of course, but if you have any favour with her, perhaps..." I trailed off.

He nodded at me discreetly just as a guard came in and told me to move on.

I went to my cell and contemplated the idea that Gracia was using Julian's body to pleasure her. It wasn't the first time Gracia had used gladiators to satisfy her lust. Phillip told me that Gold was once her favourite when he was in the ring.

I lay down on my bed and tried to sleep. Sleep wouldn't come. I saw Gold in my head, pictured meeting him in the arena. I wondered if he could kill me. He'd have to because I knew I couldn't kill him. And if we refused to kill each other, we would both die. Unless Simeon could be persuaded to let go of this obsession, there was no way out of this. No way at all.

* * * *

When I walked into the atrium, Phineas was standing in the middle of the floor being fed grapes by Jemin. Several other slaves stood around waving fans and waiting for instruction. The trainer, Horace, stood beside Phineas. He studied me as I approached and actually bowed his head to me in respect.

"Gold," Phineas said and waved Jemin away, "I am giving you to Horace. He will be your personal trainer."

"I am privileged," Horace said. "I am your servant."

"I require the service of no man."

"But I am a free man, Gold," he replied. "I give my service willingly."

"And he is handsomely paid for it besides," the lanista laughed faintly. He moved closer. "Take off your coverings," he told me.

I narrowed my eyes. It was a strange request but I did as I was told and undid the material. I held it in one hand and waited. My cock was now semi-erect. The master cupped my balls and took my cock in his hand. He stroked it and it quickly revived. "I want you to stay in a state of sexual tension." He glanced around and said loudly. "From now on, anyone may fondle Gold if he appears to have lost his..." he stroked me again, "stamina. I want him hard and ferocious."

I was not happy to hear I was to be groped at every occasion by anyone who took the fancy of it.

I bristled and I'm sure Phineas noticed. He ignored my reaction. "And to make sure he stays that way," he looked at Sullis, and trailed off.

Sullis held up some kind of a strap. As he handed it to the master many eyes looked on curiously.

Phineas lifted my cock and my balls, again stroking them until I was even stiffer. I struggled to retain composure as he wound the strap under my balls and around my shaft, pulling it snug and attaching it. I let my head go back and sucked in some breath. It was more torturous than any whip to be kept like this in a state of heightened sexual tension. I glanced down at myself to see that my cock was standing straight up at an angle and my balls were pressed up under my shaft.

"Beautiful," Phineas nodded. "Now," he held out his hand to Sullis, "give me the other."

Other?

Sullis smiled as he handed the master a round plug about three inches long, which had been oiled.

"Bend over," Phineas told me and walked around to my back. I trembled as he ran his hands over my ass then reached around in front to pet the head of my cock. One hand spread my ass cheeks and I felt the hard core of it brush across my anus. I moaned inwardly, and felt Phineas push it deep inside of me. I was at once humiliated and stimulated.

"This will keep you permanently open. And yet you will be filled. You'll never be satisfied. Stand straight."

I stood, and licked my lips. My gaze strayed to Jemin. I could have at this moment jumped him and raped him.

And from the look on his face, I knew he'd willingly open his legs for me. That was worse, knowing he wanted me.

Phineas was in front of me now. He flicked both my nipples with his fingers. "Clamps!" He called out.

"May I speak?" I asked him.

"Of course," he replied.

"Am I to wear these at all times?"

"Only during your training sessions," he replied.

One of the slave girls brought a tray with two clamps shaped like small gold hoops. "Gold for Gold," he whispered, and took his time as he pinched each nipple, shaping it, pulling on it. Then he invited Sullis to do the same. Sullis slowly moved his thumbs over them at an agonisingly slow pace, and stroked the head of my cock intermittently. I was ready to climb the walls.

Then he bent his head forward and licked my nipples. He nibbled, and pulled at them with his teeth then he clamped on the gold rings. The sensation was painful but the pain was edged with pleasure and it shot right to my groin. He pulled one of the clamps for a second, and licked it, and at the same time he reached around me and squeezed my ass a few times. *Damn you, Sullis.*

Phineas finally told Sullis to step away from me. I sighed with relief.

"He is beautiful," Horace commented, looking at me, "beautiful, and right now, extremely angry."

He was right about that. I had never felt such indignation.

"The perfect combination," Phineas smiled as he placed a hand on Horace's shoulder, "Beautiful, and deadly. The crowd will adore him."

"Train well," Phineas told me, "and you shall have any slave you want to satisfy you after your sessions."

"And we already know which slave he would choose," Sullis looked over at Jemin.

I narrowed my eyes as I looked at Sullis. Was everything calculated, and plotted, weaved together to get me to do exactly as they wanted? This was beginning to give a whole new definition to idea of enslavement.

Phineas glanced at Jemin as well, and I wasn't really comfortable with the look he gave him. He didn't look pleased. "Go now," he told Horace. "Begin your training in the courtyard. I will join you shortly."

Horace reached down and picked up my loin cloth. "Put it on," he said. "I will get you some protective gear. We train with real weapons."

* * * *

The following morning when I woke, I went to see Phillip and Julian again, to see if they were better. Only Phillip was there but he was sitting up, eating. "How are you, brother?" I asked him, glancing at the empty place beside him.

"Julian told me this morning he was ready to go back to work. He doesn't want Simeon to have the opportunity to hire on a new trainer. He's afraid it would be some tyrant," he chuckled.

I nodded. "Do you think that Julian will use his influence with Gracia to help rein in her husband?"

"I'm sure he'll try."

"And you, back to training today?"

"I'm waiting for the doctor but I believe so."

I clamped a hand on his shoulder.

"Samson," he pulled me closer.

I found myself staring into his eyes. "What is it? I have to go, the guards will be in here after me soon enough."

"I want you. I know," he put up a hand when I went to speak, "your heart belongs to Gold, but he's gone now."

Suddenly Julian came in and I turned to look at him. Maybe it was something in the way I looked at him that made Phillip let me go.

"You are free to join us, Phillip," he said. "Doctor told me earlier." He nodded at me. "Get moving now."

When he left us, Phillip said, "I see."

"What do you mean, I see?" My stomach was twittering.

"It's him now, is it?"

"Phillip!"

"I saw you. He won't lower himself to be with you. He's the trainer, and I think he is enamoured of Simeon's wife."

My eyes opened wider. "Don't be stupid. If he fucks her, it's because he's ordered to."

Phillip shrugged. "Have it your own way. First Gold, now Julian. You should un-complicate your life, my friend."

Phillip brooded most of the day and I hated it. I hated not being able to talk and joke with him. I wished we could just put this awkwardness which had suddenly developed between us, aside. But it wasn't to be.

Later in the afternoon, Claudius appeared. He stood on the sidelines and talked with Julian. I was surprised to see him. I had the impression that he'd been away for awhile.

After he left, Julian looked preoccupied and shortly after that guard came to get him. "Samson," he called out to me, "you're in charge until I get back."

I nodded at him and kept on going through my moves with one of the newcomers, a gladiator named Domitrius. He was good but eventually I put him in the sand. I extended my hand and helped him back up, and we went to get some water. As we drank, I asked him about his former master. "What was it like there?"

"Very different," he said. "The ludi was far larger, the accommodations larger. Phineas respects his gladiators, rewards them. The troupe was close, real brothers."

I'd noticed the camaraderie amongst the newcomers. It had been difficult to get close to any of them since they'd arrived. "Then Phineas was benevolent, not harsh?"

"Oh," he said, downing the water and wiping off his chin, "I never said that. Phineas is benevolent as long as you obey. Defy him, or disappoint him, and he shows no mercy. I once saw him personally whip a house slave to death for not bringing the right number of wine glasses for the guests."

I cringed.

"Why do you ask, you want to change?" He laughed gruffly.

"No. And Julian, tell me about him."

"Julian?" He lifted an eyebrow. "He's an excellent trainer. Truly, I know little about Julian. He's a bit of a mystery. He was only at the House of Phineas for a month before he was sent here with us. I wouldn't cross him. That's all I know."

I watched him walk across the courtyard.

Phillip was watching me, his eyes still filled with resentment. I sighed and walked over to where he stood. "Do we call a truce now brother, or what?"

He glanced at me, nodded. "We do."

I smiled. "Good because I've missed you."

He smiled back then lifted his wooden sword. "Then let's get to work."

We were all busy practicing when Julian came back. He was followed by Claudius. "Listen," he shouted out.

Silence loomed suddenly, and we all turned in his direction.

Claudius stepped forward. "A festival to honour certain distinguished guests is being planned. In a fortnight, we will entertain some of the finest citizens of our great civilisation. Every one of you will be called on to provide entertainment for our guests, and Samson," he walked over to me and pulled me out of the thong to stand alone beside him, "Samson," he repeated, as he yanked my arm up in the air, "will take on the greatest gladiator history has ever known. He will take on Gold from the House of Phineas, and he will win!"

There were some stunned murmurs in the crowd. I clamped my teeth together. It was official. I looked over at Phillip and he gave me a look of true pity.

Claudius dropped my hand. "Go back to your training," he bellowed then dragged me off to the other side of the courtyard where we stood for a moment and looked out to the sea.

"Is there no other way?" I asked him.

"My father wills it."

"And you? Do you will it?"

"Gold was your friend," he said, then looked at me, "your lover."

I was surprised at his sudden compassion.

"You can't beat him," he said. "He will kill you."

"Will he?" I looked at him. "Can he?"

He shrugged. "He will do what he has to. Gold is a true gladiator at heart. When I saw him in the arena as a boy, I knew he was born to it. Your only hope is if he wants to die by your hand."

I gave him a strange look.

"There is nothing dishonourable in dying a glorious death in the arena. Already sculptors pay homage to Gold. He will live on through history. He fears dying a natural death. He hopes to restore honour to his family name."

"You know a lot about Gold," I said, shivering as a cold wind blew off the water.

He nodded.

"We all fear your father is..."

"Yes," he cut me off. "His entire identity for a long time involved Gold. He must pin his hopes on another, you, Samson," he looked at me. "You are his Gold now."

"And you, his son?" I had no idea why Claudius allowed me to speak to him so but for some reason, I sensed that he had thrown off the façade of our positions and wanted to speak to me as one man to another.

"I represent hope to him only if I marry well. And he chooses my wife for me, even though I don't wish for this."

"I am sorry."

He was silent for a few minutes then suddenly, he erected the barrier and reconfirmed to me that he was my master. "I will send for you and Phillip, tonight. My parents will be gone for next three days. They will meet with the parents of my future wife. I plan on making the best of my freedom."

"Master, may I make a request?"

"You may."

"I would ask that you request Julian in Phillip's place."

He raised an eyebrow. "Julian?" He laughed slightly.

"You do not find him appealing?"

He paused, glanced over at him. "He is very appealing, but it is very daring what you ask."

I lowered my head.

"I'll contemplate it," he said. "Now return to training. You will need to train as hard as you can for the next two weeks if you are to become the new champion."

* * * *

"Magnificent," Horace commented as he stood back and watched my form. I battled the man-made post for a few more minutes then stopped, my limbs aching from the exertion. "Come here," he said.

I lowered my sword and approached.

He reached for the top of my breeches and pulled them down. Quickly he undid the strap. I breathed a sigh of relief.

"You may remove the other as well in privacy."

I nodded my thanks.

"You will face the Destroyer in three days."

I looked at him. "In a public contest?"

"No. The master will have a private party. The contest is held only to clearly hold you up as the champion of this house. You will have no trouble defeating him. Now go, rest."

The guard came and took the sword from me then followed me back inside. He took a position in the hallway and I walked through the great rooms to the bath.

Several slaves stood around the room and I hoped none of them would think to fondle me. Luckily, I was left alone. I disrobed and slipped into the water, reaching around and removing that annoying contraption.

I'm not sure that binding my cock and plugging my anus improved my fighting skills but they did leave me wanting. Even the naked slave girl looked good to me. Where was Jemin? The master had promised me satisfaction after training with the slave I chose. But the slave was nowhere to be seen.

Sullis walked in suddenly. He smiled at me. "There you are. Horace said it went very well today."

I fondled my cock in the water. "It did."

He came around to my back and reached down to stroke my hair. He pulled my head back at the same time. "I'm here to give you what you want."

I wrapped my fist around my hard shaft as he took off his toga and stepped into the water beside me.

I didn't wait for him to touch me. I grabbed hold of him and turned him around in the water. I kissed him hotly, took his hand and placed it on my cock. "I want to fuck you," I breathed.

He chuckled as he returned each kiss and played with my cock under the water. "Music to my ears," he grabbed my ass hard. "Let us go somewhere, ah..." he looked at the slaves, "more private."

I groaned at not being able to take him right there. I accepted the towel from the slave girl and followed him out of the water. He led me down the hallway to the back where our sleeping quarters were. I practically raped him when we got behind the curtain. I gave him no time to protest and there was no foreplay. I pressed his face against the wall, roughly pulled his legs apart and took his ass.

He grunted from the impact, but he thrust his hips as I pumped into him, which let me know he appreciated my efforts.

I came quickly, the sexual tension I'd been under for the preceding few hours unable to wait any longer for release. I went to lie on the bed, exhausted from my efforts. I closed my eyes, licked my lips, allowing myself to enjoy the sensation.

Hands moved up over my thighs. A tongue licked at my cock and trailed up to my chest. "You're a god," Sullis told me nibbling at my jaw.

I looked at him as if he'd lost his mind. "You're delusional," I told him.

He sat up. "No. You are a god, in bed and out. No wonder Simeon loses his mind."

I narrowed his eyes. "Simeon has lost his mind?"

"So I hear." He began to dress.

I sat up. "Tell me more about that."

"I'm not supposed to."

"Why not?"

"Because Phineas hasn't agreed to it yet."

"Agreed to what?" I insisted.

"Simeon is pushing for you to fight his champion."

Samson.

"You should see your face, brother. I shouldn't have told you."

"Why would Simeon want to sacrifice his champion this early?"

"He wants you dead."

"He thinks that Samson can best me?"

Sullis sighed. "He banks on the fact that you won't be able to kill him when the time comes." He paused. "Will you?"

"Will I what?" I knew what he was asking me but I didn't quite have an answer.

"Could you kill him if it comes to that?"

"What choice would I have?" I looked away from him.

Sullis nodded silently.

"When is this contest to take place?"

"In two weeks. It is to be closed, only by special invitation."

"You must get Phineas to turn him down."

"I'll do what I can," he said. "Rest now."

But I couldn't rest. I paced and I thought about Samson. I was finally getting what I wanted most, to be back in the arena, but to face Samson? The thought sickened me. I knew that I loved him. How could I kill my own heart, or even ask him to be the one to end my life? *Damn you, Simeon. Damn you to hell.*

Chapter Three

Well Kept Secrets

When the guard summoned me it was late. I roused myself from a dead sleep. I had dreamed of blood. It ran in deep thick streams through my head. *Gold.* The guard followed behind me as he pointed me in the direction of the great house. I was alone.

Claudius stood in the atrium, a goblet of wine in his hand. Suddenly I noticed Julian. He stood quietly behind him. My stomach flipped upside down.

Claudius waved at the guard to leave me. He motioned with his hand. "Samson," he breathed. "There you are. I was just saying to Julian how quiet it was since my father's departure. Come and have some wine. I am in the mood to celebrate."

A slave rushed forward now with the decanter. He poured some into a goblet and handed it to me with his head bowed. I took a sip.

"My father was ranting. It seems that Phineas has not yet accepted his offer."

My heart sped up. I looked at Julian. There was no expression on his face.

Claudius was drunk. He stumbled around like an actor doing pantomime on stage, and I really wasn't sure what we were in for. I regretted requesting Julian's presence now.

"May I speak?" I asked.

He glanced at me. "Go on."

"When will we know for sure if I am to fight Gold?"

He shrugged. "Whenever that barbarian sends an answer I suppose. My father grows restless. Perhaps a visit with the parents of my future wife will calm him down, stay his insanity. He is obsessed." He motioned to the slave. "More wine."

Neither Julian or myself moved.

Claudius slumped on the lounge chair, waving his hands. "Obsessed with a gladiator, both of them," he scoffed, and turned round to look at Julian. "My father is obsessed with Gold and my mother, obsessed with you. Oh, and I forgot," he glanced at me, "you're in love with Gold too."

Julian looked up sharply.

"So, let us play true confessions," Claudius laughed. "You already know how pathetic my parents are. We know that Samson here loves Gold. What about you, my fair Julian, whom do you love?" Claudius was staring at him, demanding an answer.

A shadow crossed his face. He cleared his throat. "No one," he replied.

"Did you know," Claudius announced, standing again, "that Samson here requested that I summon you tonight along with him?"

I lowered my head and flushed. I didn't expect Claudius to confess that. I felt a fool.

"Well?" Claudius demanded. "What do you say to that, fair Julian?"

"I'm sure he had his reasons," he muttered.

"It's curious," Claudius snarled. "Are you over Gold so quickly then?" He walked over to me.

"No, master," I admitted.

"Do you think Julian could replace Gold in your heart?"

"I…no," I said.

"What then? Gold was mine before he was yours. Remember that, slave!"

"I will, master," I replied nervously.

"Now, he's gone. Now, he belongs to Phineas, and that smug little slave of his that doesn't know his fucking place. They have claimed his body — as well as his glory — as their own."

The bitterness in his voice was unmistakable.

"Would you like for us to go, master?" Julian asked respectfully.

I looked over at him and I could tell all he wanted was out of this room.

"No," Claudius snapped. "I want you to suck my cock."

I have to admit, I was dying to see Julian do just that but I could tell by his face that he was not keen on the idea.

He moved closer, and picked up the glass of wine from the table that Claudius had left unfinished. He held it out to him.

Claudius took it and drained it again.

"More wine?" Julian asked. There was a beguiling smile on his face.

I knew what he was doing. He was hoping that Claudius would get too drunk and pass out before he had to complete the deed.

"Wine!" Claudius called, "more wine. Wine for everyone in the house." He pushed Julian down to his knees. "My wedding approaches. I must practice to be drunk every night so that I don't have to bed the bitch."

I felt a sudden chord of pity for the girl, whoever she was.

Claudius drank from the cup again, and encouraged Julian to do the same. He tipped back his head and poured the wine on his face.

Julian swallowed what he could and wiped his chin with his hand. He was trying hard not to show his annoyance.

"Help him, Samson. At least you know what a cock is for. Swallow me like you did the wine, gladiator."

"Excuse my inexperience, master," Julian interrupted his ranting. "Perhaps I should watch and learn from an expert." He looked at me. I made a face at him. He smiled. Perhaps it was his revenge. After all, he knew that it was I who had him brought here. Whatever it was, he sat back on his haunches and waved his arm ahead for me to begin.

Claudius swayed back and forth, and grumbled something. He didn't quite seem connected to the earth.

Julian grinned. "Come on, Samson. Show me how it's done."

I realised he was playing with me. I liked it. I liked it a lot. "I will, since you're inadequate in that task."

He laughed a little but he didn't say anything.

I lifted the master's robe and began to handle his cock. He stumbled backwards and two house slaves lowered him to the chair to prevent him from falling. His eyes were closing. It wouldn't take much.

I wrapped my fingers around his semi-erect shaft and jerked a few times. That was it. He spurted a few drops then mumbled to himself. "What do I do now?" I asked Julian.

Julian shrugged and stood up. "No idea."

I stood as well and looked at him. "I apologise. I shouldn't have requested you. You obviously don't want to be here."

"Shouldn't I be flattered?"

"Yes," I nodded.

He frowned, which perplexed me. He was very difficult to figure out.

"Did you talk to the lanista's wife?"

"We didn't do much talking, no."

I understood his meaning. "Do you have feelings for her?"

"Yes, I have strong feelings for her, but none that I would say in public."

Again I was meant to read between the lines. "I heard you say that you defied your family because you preferred men, but I think that was a lie."

He smiled, tilted his head. "What do you mean?"

"Don't tease me. You do or you don't like to fuck men. Is that clear enough?"

"Yes. That's clear." He looked around. "Should we go, or are we to stay here all night?"

I was determined. "Yes, you like to fuck men, or yes, it's clear?"

"Yes to both questions."

"And me? Do you like me?"

"You want me?" He looked down into my eyes.

"You know I do," I told him honestly.

"We'll get to it," he replied casually, as if I'd just made a comment about the weather. "Now, we need to summon a guard."

* * * *

Phineas laughed to himself as he walked into the bath. I waited to see if he intended to tell me why he was laughing so heartily. When he finally sobered, he looked at me and announced cheerfully, "This is perfect."

"Master?"

"It's Simeon," he said. "He is desperate for me to respond to his proposal."

"His proposal to put me in the arena with Samson?" I held my breath.

"Yes. How do you feel about meeting the Destroyer tomorrow?"

I'd been training hard with Horace for the last few days and doing some hard-core fucking with Sullis after every session. I would have preferred to rest for another day. "If you will it, master," but I knew I didn't sound enthusiastic.

He contemplated that. "You may have one more day if you prefer."

"I do prefer it, if it should please you."

"Doesn't please me, but I'm inclined to be benevolent. It's settled. The contest will be set up for one day from tomorrow."

"May I ask if you intend to accept Simeon's proposal?"

"You may ask. But first, I have a question for you—do you want me to accept it?"

"Against any other, master, I am most enthusiastic to fight again, but not Samson. I don't think he is ready for me."

Phineas smiled. "He was ready for you in bed, was he not?"

I lowered my head.

There was a strained silence. "You speak the truth, at least in part, but it's not your real motivation for not wanting to meet Samson in the arena. We both know that, don't we, Gold?"

When I didn't respond, he insisted, "*Don't we, Gold?*"

"Yes, master," I replied.

"I realise that it's unfortunate but Samson is the closest thing to a champion that Simeon has. We know he won't use one of those I gave him. That would be too humiliating for him. And I can think of no other better to challenge you. Can you?"

I shook my head.

"You have great feelings for this gladiator."

"He is my...friend," I said. There was no use in telling him the truth. He would only use it against me. "Is there no one else? Can you not persuade him to use one of the many fine gladiators which you sent him, convince him that they are now his? You know these combatants, one that could truly challenge me."

He seemed to contemplate that. "There is one, the trainer, Julian, but as I told you, Simeon will not use one I have given him." He paused. "I can propose it."

I lifted my head. Some hope arose in my heart.

"But if he is determined to pit you against Samson, so that he can claim a true champion from his house, I will have no choice. We could put it off but pressure from the senators will be difficult to resist, especially in light of Simeon's political ambitions. Sooner or later, you will meet Samson in the arena."

"I would be grateful to you, master. Samson would be better trained later on, and the contest much more exciting for the spectators." I knew I'd given him food for thought.

He eyed me. "Grateful? How grateful would you be to me for postponing the inevitable, my beautiful gladiator?"

"Extremely grateful, master."

Jemin came into the room now. He stood beside the bath and waited for Phineas to issue an order. His gaze stayed on me.

Phineas motioned to Jemin. "Towels for both of us. We're getting out of the bath now."

Jemin began to towel off Phineas while I used the towel on myself.

"Stay naked," Phineas told me. "We retire to my chambers."

Jemin followed us down the corridor. I knew his gaze was on me and it made me feel warm all over.

In the master's quarters, Jemin backed into the corner and waited. I kept my eyes on him over Phineas' shoulder as the master ran his hands possessively over my chest. "So strong," he whispered, "massive, muscular, what a man you are, what a beauty. You are my beauty, my whore, my ferocious blood-thirsty warrior." He took my cock in his hands and stroked it roughly. "You will enter me," he told me. "Don't hold back."

I nodded. "As you wish, master."

Phineas knelt on all fours in front of me. "Now. Do it now."

I got down behind him and spread his ass cheeks. I looked directly into Jemin's eyes as I pushed my cock up inside of Phineas.

Phineas cried out. "Yes, oh yes...yesssssssss."

I bucked into him as hard as I could, and imagined that I was taking Jemin's tender ass.

I saw Jemin placed his hand between his thighs and stroke himself.

I winked at him as I pumped the master's ass harder, sweat in my eyes. A few minutes later I shot my cum into his ass and he ordered me to pull out.

I reared back on my haunches as he turned around. He grabbed my face and kissed my mouth hard. I was surprised. Simeon had never kissed me. But Phineas was not Simeon. He didn't seem to hold the unwritten rules as sacred.

Phineas murmured something as he reached between my thighs and stroked my cock. He watched as he brought it to life again and licked his lips. "Get on the sofa."

I got up and did as he asked.

"Spread your legs." He stood above me. "Jemin, bring me the whip."

I took a breath. Was I to be punished now?

"Don't worry. It's just play," he whispered when he saw my expression. But the idea of play could take on a variety of meanings when it came to these Roman lanistas.

Jemin was back with the whip. He too looked concerned as he handed it to Phineas.

Phineas took the whip from him. He ran it down over my chest and gently folded it around my penis. With his free hand, he suddenly reached out and he grabbed Jemin by the arm and jerked him forward. "Listen to me, Jemin," he shook him, "do you see that beautiful cock wrapped in the whip?"

"Yes, master," he stuttered. He shook all over.

"It will never be yours. Do you understand?"

"Yes, master."

"It will never be in your sweet, young ass. Is that clear?"

Jemin nodded wildly.

"You will never, ever taste it in your mouth."

"Yes, master."

"Touch his cock without my permission and I will castrate him, and kill you."

I could hardly breathe as Phineas spoke. My gaze stayed on the whip which circled my cock.

Phineas let Jemin go. "Get out now."

Jemin ran from of the room.

Phineas looked down into my eyes. He tightened the whip around my cock. "I know you want him," he said through clenched teeth. "I saw him touch himself when you were inside me. He wants you too. But it's not going to happen. I didn't buy you from Simeon to have you put your cock inside some worthless house slave. Is that clear?" He pulled the whip tighter around my shaft.

"Yes. It's clear." I grunted. The pain was so intense it made my head spin.

"Jemin is not that good a servant," he laughed. "I can spare him. And you don't really need your cock to fight. Your balls will do the job."

I nodded. The threat was clear.

He untangled the whip from my shaft and threw it aside. A thin bead of blood dotted around the circumference. I knew I'd gotten off easy.

He stood. "Very well then," he actually smiled at me. "Rest. Have some food. You've trained hard today. Horace tells me it is going very well."

I nodded and struggled to find my voice. "Yes."

"Keep up the good work. You will make this house proud."

He left me. I was stunned. One moment he was threatening to castrate me and the next, he was praising my efforts. I knew only one thing about Phineas. He was dead serious about his intentions, and not to be defied.

* * * *

Finally, Claudius was conscious enough for the slaves to escort him to his bed. He waved us off with his hand which meant that Julian and I were finally free to leave.

The guard trailed a little ways behind us as we left the house. Julian and I walked side by side across the courtyard to the field where the gladiators' quarters stood.

"You were a soldier," I said.

"I was."

"A soldier in the Roman army."

He nodded.

"Of high rank."

He glanced at me. "Correct. Congratulations, Samson."

"You are no coward. Why would your father bring you to this fate?"

He didn't answer for a moment.

Julian was older than I, closer to thirty years than twenty. I had the impression he'd been in the army for a long time. "If you don't wish to tell me, I won't ask again. I know you refused to marry." We entered the building.

The solider seemed content to leave us then. He walked outside and stood guard.

Julian took a seat at one of the tables. He leant back against the wall, and closed his eyes. He looked weary. "Gracia's father, like my own, was an officer of high rank in the military. When I was a boy, Gracia and I played together, and being of the same age, our fathers decided that we should marry when we became of age."

My eyes widened. "You were to marry the master's wife?"

He laughed slightly. "She wasn't his wife then." He sobered. "Samson, I am trusting you with this. What I tell you shouldn't leave this room."

"I won't say a word. I swear."

"I didn't wish to marry Gracia. As a playmate, she was less than agreeable and as she got older, she became malicious and cruel, interested more in status than anything else. I certainly didn't wish to marry the woman."

"Did she want to marry you?"

"Yes, she did. She claimed that she loved me."

"Were you ...ah...lovers?"

Julian shook his head. "No, we weren't, although it wasn't from her lack of trying. I pleaded with my father not to go through with this stupid arrangement but he was hesitant to back down due to his association with her father."

"Were you in love with someone else?"

"Truly, I was more in love with military matters than with any one person. I was young, and wanted to be free. Finally," he said, "my father did manage to convince Gracia's father that Gracia and I weren't suited. I was relieved. Gracia was infuriated, humiliated. She swore vengeance."

I gasped. "She did this to you, didn't she? She brought you to this fate. You said that your father..."

He nodded, put up his hand. "I couldn't tell the truth. Gracia would have me killed for that. Anyway, Gracia took her time, married Simeon, who at that time was an up and coming lanista. She plotted her revenge, figured out a way that she could bring me close to her, make me her slave."

I watched his face, and waited on baited breath for the rest of it.

"My father fell in battle and I took his place. One night in Rome, we had come back from a raid and were celebrating. I was drunk and off my game, of course. A young woman—a whore—enticed me to her bed. I don't remember what happened. I only know that when I awoke, soldiers surrounded me. I was arrested, accused of stealing a large amount of gold from Gracia's father. The gold was on my person and Gracia told the authorities that she'd seen me enter the house late that night."

"What about the whore?"

"Never saw her again. She was obviously put there by Gracia to ensure that I had no alibi. It was decided, more than likely greatly influenced by Gracia, as she was the apple of her father's eye, that I be sold as a slave and used as a gladiator, due to my talents in art of war. Gracia was a newlywed at that time. Both her new husband and Phineas were at the auction. She had planned for Simeon to buy me, but Phineas bid the highest. Gracia's plan to bring me close to her failed, and for the next several years, I fought for Phineas, relieved to be at a distance."

"Did Phineas know? Did Simeon know why she'd married him?" The questions came all at once.

"Simeon doesn't know to this day why she married him. Phineas however knows the story."

"Then, why would he send you here?"

"Gracia insisted on it. When the negotiations were going on regarding Gold, she saw her opportunity. She asked specifically for me. She told Simeon that I was the best trainer there was, and a good replacement for Gold. Phineas had no choice. He wanted Gold more than he wanted to keep me. So, here I am…"

"…in her clutches and in her bed. I can only imagine how you must feel about her."

"I hate her." He tasted that in his mouth. "I hate touching her. I hate fucking her, but I don't have a choice. The first time she brought me to her, she was so smug. She could hardly wait to humiliate me, make me do exactly what she wanted."

I reached over and touched his face. "I'm sorry. Julian, did you mean it...that we would...we would come together?"

He smiled faintly. "I would like nothing better, Samson, but there is the question of Gold."

"You would have me pay you?" I teased.

"You know of whom I speak. You love him."

I bit my lip. "Yes," I said. "I do. I do love him. But that doesn't mean we can't share pleasure, does it?"

He shook his head. "No. What about Phillip?"

"Phillip?" I wrinkled my nose. "What does Phillip have to do with it?"

"He wants you, and yet you pay him no mind."

"We are friends and that's all."

"But he wants more."

I leaned over and put my hands on each side of his face. I kissed his mouth hard then reared back. "Yes," I groaned, "and so do I."

* * * *

When I opened my eyes, Sullis was sleeping on the other lounge nearby, his mouth open. I lifted up onto my elbow and watched him, with a smirk on my face. When he was awake, he was quite handsome. However, in sleep, his best profile was not revealed. I was about to wake him when I looked up to see Jemin rush into the room.

"Jemin," I said, "what is it?"

"It's the master's wife. She wants to bed me." He wrung his hands. "It is only you I would have."

"Jemin. You must do as you're told," I advised.

"I know not what to do."

"She will direct you."

"I want you," he whispered.

"You cannot have me. I would keep my cock."

"I would keep it," he smiled.

I fought the urge to reach out for him. "Stop," I whispered. "You heard what Phineas said. We must focus on something else."

"Why does she wish this of me?"

"Why do they wish anything?" I muttered as I got to my feet. "Go now. Don't let Phineas see you mooning around me. Don't fret about the master's wife. She will quickly tire of your company."

Sullis was awake now. He looked at Jemin. "Little boy," he said softly, "come and take care of my erection." He motioned to him.

I prepared to leave but Sullis held up his hand. "Wait, brother," he said. "You can't have him but I can. Don't you want to watch?"

"He does," a voice said suddenly.

I turned to see the master enter. "Jemin," he placed a hand on his shoulder, "do as Sullis asks. Gold," he turned to me, "you will bear witness."

It's the last thing I wanted to do, to watch Jemin pleasure Sullis. But what could I do? I had no choice.

Phineas walked up behind Jemin and ripped off the flimsy loin covering he wore. He threw it aside and left him naked and exposed. He clutched both ass cheeks in his hand and massaged them a few minutes while Sullis stood in front of the slave and grabbed his cock. He fondled it roughly. I heard Jemin moan and my cock stiffened.

Phineas suddenly turned Jemin in my direction. He held his hands out at both sides as he put Jemin's body on display. His nipples were hard little nubs and his cock was standing erect, straight out from his body. "I would impale his ass with my cock," he told me. He ran his hands down his chest, and slapped at his cock—hard.

Jemin gasped. He moved against Phineas and moaned with need.

"See how much he wants my cock, Gold. He begs for it, the little whore." He pushed Jemin to his knees. "Sullis, the whore is ready to pleasure you."

Sullis stood in front of Jemin now. Jemin took his cock and began to swallow it. I felt my breathing slow. My feelings were in turmoil.

After a few minutes, Jemin was pulled away from Sullis, and Phineas knelt down behind him. He lifted Jemin's legs up in the air, pulled his body into his groin, and wrapped his legs round his waist.

Jemin let out a deep cry as the master took him there on the floor, pumping him furiously.

Phineas' eyes were on me the entire time, perhaps trying to gauge my reaction. I kept my face a mask, revealing nothing.

Suddenly, Phineas grunted loudly then pulled away, dropping Jemin's legs.

"Guard," he called out, standing.

A soldier came immediately.

"Take this little whore, string him up in the courtyard where Gold will be training today with Horace. Make sure his precious entrance is exposed and ready for use. Gag him so that he can't make any sound. Every hour, have one of the soldiers fuck him, good and hard." He looked at me now as Jemin was dragged from the room. "You will go on training with your cock bound and your ass plugged. Sullis, prepare him," he said on his way out of the room, "but don't give him any relief."

"What nature of a man is he?" I asked Sullis, my voice laced with resentment.

"Imaginative?" he suggested.

"Why would he do that to Jemin? He's done nothing wrong."

A female slave brought a tray which contained the cock strap and the plug.

Sullis took the tray. "Lay down," he urged.

I was not looking forward to this stupid, humiliating ritual which I was forced to endure every day. "I fear I have brought trouble on Jemin without intending to. I don't understand the master's cruelty."

"Not cruelty," he said. "He is only asserting his ownership. You are his. He can't stand the thought that you might want that slave. And you do want him, don't you?"

I took off my coverings, and nodded. "Yes. I want him."

"Dangerous obsession, and since I suspect that it's nothing more than pure lust, may I suggest to you it's not worth it?"

"It might be," I smiled with guile.

He actually laughed. "For him, yes. But you...well...you need a real man to satisfy you."

"Like you?" I raised my eyebrow.

"Of course, like me. Not every man could handle that cock of yours, tame you, fuck you the right way."

I didn't comment but Sullis had never tamed me. When I was prone and naked, Sullis's eyes widened. "What happened to your cock, brother?" He traced his finger around the shaft where the whip had left its mark.

"Phineas happened to my cock. And I wouldn't be touching me like that if I were you."

He lifted my shaft and began to wrap it with the strap, taking my balls with it. "It's much too tempting. I'm only human," he whispered. "Now, turn on your back."

The strap tightened around my cock hurt due to the handiwork Phineas had done with his whip.

"I've oiled the plug," Sullis said softly, "but first," he whispered and leaned closer, kissing the back of the neck, "let me play."

"Sullis," I warned him but my warning was lost as I felt my ass being opened with the tip of his fingers.

"I oiled my fingers, nice and slippery." He sounded breathless as he began to move one finger deeper inside of me.

I closed my eyes, moaned inwardly. Another finger joined it and I raised my hips up as he began to instigate an in and out movement.

"Beautiful ass," he hissed. "I'd love to rape your ass, tie you up, see you helpless, and hard, um…like Jemin in that courtyard."

"Sullis stop," I begged him. It was torturous, especially with the strap binding my cock. "Put the damn plug in and let me alone."

"Not yet." He removed his fingers and replaced them with his tongue.

I pulled the sheet up and stuck it in my mouth as his tongue dipped inside of my anus and licked me there. I was going to lose my mind. I banged my fist on the sofa, bit into the sheet and moaned as my hips slammed against the bed. No release. There was no release.

He stopped and used his fingers again, two then three, deep inside me, twisting and turning. I cried out, muffling it with the material. His hand reached under me and touched the tip of my cock. I felt as if I was going to explode at any moment but I couldn't. I pulled the sheet out of my mouth. "Take it off," I growled, and scrambled to unleash my cock, "take the damn thing…" I undid the strap, threw it aside and took hold of Sullis like a madman. Within seconds, he was draped across the sofa on his face, and my cock was buried in his ass. I fucked him so hard I heard the wood crack under us. I pulled his hair brutally, dragged his head back and pushed his legs further apart so that I could drill even deeper. Finally, I came. Sullis buried his face in the leather and let out a smothered scream as he joined me in the bliss. His body went into spasms as if he was having convulsions.

I lay on the floor a few minutes to recover my breath. He glanced down at me from the sofa and grinned. "That was exciting."

I laughed a little and grunted as I sat up. "Bloody right."

Sullis sprang off the sofa and tackled me on the floor. I glanced at the slave girl who still stood in the corner. She didn't blink.

He kissed me all over and I pushed him off me. "Behave yourself," I warned, and got to my feet. "I have training to do. Horace will be coming after me if I don't go now. And the master won't appreciate us fooling around in here. Prepare me."

Shortly after, I walked through the house in the direction of the courtyard with the plug and strap uncomfortably in place. I wished Phineas would get over this foolishness. It was more than annoying, and I don't believe it improved my skills at all. It only served to make me cranky.

When I got outside, my gaze was drawn to where they'd suspended poor Jemin. They'd attached his wrists and ankles together, and spread him wide from post to post. His buttocks had been tilted at an angle and rested on a giant slab of stone. His head was resting against a piece of wood which ran the length from each post. His anus was clearly visible and at the perfect angle to be invaded. I winced.

Horace stood beside me now. "Don't worry, brother," he said. "Jemin doesn't mind. In fact he craves it. I've yet to meet a man who enjoys having his ass filled more than that one. He is a whore to the fullest."

I narrowed my eyes as a soldier now walked into the courtyard. He walked up to Jemin and began to play in his most intimate of crevices. I could hear Jemin moan, his body moving as he tried to thrust. Two other soldiers joined this one. They stood there laughing and jeering. One of them exposed his penis and began to rub the head of it against Jemin's sensitive opening. He cried out. "Yes, oh yes...um...fuck me. Fuck me."

The soldier teased him some more with the hilt of his sword, his tongue, then finally, he rammed his cock into him. He fucked him steady and hard while the others cheered him on.

"Gold," Horace said, snapping me back to reality. "Are you ready?"

I nodded and I turned away. As Horace challenged me with the lasso, I went through the proper moves but my mind was filled with Jemin's cries. At least three times during the training, a soldier violated Jemin, and each time, Jemin cried out with pleasure.

Finally, Horace told me that it was time to stop for the day. Phineas came out into the courtyard to meet us. "Splendid," he said. "You did well, very well." He glanced at Jemin. "If you want to fuck his opening, you may go ahead, but it's your choice."

He knew that I wouldn't. He'd done it on purpose, to strip Jemin of what had appealed to me most, his innocence. "Thank you, master, but I am tired."

"Very well," he said. "Take the slave down," he told the soldier. He placed a hand on my biceps and walked me back to the house. "Simeon will come for the contest tomorrow. I have invited him, and his family."

"Did you ask him if…"

"I suggested he put Julian in Samson's place. He said that he'd consider it."

"Thank you," I replied. "Is there something I should know about this Julian?"

He pondered that for a moment. "Yes. He's like you. He's never been defeated."

* * * *

Julian had taken me in the bath. While the soldier stood outside, Julian stripped us both of our clothes, pulled me into the water and filled my ass with his cock. It had been rough and fast but just what we both needed. We didn't dare take too long what with that soldier nearby. We knew that we could have been interrupted at any time.

I woke up with the taste of him on my mouth. I had managed to suck his cock some before he practically raped me. I was smiling during training which perplexed Phillip, who was able to best me at every turn today. "What's with you, brother? Gold will take your head the moment you get into the arena."

The smile disappeared. I threw the wooden sword aside and stalked off to get some water.

Julian called for a break and we went inside.

"What's with you?" Phillip demanded as I glared at him.

"Nothing. I just don't need to be reminded that I will face Gold in the arena, that's all."

Phillip shrugged. "There is nothing you can do to change it."

I was about to say something in reply but then Simeon walked in. "My fine gladiators," he called out with his hands in the air.

We all turned to listen quietly.

"Tonight, my lovely wife and I shall leave for Phineas' house where I will witness the contest between Gold and the Destroyer on the morn. The winner will fight one of you shortly. I have the list of who else will fight in the upcoming tournament." He handed the list to Julian. "It will be a grand event. Carry on," he said and turned on his heels.

"I suppose that means Claudius will be in charge," Phillip muttered.

I sighed, and nodded.

Julian called for our attention again and began to announce who would challenge who. "The contests will be between us, and none of them to the death. Only for show." There were many comments and some laughter as he read out the names. Men boasted about who would best who. It was all in fun. "Alright, men," Julian intercepted, "let there be calm. From now on, you practice your fights with your intended opponents. Remember, it's for sport and should be done in mind of entertainment. Samson, you will train with me."

I glanced over at him and smiled.

"You seem pleased about that," Phillip snarled. "Tasted his cock yet?"

"If I have, you wouldn't be told," I snapped.

Chapter Four

Torn

It felt strange seeing Simeon again, although less than three months had passed since I'd been bought by his arch rival. I wasn't sure really which master I hated most—Simeon or Phineas. They were very different, but equally deviant in their own ways.

The party Phineas held on the eve before the contest was small, with only a handful of very select guests. Simeon and Gracia obviously felt privileged to be among such elite company, even though everyone knew they hated the host. Status climbing made strange bedfellows.

Phineas' wife was gracious to the wife of her husband's arch enemy. She paid Gracia many compliments on her appearance. I could hear them as I stood there, all oiled up and on display for the onlookers. I studied Phineas' wife as she played the perfect hostess. Phineas was lucky to have such a dutiful wife however he didn't appreciate Dora at all. Although she wasn't exactly beautiful, she had an almost regal way of carrying herself. Unlike Gracia, she didn't appear to be mean and calculating but then she didn't have the influence Gracia did when it came to business either. I was starting to think that maybe women had to become calculating if they wanted to be noticed at all. Phineas basically ignored Dora, as he did his small son and adolescent daughter, who I hadn't seen since she'd been apparently sent away to 'charm' school — what parents called the place where all wayward little girls got sent when they didn't accept their lot in life.

I spied Maris now and observed how he followed Dora around like a small puppy. He looked to her as a mother, and I couldn't help but feel a pang of regret that he'd not been returned to his rightful family. However, there was little I could do about that now.

Although neither Phineas nor Simeon had approached since the party began, others had been over to examine me several times. As usual, they felt my muscles, examined my scars, and paused to argue my chances against the Destroyer, as if I wasn't there. I stayed mute, and their words waved in and out of my consciousness.

The Destroyer was present as well. He was made to stand on the other side of the room. He was also oiled up and drew a lot of attention due to his size. I had no idea what was going inside his head. Was he afraid? Did he think he was going to die tomorrow at my hands? Did he pity me, think that maybe I would be the one to die?

Phineas suddenly came to stand beside me. He motioned to the Destroyer, who walked over to where we were. Phineas called to the guests, asking them to gather round. "Tomorrow, a clear champion will be chosen. You alone will be witness to the future. Now, I would dismiss my two gladiators so they can rest before tomorrow.

Please help yourself to more wine, and food. Let us celebrate with anticipation."

There was applause, and more talk. Finally, the Destroyer followed the guard outside, and I was allowed to head down the corridor to my quarters. A soldier watched me from the end of the hall but he didn't follow.

I lay down on my bed and closed my eyes. I doubted I'd be able to sleep with all the noise. I was not concerned about the contest. There was no sense in worrying. I would either beat my opponent, or die trying. Either scenario was acceptable to me.

I finally dozed off, and somewhere in my sleep, I heard a voice whisper, "Gold. Gold. Wake up."

I opened my eyes. Simeon stood in front of me, a goblet in his hand. I sat up.

He smiled. "I have missed you. How do you fare here?"

I shrugged. "How does a slave fare anywhere?" I'd forgotten how freely I used to speak to him.

"You have been given a place in his house. It is unheard of, really, to keep a gladiator this close. He spoils you more than I did, but then I'm sure he keeps you close for a reason." He reached down and touched my cheek. "I would have you right now, my Gold, if you were still mine to have."

I said nothing, relieved that Simeon would for once have no access to my body.

"What would you wish for if I could give it to you?"

"I would ask for you to choose another to fight me, other than Samson."

"Phineas has already asked this on your behalf." He studied me. "Who then would you have challenge you in his place? Eventually, they will all want to challenge you."

I shook my head. "Samson will be dead in minutes if you put him in the arena."

"Could you kill him?"

"I'd rather he kill me."

He narrowed his eyes. "You would give your life for his?"

I nodded. I knew if it came down to it, I would. I didn't wish to dwell on the reason.

"It is not meant to be, not meant for you to die." He leant forward and kissed me on the forehead, a rare show of sentiment. "The gods have told me."

I looked at him curiously. "Then if the gods are to be believed, you would sacrifice Samson? Why would you sacrifice your future champion? What game do you play, Simeon?"

"You are still mine," he said with his jaw tight, "and either my champion will rise in the house of Phineas, or my house champion will kill his. Either way I win."

I marvelled at creativity of his logic.

He laughed sharply. "I know what you are thinking, my Gold. And yes, either way, I do lose as well. When I lost you, I lost everything." He paused. "Oh gods, Gold, I miss you," he groaned, dropping to his knees in front of me. "My cock misses you. My ass misses you. How pathetic is that?"

Simeon was on his knees. I knew he was drunk but this was unimaginable...and he'd just finished criticising Phineas for keeping me in his house.

"Please." I seized the moment, rationalising that this was the time to ensure that he didn't put Samson in the arena to challenge me. "Please choose another Gladiator, master. In my heart, know that I will fight for the House of Simeon, even if I am no longer yours. If you put up another as opponent, I will win this for you. It will be our secret."

He struggled to his feet. "One day," he shook his head, and swallowed some wine, "you *will* face Samson, like it or not, and you *will* kill him. That I know for sure in my heart."

I shook my head. "No."

He smiled. "It is inevitable. I know you. I made you." He reached down and stroked my biceps. "I will ask the gods to smile on you tomorrow."

I bowed my head in acknowledgement.

He moved away from me. "Claudius asked me to give you his regards. He had to stay behind to run things. He will prepare for his upcoming wedding."

"Congratulations," I said.

He left me.

I got up and stood at the open window. The curtains blew in the wind and the stars sparkled in the night sky. I wondered if Samson was looking at the same stars. Maybe, just maybe, I'd bought some time. But one day, I realised, it was inevitable. I would face Samson in that arena, and one of us would die. *Samson. I miss you.*

* * * *

Claudius was on his own and drunk again. This time he summoned me alone. I dreaded whatever plan he had in his head. As it turned out, more than anything, he wanted to talk, or rather, to rant. I had no idea why he chose me to do that with.

When I entered the room, he was soaking in the bath. He waved at me to join him. I lowered my coverings, walked into the water, and sat across from him.

"Slave, bring him wine," he called out.

A naked slave girl handed me a goblet of wine, and quickly refilled his glass as well.

I nodded my thanks to him and took a drink. I wondered where this would lead.

"Day after tomorrow, my intended will arrive, along with her family. They will stay for the upcoming competitions, three long weeks to endure her presence. Did you know she is ugly as a whipping post?"

"No, master," I said. I hid a smile. "I didn't know that."

"And I'm expected to fuck her after we are joined. The gods have decreed her extremely fertile, thus she's been kept under lock and key. I'm told she is quite green when it comes to matters of the flesh."

I wasn't sure what to say to that. I knew however that after he married, he would actually have more freedom to have sex with whom he chose, especially after the conception of the first child. I wondered if I should remind him, ease his mind so that he'd let me return to the gladiators' quarters. Finally, I decided that would be over-stepping my place.

"I wanted to go with father. I wanted to see Gold. Would you have liked that, Samson, to see your beloved?"

He was baiting me. It was actually painful, spiteful, but his cruelty sometimes seemed to know no limits. The thought of looking upon the face I loved more than any other filled me with such longing, I felt as if I wanted to cry. I didn't however. I swallowed the knot in my throat and remained silent.

"Answer!"

"Yes, master, I would have liked that very much," I managed.

"You still may have your chance," he laughed. "You may look upon him in the arena and then try and take his head."

I winced. No, I couldn't do that. It wasn't only because I knew that Gold could best me in the competition, but because I loved him so much.

"And Julian, my mother's whore, how will you feel if he is put in your place?"

"Julian?" I breathed. *No.*

"There is no one else but Julian. Either you go to your death against Gold, or you send Julian to his, in your place."

"You know this for sure?" I blurted out. I felt my heart slam against my ribs.

"You question me?" He downed some wine.

"No, master, I…"

"I have heard the debate. I know that Julian is the only choice, the only one certain individuals will accept to go in your place."

"He is the trainer. He…"

"That is irrelevant, as is my mother's bawling about the matter. Although she protests, she dare not protest too hard, lest my father suspect that she has a weakness for her Roman whore master. And from the look on your face, it seems you have a weakness for him as well."

I lowered my head.

"Is he good? I ask only because I want to know if he fucks my mother well. Perhaps I'll try him on for size."

I glanced down at my reflection in the water. "He is more than adequate," I murmured.

"Good. Maybe I should let him fuck me right in front of her. My mother has done nothing for me. When I asked her to save me from marriage to this cow, she turned her back on me. It would serve her right to see Julian put his cock elsewhere, other than her putrid cunt."

I heard the bitterness in his voice.

He stood now, and called for a towel. "Now, if watching her whore master fuck her own son doesn't faze the bitch, watching Gold slaughter him in the arena should."

"Please," I said under my breath.

He laughed. "Get up," he told me. "Slave," he bellowed, "throw him a towel." He glanced at the guard. "Go and get the trainer, and bring him to me. I have yet to figure out what she sees in him. And I'm anxious to tell him the news."

"Is it definite that Julian will fight Gold?" I couldn't stop myself. I had to ask.

He pushed the slave away and finished drying himself. He walked naked across the floor and stood in front of me. He took my towel and threw it aside. "From where I sit, it is."

I swallowed as Claudius raked his eyes over me. This wasn't what I wanted. I didn't want Julian to take on Gold. But then, who? If it wasn't me, it meant that someone else would have to die. I'd be responsible.

He studied me. "I am told that Phineas is very creative when it comes to his sexual games. When he was here the last time, Phineas told me about a game he loves to play with bad slaves. He has them bound, wrist to ankle and ties them in the courtyard, exposing their anus and allowing whomever to use it. I was told it's delicious."

My eyes widened.

"I'd love to see you like that. I'm sure Gold would enjoy it if he was here. I wonder if they do that to him, or who he fucks at the House of Phineas?"

I wanted to die with each word.

"Guards," he called out, "take this slave outside, string him up, wrist to ankle." He licked his lips.

"No, please," I pleaded.

"I won't hurt you. My father would be very upset if I did that. You're his next champion, after all. Anyway, it's either you or Julian I put out there. And although, as a slave, you have no choice, I will be benevolent, and give you one." He glanced around as Julian was brought in. "Make your decision."

I nodded. "I'll go."

Julian was the trainer. I couldn't allow him to be humiliated like that. And more than that, Julian would take his place against Gold, which meant he probably wouldn't make it out alive.

The guards grabbed me and pulled me out of the room. Julian gave me a curious look as I went by but I had no answers for him.

The guards lifted me up on top of a slab and attached my wrists above my head, one to one post, and one to the other. Then they pushed up my legs, dragged my butt to the front and tethered my ankles to my wrists, stretching my legs as wide as they could go. My back and head were lying flat and the only thing I could see were the glittering stars in the night sky shining above me.

I felt the air hit my exposed anus and I knew that I was completely vulnerable to anything Claudius could conjure up in his warped imagination.

Two guards nearby sniggered. One of them slid his hand between my butt cheeks and poked his finger into me. "Nice and tight," he growled. "I'd love to fuck that."

"Better not," the other said. "The Master approaches with his mother's favourite rooster."

A hand slapped my buttocks. "Well, Julian," it was Claudius' voice, "what do you think? Is it the nicest ass you've had? My mother's I'm sure doesn't compare. Does mother ever ask you to fuck her in the ass?"

There was silence.

"Answer me, Julian, or I'll flog you. And don't lie, because I know all about Mother's afternoon play sessions. Although I'm not quite sure how she got you here, I suspect you have a history. And she craves your cock like I crave Samson's ass at this moment. So, tell me, even though I know the answer. Does she ask you to fuck her in the ass?"

"Yes," he replied.

"Imagine that, my mother is a very dirty, dirty lady. And you enjoy it better than her cunt, don't you? You enjoy taking her from behind?"

"No," he said.

"Don't let her hear that." A hand moved over my buttocks. "This here is a slut. First, with my Gold, and now a slut for my mother's whore master. He needs to find his own cock to play with, don't you think?"

Several fingers plunged into me. I grunted. A hand reached up between my legs and very casually played with my cock. It began to swell. Then the hand moved to my balls and rolled them in their fingers. At the same time now, fingers moved in and out of my anus. "Bring me grease," he called out.

I was trembling as he pulled his fingers out.

A few minutes later, the torture began again. A greasy hand moved between my ass cheeks then began to fuck my hole, one finger, two, then, four.

I groaned, thrashed.

"Julian, come here. Julian will now stroke your cock. Do it slowly," Claudius urged.

I felt Julian's touch and I closed my eyes. My body rocked forward as fingers moved in and out of my ass and Julian squeezed and jerked my penis.

It went on and on until I thought I'd pass out. Every once and awhile, when I was on the verge of coming, Claudius would order Julian to stop touching me.

"Please," I pleaded. I wanted Julian to fuck me. I wanted anyone to fuck me.

Claudius withdrew his fingers. "Now," he said. "My cock."

He entered me without hesitation and fucked me frantically and for a long time, finally coming inside me. I was breathing hard but my cock was still erect and I was now suffering. "Three guards," he called out. "Line up. Take him. Take the slut, fuck him good. And at the same time, Julian," he commanded, "down on your knees. Make me hard again with your mouth, and then, Samson," he called out, "I'm going to fuck Julian's ass. Listen for his cries."

Cock after cock entered me, the first one was small, and the inserter came fast. The second one made me groan. It was large and thick, and if I tried hard, I could imagine it was Gold.

Claudius was moaning as were the soldiers, and Julian let out a cry which told me Claudius was fucking him there on the ground a few feet away from me.

The big cock was long lasting. I could feel each thrust intensely, and I was desperate for release. I pleaded as I heard Claudius release inside of Julian.

The big cock let go as well and shouted. Another cock quickly replaced it and I was like a coil. If someone didn't give me release soon, I was going to lose my mind.

The last one came inside of me then Claudius murmured. "Enough." He slapped my ass again. "How was that?"

"Please," I moaned.

He chuckled. "Julian is as hard as rock. Should I let him have you?"

"Um, please, yes. Yes." Would he have mercy?

I felt Julian's hand on my cock. "It's okay," he said softly, "breathe. Close your eyes." He moved his hand over my cock in long smooth strokes, while soft fingers tips flirted with my entrance. I started to hyperventilate. My hips lifted up. I pulled at the constraints like a crazy man.

I could hear Claudius laugh. I didn't care. "Fuck me," I cried out to Julian. "Fuck me, please."

He was inside of me, moving, his hand still fondling my cock and within seconds, my cock pumped into the air. I gasped, the orgasm so strong, I thought the top of my head would blow off.

I lay there spent, exhausted. My tongue moved over my lips and I sighed with pleasure as Julian came in my ass.

"Just a receptacle, nothing more," Claudius said, "a hole to play in. You are a real slut, Samson, born to be a slave. Cut him down," he commanded. "Take them both back to the ludi."

When I was lowered to the ground, my legs were so cramped, I could hardly walk. Julian put my arm around his shoulders and led me back to the gladiators' quarters.

The soldiers leered at me before they left us, chuckling and talking among themselves as they went back outside.

"Are you all right?" Julian asked.

I sat down, then winced and stood back up. "My ass is sore."

"No doubt. I have something for that."

I nodded gratefully. "Julian?"

"Hmm?"

"They are intending to put you in the arena with Gold, in my place."

He didn't react.

"Julian, say something."

"What do you want me to say?"

"I don't want you to die. It will be my fault and…"

"You have little faith," he smiled.

"I know Gold. He's fierce. He's the best and…"

"And, is he the best at everything?" He met my gaze.

I lowered my head.

"You love him. That's why you can't fight him. And there is no one else that comes close. They need a show. I can give them one."

It was impossible. I couldn't see either one of them dead. "I will face Gold."

"It may be too late. You need to understand something, Samson," Julian said, leading me through the passage to his cell, "you are not in control. They can do whatever they want with us."

"Then we must leave here, be free."

Julian raised an eyebrow. "A revolt?"

I nodded.

"Lay down on your stomach."

I did as he asked and he very gently applied a soothing balm between my ass cheeks. I closed my eyes.

"Sleep now," he said. "We can talk tomorrow."

Blackness moved in on me. I saw Gold in the arena. *Gold will now face the Destroyer…Gold. Gold. Blood soaked the sand. The Destroyer stood, a mace over his head and there was Gold, still, dead. Gold? No. No!*

* * * *

Horace hadn't stopped talking at me since I'd risen that morning and frankly I wished only for peace. "Horace," I said suddenly, "I need to rest my mind. I know all that you tell me, and I thank you for your care. Now I need solitude before the battle."

He nodded and left me.

I paced in the place under the arena. It was quieter than I was used to. The general public hadn't been invited so the crowd would not be a distraction. I also couldn't use it for energy. The chanting and the encouragement of the crowd sometimes could refocus your concentration.

It would be easy just to let the Destroyer kill me today. I'd have all that I wanted, a gladiator's death, and a way out, so I wouldn't have to meet Samson in the arena.

And as I walked into the ring, that was, of course, in the back of my mind.

* * * *

I was a little stiff today, but the cream Julian had applied to my anus the night before had helped. It was not my physical condition that plagued me, however. It was my emotional health which was the more fragile of the two.

Gold was in the ring with the Destroyer. Although I didn't know the exact time of the competition today, I could feel it. It made me nauseous.

My fighting was off, but Julian knew why, and he went easy on me.

When it was over for the day, I sat outside quietly, looking out at the water. *Was he all right? Did he live?* I would hear nothing until the master returned.

I spent a sleepless night. The next day, in the early afternoon, the master and his wife returned, along with Claudius' intended and her parents.

"Julian," I said when I could no longer contain myself, "please, can you not go to the house to ask how the contest went?"

231

He nodded at me. No emotion showed in his face but I knew there was a lot going on inside of him. Did it pain him to know how desperate I was to find out about Gold? I never promised Julian love, nor him to me.

I was left standing in the courtyard, the wooden weapon at my side. *Please, let him live.*

Suddenly, the guard approached. "You are to go to the house, immediately. The master wishes to speak with you."

I almost ran across the yard to the door. When I arrived, Simeon, Gracia and Claudius sat around with an older couple and the young woman who must have been Claudius' future bride. Claudius didn't look very happy. Julian stood off to one side.

I bowed my head. "Master."

The guard backed away.

"Samson," he stood. "I have an announcement to make, to all of you," he looked around the room. "Samson, you will not be fighting Gold in the arena."

I tensed. *Did that mean Gold was dead, that he had lost the fight?*

"Julian will face Gold," he said. "You will face Gold at another time in the future."

I let out of breath. Gold lived.

Gracia jumped to her feet. "That can't be!"

Everyone turned their attention to her.

"That is most absurd. Julian is our trainer. He is not a gladiator for the ring. If he falls, who shall train them?"

"We've had this conversation before," Simeon sighed.

Claudius suddenly looked amused.

"Yes, well apparently you didn't hear me," she snapped. "Julian will not go into the ring with Gold! We will not waste our best trainer for sport!"

There was dead silence for a moment then the father of Claudius' intended spoke. "My gods, Simeon. Control your wife."

Simeon looked at Julian and me. "Go," he said, motioning to the guard.

As we walked out, we heard Simeon shout. "I am the master of this house. What I say shall be, woman!"

I looked at Julian as we crossed the courtyard. "Are you all right with this?"

"Do I have a choice?" He asked me. Then suddenly, he said, "I will say, however, I have to wonder who you will be cheering for in that ring, Samson."

I balked.

Julian walked inside.

* * * *

I had come close to surrender in that ring with the Destroyer. Then I thought, if the Destroyer meets Samson, he won't show mercy. Maybe I was Samson's greatest chance, aside from using myself as a human shield in the ring. I knew I couldn't protect him forever but I'd take one challenge at a time.

I brought the sword down on the Destroyer's neck. As he looked up at me, waiting for death, images of Phineas, Simeon, and Claudius, and every prominent citizen who'd ever used and humiliated me, stared back at me. The victory was therefore sweet.

I noticed that Phineas and Simeon seemed to bond somehow over this at the party the night before. They held up each other's hands, and walked around the room, shouting. "I consider this a shared win," Phineas had said, toasting his rival. "Simeon's champion, in my house."

I had stood by silently, thinking how trivial and meaningless it was. A man was dead and it was of no importance.

Others moved around me and I was subjected to a great deal of admiration and praise. I couldn't wait for it to be over.

"In three weeks' time," Phineas had announced, "Gold will meet Julian, my former trainer, the unbeaten foe, and then a true champion will reign."

There was applause. I closed my eyes, breathing deeply. Finally, I knew I wouldn't face Samson in the arena. I had been given a reprieve.

Simeon smiled over at me, and I nodded my thanks.

Sullis came up and stood beside me. "Congratulations."

I nodded at him.

"You were superb today," he'd told me, "so beautiful, so masterful. You pleased Phineas, made him very proud. He will reward you."

"He already has."

"It will only buy time," Sullis warned, reaching out to pinch Jemin on the ass as he walked by.

"I'll take it."

Maris had come running over as well. He hugged me tight. "Gold, you are my hero. You are the best there is."

I smiled at him. "Thanks, boy."

The next day, Phineas pampered me. The slaves bathed me and fed me by hand. I was excused from training that day. Sullis lay with me and I fucked him all afternoon. And that night, as I sat drinking wine and eating at the master's table, Jemin was sent for.

My gaze drank him in as he walked up to the master, his head bowed. He was naked, adorned only with nipple clips and a cock ring.

Phineas looked at his wife. "Retire to your room, woman."

She quickly rose and disappeared.

"Does he please you, Gold?" he asked me as he sat back in his seat, grinning.

"Yes." How long I'd wanted that ass.

"Before I was jealous, but now I know it is mere lust you hold for him. And tonight, I would give him to you. I do wonder, however, who has your heart, Gold?"

I didn't answer that. I would never tell them who it was, although it seemed more than obvious.

Phineas stood. He pulled the cloth from the table. The dishes clattered to the floor. I looked at him curiously, as did the servants.

He chuckled. "Jemin, get on the table, on your back."

Jemin obeyed immediately and lay down.

The master shouted for wine. He ran his hand over Jemin's nakedness, pulled on the clamps hard and handled his cock roughly.

Jemin whimpered as Phineas ordered him to place his hands behind his head.

Phineas poured the wine over Jemin's chest and over his groin. He yanked him to the side of the table. Reaching out, he pulled Jemin's legs wide apart and placed a bowl of grapes on the table between his thighs. "Lift his legs," he told me, "and insert the grapes into his anus, as many as you can. Then take them out with your teeth and your tongue."

I lifted Jemin's legs, met his gaze. Jemin licked his lips, his cock already hard. I pressed the grapes into his anus — three, then four.

"Um," he nodded. "I'm so full."

I lowered his legs and started to lick his clamped nipples. I removed one clamp, bit his nipple and put it back on. He squirmed on the table. My cock leapt for joy. I licked down his chest to his groin and savoured the wine there, then lifted his hips and rolled him onto his side.

I dug my tongue inside of him and fished out the grapes. He let out a cry as I continued my exploration. I massaged his firm little ass and slapped it a few times.

"You want him, Gold?" Phineas insisted.

"Yes," I looked at him for permission.

"Plug his ass again then tip his head over the side, and feed him your big, hard cock. He's a supreme slut. He loves it."

I pushed four more grapes into his ass then yanked his head over the side. I poured wine on my cock and lowered it into his mouth. He licked and sucked me almost violently. I was on the verge when I backed away. I reached out and played with those clamps, pulling on them with my teeth and stroking his cock until it stood up straight in the air. Then I pulled him off the table and pressed him down to all fours.

I took my time. I massaged his cock again, removed the clamps, threw them aside and pulled and pinched both nipples. Then I sucked out the grapes and inserted my fingers, fucking him like that until his anus felt ready. I plunged into him and shouted out with joy as I took his tight, needy little ass.

He was sobbing, yelling, "Yes, oh yes. Fuck me. Fuck my ass, Gold! I'm your whore, your slut."

When I came, I jerked him to come with me. When I reared back, the master reached out and grabbed Jemin by the hair. He pulled him to his groin, and lifted his robe. "Suck it, bitch."

I tried to get my breath as the master used Jemin's mouth. "Back on the table," he ordered after a few minutes.

Jemin scrambled back onto the table.

"Bring your ass to the edge, legs up in the air."

I watched, my cock hard again.

Phineas smiled at me. "Take him, and while you do, I'm going to fuck your ass good and hard, ride you like a fine stallion."

I grabbed Jemin's legs and pushed them up onto my shoulders. I stabbed his anus with the head of my cock, moving it in and out a few times before sinking into the depth of him.

Phineas seized my hips. "Grease," he called out. "Grease him," he commanded one of the house slave, an older man with blond hair.

I slowly stabbed into Jemin's ass who pulled on his own nipples as I fucked him slowly.

Slippery fingers were now preparing me for the master. I licked my lips. The sensation was sending me to Nirvana.

I kept up the slow, rhythm as Jemin moaned and groaned, and I began to make some noise as Phineas pulled at both my nipples and the slave continued to delve his fingers up into my ass.

Four fingers stretched me wide and the muscles had now surrendered. I actually craved his cock.

Phineas pushed the slave away. "Withdraw." He grabbed my hair, yanked back my head and pushed into me, his cock going in all the way so that for a moment I couldn't breathe. I felt his balls slap my ass and he began to control the movements. I moved as he did. Jemin cried out as I did. The room was filled with our passion.

Jemin came, his hand on his cock. I came almost at the same time but the master wasn't ready. He pulled me from Jemin and pushed me face down on the table, slamming into my ass like a tidal wave. I groaned with each slam of his hips then clamped my teeth shut when he let loose, shouting as a soldier would after a great victory of war.

He pulled out and slapped my ass a few times. Then he pulled me up, turned me around and pressed me down on the table on my back. "Spread your legs," he ordered.

I was covered in sweat and cum. He stood there and looked at me, ran his hand through his hair. He reached out and fondled my failing cock, massaged my balls, moved his hand up over my belly and slowly twisted my nipples hard.

I was erect again.

He smiled at me, again slapping my cock back and forth. "You are incredible. So hard, so fast. Don't move."

It wasn't the most comfortable of positions but I had no choice. I had to remain there.

The slaves were all watching me as well, waiting as if to see what he'd do next.

"Jemin, get off the table," he ordered. "Play with his cock, his balls, his nipples. Only your hands."

Jemin came to stand in front of me. My cock leapt. He ran his fingers over my shaft. I closed my eyes. He lifted my cock, let it fall, rolled my balls in his hand then slapped my cock a few times as the master had done.

I groaned.

Phineas went to sit on his sofa. He watched quietly, rubbing himself.

Jemin's hand left my cock and went to my nipples. He licked his lips again and moved both thumbs over my hard, dark nubs.

I swallowed, my cock standing out straight. He brushed my cock with his and played with my nipples, his gaze stroking them as he watched his fingers build them into even stiffer tips and pulled and pinched them hard. I winced.

Phineas laughed.

"Please," I looked at him.

The master stood, motioned to me.

I walked over to him, my heavy cock swinging like a club between my thighs.

He got down and knelt over the sofa. "Fuck me," he invited. "Jemin, you may fuck Gold, but only with your fingers while he fucks me."

I leaned down and gripped Phineas' hips then fucked his ass like a man gone mad. Jemin put his fingers inside me but he couldn't keep them there. I slammed Phineas hard on that sofa then took him down on the floor. He pounded his fist on the carpet and cried out as he grabbed my hand and led it to his cock. "Oh yeah, yeah. My champion! My champ!"

Finally when the master had recaptured his breath, he told Jemin to get out.

Jemin left the room, a smile on his face.

"There," Phineas said. He covered himself again and called for wine. "My gift to you. Now, you will stay with me tonight." He glanced down at me, his gaze assessing my cock again. "I want it. I want your cock again tonight. Clean yourself and come to my bed."

I nodded and got to my feet. He was insatiable. "Yes, master," I muttered.

* * * *

Several house slaves had been whipped which meant Gracia was in a foul mood. Julian had said nothing to me about it, but he'd been summoned to the house by Gracia three times.

Finally I had occasion to speak to Julian alone. "What is happening with Gracia?"

He looked sullen. He heaved a sigh. "I have no idea what to do with her. She flies into a rage and breaks into tears. I've told her it is of no consequence and that I want to meet Gold in the ring, but she is determined to put a stop to it. Samson," he looked down into my eyes, "she told me if she can't stop this contest, she will find a way to make sure Gold loses."

I narrowed my eyes. "Loses? You mean, she will..." I gasped. "Why would you tell me this?" A feeling of utter helplessness made me angry suddenly. I knew if she was determined to do something to fix the fight, I would have no power to stop her. "It's in your interest."

Julian looked shocked. "What kind of a man do you think I am? There is no honour in facing a man that's been drugged."

"Drugged?"

"It is her plan," he nodded. "She has told me not to worry, that Gold will be weakened before he goes into the arena, and that he won't feel anything when I kill him."

"When...how does she intend to do this?"

"They will come here, Phineas' troupe, be housed here as Simeon's guests during the contest since it will be at the local arena. She will have a servant do it, I'm sure."

"We must warn Gold."

He nodded. "Yes, but it will have to be you. I will not be allowed to see Gold before the contest. Simeon told me I am to be housed in a separate place."

"Then I will see him, Gold? I will talk to him before the..." I trailed off. Tears lit my eyes.

"You will," Julian turned away.

"Julian," I put a hand on his arm. "I'm sorry. I..."

He shook off my hand. "You cannot help who you love."

"I thank you for..."

"I didn't do it for you. I will not fight a man who is at a disadvantage." He walked outside, and left me to ponder this. I would see Gold, but at a price that was already too high. Gold and Julian fighting each other seemed like a nightmare to me. And I wished I could change things, meet Gold myself in that arena, just let him kill me and put me out of my misery.

Outside I could hear the sound of the men practicing with their wooden swords. I knew Julian waited for me.

I walked out into the sunshine and joined him. He smiled at me. "Don't despair. You must practice. This morning, the lanista told me you will be profiled against several gladiators here, to show your potential for champion." He raised the stick. "He doesn't expect me to survive this."

I met his stick silently with my own. There was nothing to say.

The next weeks were hectic. Simeon had decided that his son's wedding should take place on the eve of the contests, a kind of lead in to the celebrations. Thus, the preparations were already in hand.

Claudius was drunk almost every night, but thankfully didn't call on any of us to serve his lust. Several times however, he came into the gladiators' quarters in the middle of the night, singing at the top of his lungs, and shouting out crude remarks. The master had the guards remove him.

On the day Phineas and his troupe were to arrive, I rose to see Gracia standing outside the gladiator quarters. She clung to Julian, in the early dawn, her head pressed against his chest.

He stood there quietly while she carried on.

I watched from the doorway, and waited until she hurried away. The sun hadn't even come up yet.

I walked outside to meet him. "What did she say?"

He shook his head. "Nothing of importance."

"She's not going to go through with her plan, is she?"

"I have no idea what is going on in her head. I've asked her not to interfere. All we can do is warn Gold to be careful when he arrives. That's all."

* * * *

As we were led though the courtyard in the direction of my former home, I had flashbacks of my capture. I remembered when I was first brought here, how I'd fought, the final taste of freedom still fresh on my tongue.

My heart pounded in my chest as I scanned the horizon for a glimpse of him. *Samson*. It would be worth dying just to see him again. As we rounded the corner, I heard the familiar sounds of wooden sticks battling. And there were the gladiators, not numerous like Phineas' ludi, but some fine specimens nevertheless.

Then I saw Samson. He stood just a few feet from me, looking at me. I paused, caught my breath, and smiled faintly at him. I wanted to touch him, kiss him, but of course that was impossible.

I wondered which one was Julian.

Phillip came over immediately now. He clamped a hand on my shoulder. "Brother," he said. "Good to see you looking so well."

I gave him a hard hug. "Phillip. Gabien?" I called out, as he too came to meet me.

Samson wandered over slowly, as if it was difficult for him to walk. The other two stood aside as he approached. "Gold," he said. His eyes were glistening with unshed tears. Mine were hiding in my throat, making it ache.

242

"How are you?" I asked him as my gaze met his. He looked wonderful, fit, and handsome. I felt desire, as always, and—love? Yes. Oh yes, love.

He just stood there looking at me, as if he couldn't actually form words.

I placed a hand on his forearm. I saw his throat work.

I nodded again and walked past him as the guards shouted at us to keep moving. He reached out and clutched my forearm. I looked at him. "Gold," he said, something desperate in his voice. "Gold, I have to tell you something. Listen…" Then the guards yelled again, drowning out his words and someone pulled me forward, away from him. Whatever he wanted to tell me would have to wait.

Chapter Five

Reunions

Samson and I saw each other only from a distance. We were told not to socialise with the members of Simeon's troupe, and we were relegated to separate ends of the courtyard. At the house, there was great activity as Simeon and Gracia prepared for their only child's nuptials. I hadn't seen Claudius' intended but I was told she was no prize, and the thought made me chuckle to myself.

Sullis had been in a nasty mood since our arrival. He complained about having to sleep in the gladiators' quarters. Today was the eve of the wedding. It was also the beginning of the three day ritual which would climax with my battle with the trainer called Julian. Sullis marched around the courtyard assuming an air of authority which was irritating the guards.

At one point, he walked over to where I was sparring with Horace and demanded to know why Horace got to sleep in the master's house, while he was excluded.

Horace paused and looked at him. "You take me away from important work to ask me this ridiculous question, while I must challenge Gold with toy swords?"

I hid a smile.

"It seems Simeon is less trusting than Phineas when it comes to weaponry," Sullis cleared his throat.

"Yes," he wiped the sweat off his brow, "but he could at least provide us with thicker wood." He glanced off to the side where several broken makeshift weapons lay. "Gold breaks them in half."

Sullis started to laugh.

Horace gave him a stony stare. "Is that all?"

"No," he sobered. "I should be staying at the great house as well. Why you, and not me?"

"Simple," he shrugged, "I am now a free man. You are not."

"A very minor detail," Sullis muttered.

Horace ignored him and lifted his weapon. He looked at me. "Again!"

As I fought, I saw Samson out of the corner of my eye. He'd been watching the interaction between Sullis, Horace and I. I looked at him. His gaze held mine.

Horace threw me to the dirt, the wooden weapon at my throat. "What distracts you, boy? You're dead."

I grinned at him. "Good thing that weapon is wood then." I held out my hand.

He took it and pulled me to my feet.

"Laugh, my friend, but you won't laugh in the arena."

I slapped him on the back. "You are far too serious." I wiped the sweat off my face and my chest, again looking over to see that Samson was still looking back. Our gazes held and I felt my lust rise. I wanted him. I *had* to find a way to have him.

Gold moved the piece of cloth down over his chest, absorbing all the sweat on his flesh, and I wanted to drop to my knees. What an impressive man he was—his chest so well muscled and defined, his thighs and calves so powerful. He was so beautiful, and I craved his body. He lifted his head now and smiled at me as if he knew where my thoughts were. I gave him a flirtatious smile back then sobered. There were more pressing matters than having him again, although right now, I had to prompt myself to think of what they were.

Gracia. I was hoping that with the wedding plans, she'd given up on her diabolical plan, but last night I overheard two guards talking about how Gracia had snuck into Julian's quarters twice during the night.

"The cow is getting her udders suckled good," one had chuckled.

"She appreciates Julian's fine Roman cock," the other responded, *"twice the size of old Simeon's I hear."*

As the wedding guests began to arrive, extra guards were positioned around the ludi, probably to assure the guests of their security from us ruffians.

One of the guards, Romulas, had slapped me on the buttocks a few times during training today. He was a guard on loan from Phineas, and I believed he'd taken a shine to me. I waited until I saw him do his walk past my cell.

"Romulas," I called out.

He paused, came to stand in the open door of my cell, looked at me. "You know my name?"

"Come in," I invited. "I want to show you something."

I had taken off my coverings and I lay sprawled out on the straw pile. I spread my thighs wide and casually played with my cock.

I saw him lick his lips, his eyes shining. He moved in closer. "Nice," he whispered.

"You like my cock?"

"Um," he nodded.

"You want my ass?"

He laid his weapon aside and closed the door. "I'm going to make you scream."

"I hope so," I growled. I stood, waited until he began to disrobe. I walked around him as if to inspect him then just before he caught on, I wound my arm around his throat and tightened it, cutting off his air. I knew that no matter how I played this, if I was discovered, I'd be put to death. Gold was more important.

The soldier grunted, struggled, tried to call out. He went to his knees and I snapped his neck. I pulled his body over to the corner and covered it with straw. Then I carefully made my way down the corridor to the other side where I knew my Gold was.

As I got round the corner, I could hear the party goers yelling and singing. The guards were still all around but distracted, thinking that they could slack off due to the fact that the masters were all drunk.

When I got to his cell, Gold was sitting on the floor, his head against the wall. He jumped to his feet when he saw me. I put a finger to my lips and closed the door.

We came together without words. I grabbed his face and kissed him hotly while I tore at his coverings like a mad man, desperate to touch his cock, to taste his balls. I wanted his cock inside me so badly, I was hyperventilating. And by the way he pulled at my clothing, I knew his impatience could easily rival mine.

"Gods, yes," he hissed, his mouth coming off mine as he whirled me around and pushed my chest against the wall. He wrenched my legs apart and went to his knees behind me. I felt his tongue laving my opening as he reached under and played with my balls, teasingly brushing the head of my cock with his knuckles at the same time.

I trembled with need. He kept licking me and he grabbed my hard rod and stroked it aggressively. I moaned, and pressed my forehead against the cool adobe. I pumped against the wall a little and his tongue got replaced by one finger then two. He fucked my hole very well with his two fingers then inserted a third, as his chest crushed my back and his lips found my ear. "Like that? Like my fingers up your ass?"

"Um, yes," I moaned.

The other hand moved up my chest. I winced as he brutalised one nipple then the other with his thumb and forefinger. He played with my nipples for the longest time while he went deeper inside of me with those fingers, and found the spot that made me beg him to fuck me.

His hand left my chest and went to my dripping cock. He squeezed the shaft, and jerked it then feathered his fingers across the head and around the sensitive tip. "Please, Gods, Gold. Please! Please, your cock."

The fingers came out and I felt the head of his shaft push up into me. I gasped. He pulled me backwards and with both hands pinched my nipples. He twisted and tugged at them as his cock divided my ass in two. I felt impaled, I felt filled. I felt as if his cock would at any moment slice me in two. I moaned with pleasure. "Fuck me," I hissed as he paused, and waited for me to settle in to the sensation. His fingers still on my nipples, he drove up into me, hard and fast, grunting with each push.

My tongue wet my lips. My head went back on his broad shoulder. I was his, completely. He reached down with one hand and slapped my cock and immediately jerked it as he pumped harder and I groaned loudly, no longer caring who heard. He slapped my cock again, then cupped my balls as he withdrew his cock and pushed me to my knees. He drove into me as I rested on all fours. The sensation of his rock hard cock sliced into my ass again wrenching a sharp cry out of the core of me. "Fuck me," I grunted and he instantly obliged. He grabbed my hair, yanked at it as if it was a slave collar and slammed my ass over and over until we both collapsed face down on the floor, and struggled for air.

"Gold," I whispered finally, as I crawled closer and touched his cheek. "Gold," I moaned.

He pulled me close to him, kissed the top of my head. I was in paradise but something nagged at me, and I finally used all my strength and moved out of his reach. I couldn't speak when he was this close. "Gold."

He looked at me, silently. He waited.

"Gracia intends to drug you."

He narrowed his eyes. "Drug me? Why?"

"She is in love with Julian, your opponent. He has told me to warn you."

"He has honour."

"He is a very good man."

Gold looked at me.

I looked away.

"You care for this man."

"Yes." I turned back to him. "I tried to care more, but you were there in the way. I don't love him. I'll never love him like I do you."

Gold nodded. He was quiet.

I touched his forearm. "I'm sorry."

"Don't be," he shrugged like it didn't matter. He stood. "We cannot be together, and if he defeats me..."

"No," I jumped up as well. I shook my head at the horror of it. "I can't bear the thought of either one of you..." I trailed off.

"One of us has to die, Samson."

A single tear rolled down his face. "Kill him quickly then. Don't let him suffer."

"Are you so sure he would show me the same, given that he probably knows how you feel about me?"

I blinked. "I don't think I want to talk about this. In fact," I looked at him, "I don't want to talk at all." I pressed him now against the wall and slid down to my knees. I took his cock in my hands. Gold placed his fingers in my hair.

"Go on," he urged. "Yes. Yes."

As Samson's tongue and lips devoured my cock, I couldn't get the thought out of my head that the man I was to fight to the death had been inside of Samson. Although Samson hadn't directly come out and said it, I knew it to be true. I couldn't help feel a little possessive at the moment given that Samson was pleasuring my cock into a frenzy, but I knew I didn't have the right. Gods only knew that I certainly had not led a chaste life since I'd been sold to Phineas, that I'd lusted after the house boy without conscience or regret. *Still.* It would have been easier if this Julian hadn't been shown to be so honourable.

I collapsed against the wall now. My eyes closed as Samson lapped at the cum on my shaft and moved his cheek against my groin. He reached up and pulled me down to him, his mouth capturing mine aggressively. He was hard again but I began to worry about getting caught by the guard.

Suddenly a question arose in my mind and I broke away from him.

"What's wrong?" he demanded. He sounded annoyed I had separated my mouth from his. "Kiss me, Gold."

I held him away. "How did you get to me?"

"What?" He seemed to shake himself.

"How did you get to me? They've increased the watch, and—"

"I have a dead soldier in my cell. I offered him my ass," he shrugged, "and he gave me his neck."

"Are you insane?" I demanded and yanked him up on his feet. "They'll take your life for this."

"It was worth it," he whispered.

"Do not be stupid," I snapped. "Nothing is worth that. Come on, we have to dispose of the soldier before someone realises he is missing."

I hauled him down the corridor while he protested that I was getting carried away. I shushed him. He didn't seem to have any idea of the consequences of what he'd done. I'd enjoyed fucking him well enough, but I wasn't sure it was worth our lives.

When we got back to Samson's cell, I pushed away the straw and looked down at the frozen face of the dead soldier. "Zeus's cock," I muttered.

"Yours is nicer," he whispered.

I stared at him. "Are you a fool?" But the smile on his face was contagious and I smiled back. "Damn you, Samson."

He pulled me close to kiss me. "It's your fault. You're so irresistible. Gold, let's get out of here, run."

"Where?" I asked him. I held him close, rubbed my cheek against his. If I thought we could get away with it, I would have gone in a heartbeat.

"Anywhere," he groaned. "I love you."

I swallowed.

"Gold," he looked into my eyes. "Say it. You do, don't you? You love me."

I nodded. "Yes, I love you."

He held me tight for a minute then released me. "So, handsome, what do we do with him?" He looked down at the dead man.

"I have an idea," I said.

It took some creative thinking to cover up Samson's dead soldier but I did it. While Samson distracted the guards outside by making small talk, I reached for a vat of wine that sat beside the entrance and dragged it inside. After dousing the dead man with the contents, I quickly hoisted the body over my shoulder, dashed around to the back of the compound and hauled him over the embankment. I didn't wait to see the body hit the water.

On the way back to my cell, Samson met me in the corridor. I cautioned him to keep his voice down, and not to wake the others. "What did you do with him?"

"Me, nothing?" I grinned. "He was just a drunk soldier who fell over the side."

Samson kissed me softly on the mouth. I melted against him, wanting to hold me in my arms again. Then suddenly we heard footsteps. I pushed Samson back away in the direction of his cell and raced to get back to mine. I was out of breath when the guard walked in. He looked around curiously. "Why aren't you asleep?"

I shrugged. "I have many things on my mind."

He paused, narrowed his eyes, and studied me for a moment while I held my breath. Then he said, "Yeah, Samson's cock, no doubt."

"There are many nicer cocks at Phineas' house."

"So I've heard," he said. "You could always try me," he gestured in a lewd way.

"I'd prefer not," I snorted.

He turned to go. "Don't know what you're missing. By the way," he glanced at me, "my money is on you for the contest." I nodded my acknowledgement.

He left and I finally started to breathe again.

The next day, aside from a few disgruntled soldiers who would have preferred to be watching the chariot races they'd put money on, I found myself practically alone. One performance after another was taking place in the arena today but neither Julian nor I was permitted to be present. Slaves weren't allowed to be spectators at events unless they were in the wait to compete.

Julian and I were to be the grand finale. The crowd was supposed to anticipate our arrival and be delighted to finally see us walk into that arena on the final day.

As I ate alone, I watched the sun go down in an almost purple sky and wondered how Samson had fared in the contest today.

When Claudius walked in, I stood, looking at him curiously. Had he come to do his mother's dirty deed, come to poison me before I met her lover in the arena tomorrow?

Claudius waved me back down. "Go on, eat." He came closer, smiled.

I warily awaited his next move.

"It's so nice to see you, my beautiful Gold. Are you lonely?"

"Actually, I am enjoying the solitude."

He sat opposite me. "Of course you are. I have missed you. I've missed your cock."

I assumed by that statement his wedding night was a disappointment.

"I came to wish you luck."

"I appreciate it," I nodded respectfully, hoping that's all it was.

"My mother does not wish Julian to fight. Did you know?"

"I have heard rumours."

"She enjoys his cock too much."

I was not supposed to comment so I didn't.

"I am miserable. My cock is miserable. We are alone, you and I."

I looked at him. I had a feeling he was being philosophical.

"I want..." he stood, "no, actually, I need your masculine touch." He met my gaze.

I sucked in some breath. "You are not my master," I told him.

"You would refuse me?" His voice was enraged.

"Claudius, I have to—" I hoped to make him see reason.

"Guard!" he cried out. The expression on his face seemed quite crazed.

I stiffened.

A soldier came in on a run.

"Bind and gag him and hang him in the courtyard."

My eyes widened.

The guard froze.

"What in hell are you standing there for?" Claudius demanded.

"You...you want...are you sure you want me to hang Gold in the courtyard?"

"Do you have a problem with your ears?"

"No, but...I mean, it's... Gold. He is to fight for the championship tomorrow and...if your father..."

"My father isn't here, is he?" he sneered. "You will do as I tell you!"

The guard nodded and nudged me with the edge of his sword. "Move!" he barked.

* * * *

I trudged alongside Phillip and Gabien as the guard ushered us all from the wagon. Suddenly, I felt the full impact of where the sword had come down on my shoulder. I'd been certain at one time in that arena that my opponent had been trying to cut me in half. But it was only a bruise, one that seemed to have gone straight to the bone.

We'd all done well today, and Simeon had been pleased. He'd rewarded us by personally handing us laurel leaves and small pouches of coin. Money was hard to appreciate, however, when you weren't a free man. *Freedom.* It was funny how the idea of freedom had reached out and grabbed hold of me once I'd seen Gold again.

When I saw him in the courtyard, I couldn't believe my eyes. Phillip reached out and grabbed my arm. Even the guard said something under his breath. I trembled all over. His wrists had been tethered to the whipping post and they'd laid the whip to his back. I let out a cry and ran to him. His head hung forward.

He mumbled something I couldn't quite understand. I lifted his head and pressed my cheek to his. "Gold, Gold. Good Zeus, how did this happen?"

"Step away from him," a voice bellowed.

I carefully lowered his head and looked around to see Claudius. I didn't think about the consequences. The anger flooded through me. "Why in hell would you do this? Why would you do this when you know tomorrow he will fight? It is you, in conspiracy with your mother to stop Gold from fighting Julian!"

Claudius came close to me. "How dare you!" He reached out and grabbed me by the hair and yanked.

I could have taken him. I could have laid him out on the ground and stopped him from breathing. But I held myself back, knowing that not only would I be put to death, I would be putting other slaves' lives in jeopardy as well. I allowed him to push me to my knees.

He glared down at me. "He isn't yours," he clenched his teeth.

"He isn't yours either," I grunted as I met his eyes defiantly.

He struck me hard in the face. I tasted the blood in my mouth. Claudius motioned to the guard. "Twenty lashes. Do it, now."

The guard reached down and yanked me to my feet.

"Gold might not be mine, but you are," he sneered.

The guard wound my arms around the post and tied my wrists together. I faced Gold, so at least as the whip came down on my back, my vision was filled with him, and it distracted me.

He was still limp, his head lowered, and I couldn't help but wonder if Gracia had gotten to him, given him something to drug him. Gods, was it fatal? Was I losing him? Why would Claudius have whipped Gold? It made no sense given that the contest was tomorrow. What would Phineas say when he returned, or Simeon for that matter? If the main event didn't take place, Simeon, who was the host, would never live it down.

The pain was intense. Eventually, I stopped counting the lashes. I left my gaze on my beloved, and thought that death wouldn't be so terrible as long as I could look at him as it claimed me. Blackness overtook me finally, almost mercifully, and in my mind's eye Gold remained.

* * * *

Samson. My eyes blurred with tears when they finally focused again, unusual for me because I'd never been prone to them, even when an opponent's blade tore into my flesh and drove me to the dirt. It was seeing Samson which caused my eyes to fill. He lay in the dirt on his face a few feet away from me, his back a bloody pulp, and it was because of me.

I struggled against the cords which held my wrists but I was held fast. Suddenly I realised I couldn't feel my back. I was numb from the waist up, probably preferable to the alternative. My arms ached from being suspended for so long, and I was desperate to get to Samson, to see if he was all right.

The loud cry suddenly pierced through the early morning dawn. I pulled again against the restraints and felt one give as it dug into my flesh, causing blood to flow down my arm. I had one arm free when Phineas came on a run, with Sullis at his heels. "Who did this?" he bellowed, looking around at the guards who stood in the distance. "Who is responsible for this? Get him down! Get him down immediately!"

Sullis helped the soldiers and they released me. I dropped to my knees not realising how much blood I'd lost. I struggled to my feet, however, pushing off Sullis's curious hands and managed to get to Samson. I fell in the sand beside him, lifted his head. "Samson," I coaxed. "Samson, please, open your eyes." I turned him gently and placed his head on my lap.

He moaned in pain.

The other gladiators were standing around now. Phillip ran over with some water.

"Take this man and get him attended to," Phineas barked. He grabbed my arm and attempted to pull me to my feet. I pulled my arm away and looked down into Samson's face, stroking his hair. As I looked down into his face, it made me realise that my life was nothing but hell and misery, the threat of death and punishment my constant companion. I suddenly realised Samson was all that mattered in my world, and if he was gone, I would have nothing. We couldn't be together, but as long as he was still in this world, it would give me the strength to go on.

Soldiers tried to take Samson away and I held onto him until I felt him slip from my grasp.

Phineas marched around the courtyard and as I lifted my head, I saw my former master coming across the field, his long white tunic flowing out behind him. Gracia stumbled beside him, as she struggled to keep pace. Claudius was nowhere in sight.

The doctor was there now. He poked and prodded my back and tried to coax me to my feet. I lifted a fist full of sand and gripped it tight in my hand as Sullis stood by, watching me like an anxious mother.

The two lanistas met as if they were two gladiators in the arena. Simeon's body was tight and stiff, and he was on the defensive. Phineas was practically on top of him, his red, angry face almost pressed to his. "Who gave you the right to beat my slave, my champion? I want to know who is responsible for this! I want them punished. Gold can't fight like this!"

Simeon's stance changed. Now he was thinking about the loss of money, and more importantly, the destruction of his credibility. He pushed past Phineas and stared at me, his jaw slack. "How? Oh great Zeus, how in the…" He came close to me, lifted my chin, walked around and inspected my back. His voice rang out in a roar that might have shaken the heavens. "Which of you did this to him?" He eyed the soldiers. "Who was it? Step forward."

Phineas placed a hand on his arm. "They were following orders. You can't blame the soldiers. Who gave the order?"

"Perhaps no one," Gracia stepped forward now. "Perhaps one of the soldiers found Gold to be disobedient and decided that he needed discipline."

"And they would whip him before the contest knowing they would earn my wrath?" Simeon stared at her as if she'd lost her mind.

"Earn your wrath? You forget, my friend, Gold is not yours," Phineas protested. "He is mine."

"Don't stand there," Simeon screamed at the doctor, "heal him so that he may fight."

"Don't be insane," Phineas scoffed, "he will not fight. He is in no shape to fight."

Simeon met his gaze. "Will not fight? What in hell do you mean by he will not fight? He has to fight. It will ruin me."

"That was for you to think about before one of your idiot guards decided to strip the flesh off his back," Phineas thundered as he pointed at him. "And you will pay."

"He is right, Simeon," Gracia intercepted. "Gold can't possibly fight in that condition. Just look at him."

"Shut up, woman," Simeon told her.

Phillip helped me up off the ground now as the doctor fussed over me and tried to coax me inside the gladiators' quarters.

Gracia actually smiled at me. She had gotten what she wanted. I had to wonder what she'd promised her son, perhaps to get rid of his nubile new bride.

Simeon and Phineas continued to fight as I was led inside. Phillip and Sullis trailed after me like anxious chicks.

When I was led into the sick room, Samson was awake but I could see the pain in his eyes. I slipped over beside him and took his hand. He squeezed it in mine. I smiled at him until I was wrenched away and made to lie on my stomach. I turned my head in Samson's direction. Our eyes met and held. I flinched a little as the doctor tended my back. He cleaned it then rubbed some terrible smelling ointment into the wounds.

I fell asleep looking at Samson.

When my eyes opened, Phineas stood there. He looked anxious and when he saw my eyes had opened, he came closer.

"How are you?" he asked.

I nodded. "I'm sore, but I'll live."

"What did you do to earn such treatment?"

I sighed but didn't rush to answer.

"Talk," he barked. "I insist. I want the truth."

"I believe it was calculated. There are rumours that some people prefer me not to fight Julian."

"Gracia," he hissed.

"Ah yes, you know the history."

He nodded. "Who gave the order in her stead?"

"Claudius."

"And what pretence did the little prick use?"

"I refused to serve his sexual needs. He accused me of defiance."

"That little...fucking..." he sputtered.

I held out my hand. "I will fight today."

"No. You're not in shape. Julian could..."

"Let it be in the fate of the gods."

"Sullis told me you're a non-believer."

I grunted and moved into a sitting position. "Let me do this, if just to show Gracia that she has lost."

"And Claudius," he lifted an eyebrow, "what shall we do with him?"

I grunted, and hopped off the slab. "I think he has been punished by marriage."

Phineas laughed. "Hmm. But in case Gracia promised to help him in that matter, I think I'll have a little talk with her, let her know that I'm aware of her mischief and also her son's. Any attempt to reward him in this matter will bring exposure. This way, neither of them, gets rewarded for their bad behaviour."

I nodded.

Phineas ran a hand over my biceps. "Are you sure you're ready? I can call it off, let Simeon fall on his face."

I shook my head. "I will fight Julian today."

Phineas left me, and I was left looking at Samson who'd been listening quietly to the conversation. "Why?" he said.

"Why what?"

"Why insist on fighting Julian?"

"If not today, then another."

He closed his eyes.

I walked over and leaned down to kiss him. I let my lips linger on his a few minutes then lifted my head. "I still have to wonder," I whispered, "which death you will regret most."

He made a sound as if he was in pain and grabbed my arm. "Don't, please. I can't bear the thought of either one of you..." He paused.

"He was inside you," I looked down at him. "How do you think I'll feel when I face him? How do you think he will feel knowing that you love me, not him? You do love me, don't you, Samson?"

A single tear spilled onto his cheek and rolled down his face. "You know the answer to that."

I touched his hair. "Sleep," I said. "When you awake, it will be all over."

Simeon hadn't stopped talking since Sullis and Horace started to outfit me in the courtyard. You would have thought that I was his champion still. Phineas stood silently in the background looking deep in thought. "I believe that due to Gold's recent experience, he should wear the oblong shield that covers his body from shoulder to calf."

"Then I shall have to have Julian wear the shoulder guard on his left shoulder," Simeon protested. "I thought Gold was to be the challenger here, the one with something to prove."

"The small square shield which covers the torso would be a better choice for Julian," Phineas claimed.

Instead of the calf-length greaves, I wore leg protectors which came well above the knee. They were cumbersome and I would have preferred to do without them. Although the retiarius, or net-fighter, as they were called, had only a shoulder guard on his left arm, he was relatively unencumbered and could move nimbly to inflict a blow at a long range, and cast a net over his opponent, before finishing him. I told Horace as much as the two lanistas argued.

"Gold prefers the role of the retiarius," Horace spoke up, being a free man, and considered an expert in the area. "He has permitted Julian to take the role of the secutor, if you wish." He bowed his head to Simeon.

"That is very generous of you, Gold," Simeon said, probably knowing full well that it had nothing to do with generosity. The heavily armed secutor, although virtually impregnable, lumbered under the weight of his armour. It was an advantage only to one who knew how to use it.

Phineas came over to me. He nodded at Horace. "Give him what he wants. Make him the retiarius." He turned to Simeon. "Outfit Julian the way that pleases you and will please the crowd."

Simeon considered that for a moment. "Very well. Gold," he said, "you will face the secutor."

I nodded at him. He had just handed me victory.

Chapter Six

The Contest

The crowd roared as Julian and I stood side by side at the entrance to the arena, with our swords in hand.

My opponent wore the heavy armour with a full face mask and helmet. I, on the other hand, wore nothing save for my breeches, and had even abandoned the leg protectors altogether, which caused Horace great alarm.

The trumpets sounded, the crowd screamed louder and we both walked out into the arena, me with my hand in the air. The citizens chanted my name and I was lost in the noise around me for a moment as I walked around the ring and roses flew into the air. "Gold, Gold, Gold..." I smiled, my hair blowing around my face in the breeze.

Julian took his place opposite me and waited. He knew he wasn't favoured by the crowd but it was the least of his worries. He eyed me from behind the mask, and I wished I could see his face. Was he handsome? Did Samson's desire for him reach a frenzied pitch in the quiet moments of the night? I wanted to turn my jealousy into strength, try to forget that Samson had asked me to show mercy.

The Emperor spoke. I glanced up to see him, surprised that he had taken such a personal interest in this battle. Of course, spectacle entertainment assured him he would be remembered in history, would distinguish this time with his reign.

I squinted up at him as he spoke, Phineas and Simeon on each side of him. I searched the stands for Gracia and Claudius but they were nowhere to be seen.

The referee was standing between us as I moved closer to my opponent. I could see the whites of his eyes now, almost hear his laboured breathing through the mask as he clenched his fist around the handle of his sword.

"...and here we stand, the great citizens of Rome...prepared to witness a battle between the greatest gladiator of them all, Gold from the House of Phineas, once a trainer at the House of Simeon, put back into the ring by popular demand. And Julian, another trainer, formerly of the same house, a trainer at the House of Simeon now...Julian, who has never been defeated. These two gladiators will battle for the status of champion. It is by the grace and generosity of these two lanistas, and Rome itself, that this be a battle to the death. Two men have entered but only one man will leave alive. Let the battle begin!"

The referee stood aside and I didn't hesitate. I swung my sword over my head and let it come down on his chest. It hit the metal armour with a heavy thud, echoing throughout the ring. It had begun.

The doctor was fussing over me. I shooed him away. He was really getting on my nerves and I didn't have very many left. When I opened my eyes, I was in pain but it faded into the background the moment I realised that the sun had started to go down in the sky, and the contest between Julian and Gold was most likely over.

There was no way that anyone would have word yet. The soldiers who'd gone to the fight would mostly stay for the night whoring and drinking in town. Phineas was not expected to return. He had already sent his gladiators home, and after the contest, he would return home himself.

Gracia and Claudius had not gone to the contest. And as I sunk down into the bath, and sighed with relief as the water covered my back, I heard some of the guards say that Simeon had ordered them to remain at home.

No matter which way it went, one of the people I cared about would be dead. I knew if given a choice, I'd sacrifice Julian, but thinking about the pain of that loss was suddenly overwhelming to me. Even if Gold lived, I might never see him again. At least Julian would be here, with me. I could touch him, even make love to him, when an opportune time arose. What good was Gold to me, except as a distant longing?

"How are you feeling, brother?" a voice asked and I looked up to see Phillip.

He slipped down into the water beside me.

"I'm in hell," I told him.

He nodded. "I'm sorry." He reached over and placed a hand on my thigh and I didn't push him away. I wanted, needed his touch suddenly, something to make me feel alive, to make me endure the waiting.

He met my gaze, questioning, and I nodded. "Yes," I urged, "touch me."

The crowd was incensed now. The smell of blood was all around me and I could hardly stand anymore. This is what I wanted, to die in this arena, to leave this world with dignity and pride. Samson didn't want me to kill Julian. I knew that, and that's why I'd given up at least three chances to take his head.

At one point, Julian realised what I was doing. He whipped off his mask, pressed hard against my chest, our swords straining against each other, and demanded breathlessly, "What in the name of Zeus's cock are you doing, brother? You trying to lose deliberately?"

I pressed back and managed to push him off before I had to answer him. We went at it again, our swords sliding off each other causing sparks to fly in the air. Julian was a good fighter but I had one advantage over him, aside from the lack of armour, I was very good at sizing up my opponent, and he was distracted by the fact that Samson had been my lover. He couldn't get past it. It was in his eyes, and he wasn't sure what to do with his jealousy which contained just enough admiration for my skill and reputation as a gladiator, that it did him a disservice.

I don't know when I decided to allow Julian to win this thing. The battle had gone on far longer already than it should have, and the crowd was growing restless, turning on me for showing mercy when I could have had Julian's head.

"I will not kill you," Julian announced between clenched teeth as he took a swipe at me with his sword. I raised my left arm and he caught me there against the guard. "I will not kill you!" He screamed out again. Only I could hear him against the noise of the crowd. Women tore off their clothes and men fought among themselves in the stands. "Kill, kill, kill!"

Julian swung the net and I ran from him, swirling around him and slicing him across his upper thigh. It was enough to enrage him and that's what I needed to do. He was a good man. He would love Samson, protect him, stay close to him. I, on the other hand could do nothing for Samson anymore.

The crowd was on their feet. Julian moved quickly and I deliberately went in the wrong direction and allowed the net to fall over me.

I blocked out the noise. I waited for death, welcomed it really. Julian looked down at me, his handsome face a maze of sweat and blood. "Please," he pleaded. "Don't make me do this."

"Do it, do it, brother. He's yours. I will soon be a memory."

The crowd chanted and I made an attempt to free myself in order to make it look authentic. Then the sword came down...

Phillip's hand massaged my cock slowly and I leant back in the water and closed my eyes. I swallowed. "Don't stop," I pleaded. "My cock aches."

Phillip's lips pressed against my throat. "I want to fuck you so badly," he groaned.

I nodded as I pushed away from him. "Come," I invited getting up out of the bath. As we practically ran down the corridor to my cell, I felt a deep pain. *Gold!* Phillip pushed me against the wall and spread my legs. He yanked me forward, my ass against his groin and positioned his cock at my entrance. Without delay, he pressed his hard cock up into my ass, and I gasped. The pain in my back intensified from the friction of his body, but his cock filled the emptiness, and I begged the gods to resurrect my Gold.

Phillip pumped into me hard and I let my head go back, my nails dragging along the walls. His rough hands prowled my naked body and I pushed back against him as he rode me harder and harder until I felt my body shudder and surrender its release.

When I turned around, it was Gold's face I saw in the semi-darkness. "I'll always love you, Samson," he said softly. "Don't ever forget that."

I blinked, reached out as Phillip's face blurred before me.

"What's wrong?" Phillip asked me. He covered my hand with his.

I withdrew from him. "It's Gold," I said. "He's dead."

Phillip laughed slightly. "Samson, Gold isn't dead. He's unbeatable. Don't worry. He'll be fine."

"Julian, Julian, Julian," the crowd chanted as Simeon held my arm up in victory, all the while screaming out his claim to victory and chastising me gruffly at the same time. "You were supposed to take his head. Why in the hell didn't you take his head?"

I couldn't believe Simeon's callousness towards someone who had brought the little worm such glory and prestige. How could he just throw Gold away like yesterday's garbage?

Out of the corner of my eye, I saw Gold being carried out of the arena on the slab of wood. One arm hung limply over the edge. I hadn't taken his head. I couldn't, no matter how the crowd demanded it. I simply put the sword straight through him, saw the blood and turned away.

I couldn't move for the longest time. And there was complete silence, an almost collective mourning which I too observed. Then when I made no move, the Emperor stood and declared the contest over. "Julian is the new champion of the House of Simeon," he cried, and a cheer went up. Roses and laurel leaves and music from the band rained down. People in the crowd threw gold coins as well and finally Simeon came down to share in the praise.

I looked up to see that Phineas was no longer in the stands. He'd sacrificed his best, gambled — and lost. And here I was, the champion, a title I never wanted, going back to face the man I loved, a man who wished that I was someone else.

My admiration and respect for Gold turned to bitterness, and I felt that he ultimately remained the victor. He would forever stay in Samson's heart, a memory, and I couldn't compete with a dead man. They never did any injury.

As I was ushered through the victory gate back under the arena, I saw Phineas and Sullis at the end of the corridor. "Why?" Phineas asked me.

Sullis kept his head bowed.

"I don't know," I replied. I was bloodied and broken, both in body and soul.

"It is a hollow victory, isn't it?" Sullis snapped suddenly, daggers in his eyes as he glared at me.

Phineas placed a hand on his arm. "Sullis, enough. Gold wanted this."

"Yes, and aren't I the lucky one? He had to choose me to fulfil his wish." I sneered.

The Emperor had a big party and I was, of course, obligated to be present. Simeon was so smug that if I had been in any position to, I would have put my hands around his throat and strangled him. What made it worse was, at every turn, his dragging me front and centre and calling out, "Julian, my new champion, the gladiator who finally defeated the undefeated, the one to finally kill Gold."

I felt sick to my stomach every time but I had no choice but to endure. I could almost understand Gold's surrender at these moments, it was freedom. Death was freedom. Death in the ring was freedom with honour.

Phineas took his defeat with dignity but I could tell that both he and Sullis were sincerely in mourning for the loss of Gold. I, too, was in mourning, although I'd known him for so short a time. But perhaps in that ring I knew him better than I would know any man.

Finally, Simeon told his soldiers to take me back to the ludi. I was shackled and put into the wagon, reminded that no matter how many people screamed my name, I was still enslaved. I fell asleep on the way back and was awaken by the sun burning into my face.

A soldier pushed me out of the wagon and told me to go inside. "Congratulations," he slapped me on the back. "Finally, the Romans have a real champion, one of their own."

I swallowed that. Said nothing. I wandered into the ludi, half asleep, blindly found my cell and fell onto my bed. I was asleep again within minutes.

* * * *

When I saw one of the soldiers who'd been absent yesterday, I knew that he had the answer. And although I knew it, I had to hear it to make it real. I walked out into the morning sunshine. It felt different, surreal. I knew it would never feel the same again.

I waited for him to turn around. He stood drinking water from a cup, looking out at the water. When he saw me, he grumbled something. I really didn't hear him, although I understood him. "Does Gold live?"

Those three words were the most difficult I'd ever utter. I swallowed, waited. His words came out distorted. I felt my knees weaken and yet I remained on my feet. I nodded, my throat aching. He was still talking. I turned and walked away. I stopped at the entrance, placed a hand on the door frame. I closed my eyes and trembled, feeling cold although the heat was intense on my back. Why?

Why did he do it? Why did he sacrifice himself for Julian? Maybe I'd never know.

I felt soft lips on my cheek, and the pressure of a warm body against mine. When I forced open my eyes, I heard a soft sigh and looked up into the face of Gracia. "Julian, oh Julian," she stroked my face, "I thought you were dead. My love. My love." She turned my face and kissed me hard on the mouth. I recoiled but she held fast, her hands moving down over my body and grasping me between the legs. "You are mine, this is mine," she let some air free from between her teeth as she tightened her fist on my cock. "We'll be together forever. Champion. I always knew you were my champion."

I wanted to push her off but I couldn't. She owned me. I didn't have a right to push her away, didn't have a right to my own body. *Champion. Champion of what?*

"I can't stay," she stood. "We'll be together soon. Just remember, Julian, I love you."

I turned away, closed my eyes, tried to escape into sleep again. When I finally did find the strength to leave my cell, I could hear the gladiators practicing outside. Would I still be the trainer, or would I just be expected to win one competition after another? I was the new champion, in a role I never expected to be in, never wanted to be in.

I wandered down the corridor, and headed to the bath. I didn't want to see Samson now. In fact, I wasn't sure how I'd face him. I felt guilty for being alive. I felt guilty for not being the one he wanted. I couldn't bear to see the disappointment in his eyes.

* * * *

Gold was gone but Julian was alive, and he was all I had left. I wondered. Did Gold suffer in the end? Did Julian show him mercy? Did he take his head? I shuddered at the thought of my Gold dying in that arena. And I couldn't even be there to perhaps give him comfort in his final moments.

Julian was lying in the bath, his head back, his eyes closed. And when I saw him, I felt the bile rise in my throat. I swallowed it. I tried not to hate him in that moment. I had great feelings for this man, and if I'd never met Gold, I would have found myself crazy in love with him. But now all he was to me was Gold's killer — *murderer* — even though I knew the title was not realistic. He'd had no choice. The real killers were the lanistas and the blood thirsty crowd.

Julian was aware now of my presence. He was looking right at me and I met his gaze. "You fought bravely," I choked.

"I didn't want to take his life," he replied, his voice hushed. "He wanted me to."

Julian's eyes were filled with grief.

I swallowed the pain.

"He had the chance to win, more than once, but he chose not to."

I closed my eyes, felt tears spill down my face. I wiped them away hastily. "Did he die right away? He didn't suffer?"

"I don't know. I didn't take his head."

I sucked in some air.

"He was caught in the net and I didn't really look. I just...I just brought down my weapon. They carried him away. He was still, his body limp. They did none of the tests, just took him away."

"He was dead?" I insisted.

Julian nodded. "I'm sure of it. Please, Samson," he looked at me, "don't hate me."

I came closer. He stood. His naked body gleamed wet in the dimly lit room. "I don't hate you," I replied softly. "I couldn't. I know you had no choice."

"It wasn't fair. It wasn't fair for Gold to make me do this."

As he came out of the water, I opened my arms to him. I held him, stroked his wet hair. "I'm sorry, Julian. I'm so sorry."

* * * *

A warm breeze blew in through the window. I lay on something soft. I moved my head to see that my arm was bandaged and there was also a bandage wrapped tightly around my waist. I took a painful breath and struggled up on my elbow. I looked around the room, large, tastefully decorated, the walls and ceilings well made. The house belonged to a nobleman, but whom?

I felt weak and I lay back down. My eyes closed and I imaged that this was a dream. Do the dead dream? I should be dead. Why in the Hades wasn't I dead?

I don't know how long I slept but when I awoke, a young woman stood at my side. She lifted my head and bid me to drink. "The master will come to see you shortly. Eat," she urged. She held out grapes to me and fed them to me one by one.

"Enough, woman," I pushed her hand away. "Who is this master you speak of?"

Suddenly I heard a deep voice say. "She speaks of me."

The slave girl left my side. A man stood in her place, tall, dark haired. He was a young man with a cultured voice. There was something very familiar about him although I knew we'd never met before. "How are you feeling, Nicolaus?"

I stared at him. "You know me?"

He smiled. "Yes. I've been looking for you for many years."

"Why? Who are you?" I asked warily.

"My name is Mitrius. I am your brother."

I blinked. "Brother. I have no brother."

"No brother that you knew about." He walked to the window and looked out. "We share the same father."

I allowed myself to digest that. "Then I guess you should know that I murdered the bastard."

"I do know." He turned to look at me. "It was the reason for your enslavement. You need not worry about that. I never knew him, only by reputation. He raped my mother, who never told anyone except me on her deathbed. I grew up believing that a member of the Spartan royal family was my father. "

I narrowed my eyes. "What am I doing here, Mitrius?"

"I bought your freedom."

My eyes widened.

"I know what you did. You tried to save your sister from a savage man. I only recently discovered who you were, that you were Gold, the greatest gladiator who ever fought in the arena."

"But... How did you...you arranged all this? The fight was real. Julian brought his sword down on me and..."

He nodded. "It was a risk. There was a chance that he would kill you. We were lucky that your opponent was reluctant to take your head, giving us time to remove your body from the ring before the final blow. What possessed you to surrender in that way?"

"Perhaps I was tired of living."

"You should have never been a slave. Your mother and your uncle should have protected you. They turned their backs on you."

"I have no family," I said.

He smiled at me. "You do now."

"And I'm really free?"

He nodded. "I had already paid those who remove the bodies to go immediately and take you out, if you should fall. When I saw your body and determined that you were still alive, I bought you from Phineas."

"I am surprised he allowed it."

"I convinced him that you would be of no asset to him in the ring, or wherever else he desired to use you, and I gave him more gold than he'd seen in a year. It wasn't so hard. He told me you wouldn't live the night, but you come from strong stock, and I knew better."

"What if I'd won?"

"Then I would have still tried to buy you, and if he refused," he shrugged, "there are other ways to deal with those Roman slave owners. They are common." He came over and perched on the bed beside me. He touched my cheek. "It is amazing how much we look alike. We must look like our father. My mother did tell me that in spite of his sinister nature, he was a handsome brute."

I nodded. "My mother was insanely jealous of him, and I never understood why she gave a damn, given his cruelty."

"Women are a strange breed," he laughed.

"Are you married? Do you have children?"

"Yes. I have two sons. I am a magistrate. My parents are both dead now and I have inherited more than I could ever need in a lifetime. I want to share it with you." He smiled.

"Why? Just because we share the blood of a madman?"

"Yes, for that, and because I want you teach me how to be a gladiator."

I started to laugh. Then it hurt and I stopped.

He stood. He looked offended.

I put up a hand. "I didn't mean to laugh at you. I just don't understand why anyone would want to be a gladiator. You'd have to surrender your freedom for five years and...your family...what of..."

"I know what I'd have to do. It's been a dream of mine. And even more so when I discovered that you were my brother. Teach me and for the next five years, all this can be yours until I return, as long as you look after my family for me."

"If you return," I said.

He nodded. "I know the risks. I've discussed them with my wife. If you'd do this for me, Nico, I would feel secure in knowing that my blood is here looking after my children, their uncle, whom I can trust."

"And your wife, would you have me be husband to her as well?" I scoffed.

"Do as you wish," he said. "It is an arranged marriage, no love between us."

I sighed.

"Think of what I offer you brother," he insisted, "and yet ask so little in return. You will have a home here, wealth, freedom, instant standing in the community, and all you need do is train me well and then be the guardian of my family."

His eyes pleaded. I was grateful to him, and started to like the idea of having a brother, but if it was only to be to lose him again, I was reluctant. "Let me think about it," I concluded.

"Of course," Mitrius said. "Rest now, get well. There is plenty of time to think it over."

* * * *

Three months later

Julian held me for a long time tonight. He didn't say anything. I think he'd been worried about the outcome of my competition today with one of Phineas' new gladiators. I took his head quite easily, and along with it, soaked up the worship of the crowd as I stalked around the ring with my laurel leaf crown. We'd had no party to attend tonight. Simeon was not feeling well, and there were rumours he was failing. As the weeks went by, there were only three contests, all of which both Julian and myself won. I held my breath knowing that one day, given my success in the arena, Julian would be expected to fight me to defend his title as champion, a title, he made clear to me often, he never wanted. "If I could hand it to you, I would," he said.

Simeon had not found a new trainer, so Julian continued on in his role, finding it awkward to train men he may one day come to fight.

It was right before the autumn when everything was colourful and crisp that Simeon died. A quiet funeral was held and a semblance of a mourning period attempted. But no one truly mourned him.

Claudius was dubbed the new head of household. He held dominion over everything, his wife, his mother, and the gladiators. This was a Claudius who'd grown bitter in a loveless marriage, bitter to everything around him. With his wife now expecting their first child, he was at the same time trapped, yet free to indulge his sexual proclivities. He instantly began to engage in excessive abuses of power that would have horrified his father, while Gracia was free now to indulge her lust for Julian, without limit or obstruction.

The night Simeon died, Julian looked sullen. He warned me of the future. "Our lives will change."

"Not so much," I scoffed.

"Claudius is a fiend. He enjoys excess and torture. Expect to be his plaything. And Gracia, she has longed for this day. Without Simeon in her bed, she will seek me out every night. And Claudius will do nothing to curtail her as long as she doesn't interfere with his own desires."

We would know just how right Julian was in the coming weeks. Simeon's death was about to begin a whole new reality for all of us. Claudius' descent into corruption and total self indulgence would lead to excessive rounds of gladiator contests where we would be used like horses in a race, and bizarre adventures into sexual games designed to feed Claudius' endless lust. And through it all, we would have no choice. *Let the games begin.*

* * * *

As my health improved, I began to train my brother, even though everything in me screamed it was wrong. He imitated all the right moves, but I knew he didn't have what it took. I don't think he had that killer instinct. He would hesitate, and it would be his undoing.

His two sons took to me immediately, and I to them. Two fine boys which favoured their father in looks. And Lacia, my brother's wife, surprised me for not protesting more when my brother insisted on giving away his freedom for five years in order to face death in the arena. *Lacia.* Her answer when I asked her this question was, "He is the man. I am merely a woman. I am his slave." She'd looked at me now with clear blue eyes. "I give him everything he needs with my body. He takes me in front, in back. He loves to watch me with other men, watch my body being possessed."

I didn't know what to say. I wanted to shake her actually. This was a serious matter.

"You may have me, Nicolaus, when he is gone," she said. "He would approve of that."

There was nothing I wanted from her. I was actually insulted and offended, but I held my tongue. Instead, one of my brother's slaves interested me far more. They called him Pleasure, and I could imagine why. He was ebony skinned with big brown eyes. And he served completely naked which was a distraction. I was tempted more than once to pull him aside and ride his fine ass but I hadn't had the opportunity.

It was my brother who announced that he was ready and when he gave up his freedom to a local lanista, I had tears in my eyes. During the few months we'd had together, we'd grown close. And he'd given me so much, my freedom, a new life. How could I repay that except by taking care of his family, as he'd asked me?

As they took him away, his two boys, only seven and nine, clung to me. I stroked their hair. It was if they too knew their father would never come home again.

I went back to the house and sat in the garden. Pleasure came to ask if there was anything I needed. He smiled at me. "Yes," I stood, "as I matter of fact..." I ran my hands over his flanks and gripped his ass.

He licked his lips and let his head go back.

I stroked his fine cock and licked his nipples. Lacia had taken the boys to her room to rest and tell them a story. We were alone except for two female house slaves.

I tore off my toga and pushed him against the garden wall. I lifted his legs up around my waist. He was a little slip of a thing, easy to heft. Without hesitation, I held him up with one hand and pushed the head of my cock up into his ass with the other.

He grunted and cried out.

I grasped his hips with my hands and pumped up into him. "Gods, you feel good," I grunted between clenched teeth. I wanted to go deeper. I wanted to impale him, spread his ass in two, but like this, I couldn't get leverage. I whipped him around and pulled out of him. "Down on your knees, all fours." I pushed him down.

He held up his ass to me and I slapped it a few times which he seemed to enjoy. He moaned. "Bitch." I slapped him again, reached around and played with his hard little nubs. I reached between his legs, brutalised his cock until he sobbed with need. Then I took his ass again. I rode him hard and long, slapping his ass occasionally and alternately pulling on his shaft.

Pleasure humped back up against me. "I'm a dog in heat!"

"Bitch. Slut. Gods," I called out. I pulled out of him and turned him around. I came on his lips and he licked at the juices furiously, grabbing my cock and lapping the cum. "Suck it," I demanded.

He took it into his mouth and brought it to life again and I fucked his fine mouth until again I came. I stood after, left him there moaning on the ground. I put my toga back on and walked back into the house. I closed my eyes. *Samson.* It was best I try and put him aside for now, leave him with his Julian, who I was sure was quick to comfort him.

* * * *

The crowd cried out my name as I entered the ring. I was paraded around, my hands in the air, favoured to win. In fact, I had won all the competitions that Simeon had put me in over the last year.

I met one of Phineas' gladiators and made short work of him, holding his head up on the edge of my sword, grinning at the dripping, bloody head. I was officially the next in line for champion now, undefeated, and responsible for bringing glory and honour back to the master's house.

I looked up at Claudius and his mother as people threw flowers. I showed them the head. Gracia gave me a cold smile. She would have liked nothing more to see my head in its place.

When I returned to the ludi, Julian was waiting. There was no great party to celebrate in the house tonight but we were both always on alert.

"Claudius will bring this house to its knees."

Julian shrugged. "Yes."

"I shudder at the thought of what might happen."

Julian drew me around the corner into the corridor and pulled me close. "You will always be safe as long as I am close, my champion."

I kissed him but it didn't ease my mind. Julian moved his hand down over my thigh then reached under my toga to handle my balls. I sucked in some air, groaned. "Fuck me," I breathed.

Julian chuckled, checked around him and dragged me into his cell. He pushed me face first against the cold wall and lifted my toga. He slapped my bare ass a few times then inserted a finger up inside me. I licked my lips as he pushed it deeper, crooking it and finding the right spot.

I gasped.

He inserted a second finger. He started to fuck me with them, stretched them at a V to stretch my awaiting tunnel.

"Um, yes, yes," I panted. "Your cock, Julian, give me your cock."

He slapped my ass again, withdrew his fingers. "You are so tight. I will lubricate you with my cum." He rubbed his cum around my asshole and pressed the tip of his cock there. He nibbled my neck then rammed himself inside me.

I muffled my cries with my hand.

He pulled my hips out at the waist and went deeper, pumping me until my entire body was one trembling mass, in desperate need of release. He stroked my cock hard as he came and I came soon after, my forehead pressed against the wall.

He turned me around now, held me tight and, kissed me deeply, his tongue playing with mine. I sighed, melted against his hard body. "Julian," I whispered.

I was happy for any time I got to be alone with Julian. Every day, Julian trained us, and every night, he went to Gracia. He was exhausted in the morning, and it galled me to know why.

At one time, I pulled him aside and asked, "Can't you put a stop to this?"

"How?"

"I don't know how." I shook my head. "I can't stand it."

"You think I can?" His expression softened. "She'll grow tired of me eventually."

"Don't count on it."

That night, I closed my eyes and I felt hands move over my naked body. I lifted my hips in surrender as a warm mouth closed over my cock. My hands held high over my head, a big, thick cock impaled my ass, and I cried out. "Yes, oh yes, fuck me. Fuck me!"

A voice said softly. "Do you still love me, Samson?"

"Yes, oh yes," I whispered back. "Gold."

* * * *

"He is not ready to meet the champion of the House of Claudius," I told the lanista who owned my brother. "Is there no one else you can put in his place?"

Casus sat back on the sofa. "You have great balls, Nicolaus. You come here, a former slave, with no title of your own, and tell me how to run my ludi."

"I am not telling you anything except that my brother is not ready to fight a champion. You are sending him to his death. He's a volunteer in this."

"And as a volunteer, he belongs to me. He signed the paper."

"I beg you to reconsider."

"Do you know who the present champion of the House of Claudius is?"

"House of Claudius?"

"Yes, poor Simeon crossed the river."

"He's dead?"

"Yes. Claudius' champion is Julian but your brother will fight Julian's contender, Samson."

My jaw fell. Samson would kill my brother. I made another attempt to convince him, but it was in vain.

I struggled with the decision and in the end, I did not attend the fight. When the soldier came to the door, I knew what the announcement would be. Mitirus was dead. There was more. I was now head of the household. Everything he had was mine, and I would pass it on to his sons upon my death.

It was a big responsibility. I had two boys looking to me, as their uncle, to raise them, and a sister-in-law who was more concerned with accumulation of wealth than with the fact she'd just lost her husband. And as time went on, I realised that Lacia not only expected me to be a father to her children, but also to substitute for him in her late husband's bed.

My head was in a spin. The sadness over my brother's death, a brother I barely had time to know, and the fact that Samson had taken his head, gave me horrible nightmares. And just as I was trying to adjust to running my brother's household, a member of the council came to visit.

Lacia was very excited about the visit. She insisted that everything be perfect for his arrival. I was wary, wondering what in hell a member of the council could want with me.

"Maybe they want you to become one of them. There are twenty-eight, especially appointed by the Kings and —"

I raised my head. "Lacia. They are not coming to make me a member. They want something."

"It's exciting, special to be singled out," she gushed as one of the slaves arranged her hair.

I remained quiet, and took my youngest nephew on my knee. He's been clingy since his father was killed. I hugged him to me and tickled him until he laughed.

When the councilman arrived, a white haired man called Marius, the servants offered him wine and fruit. He kissed Lacia's hand and gave her his sympathies. "I was sorry to hear about his death. Many young men wish to be gladiators nowadays. At least his death was a glorious one. And here," he turned to me, "we have the best of them. Your reputation is well known. You deserve this freedom."

I held my breath. I knew that at any moment on a whim, it might be taken away. I could still be considered an escaped slave, even if my brother paid for my freedom.

The council could do as they chose. I smiled at him, nodded. "Thank you."

"I do have a matter to discuss with you." He took me by the elbow and steered me down the corridor.

I met his gaze. "Yes?"

"We need you, Gold. I mean…Nicolaus. We need you as a trainer, to make Spartan gladiators the best. You can do that."

My eyes opened. "I…no," I shook my head. The last thing I wanted was to train young men to fight to their deaths. I'd been lucky to get out alive, but most were not.

He didn't seem to hear me. "We want you to open your own school, the biggest gladiator school ever. You would train the gladiators of the Monarchs. It is a great privilege, coming down from the Kings themselves."

"I can't," I replied.

"Gold," he said sternly, "don't you have any pride in being a Spartan? It is not a request."

Six weeks later, after watching the slaves who were appointed by the monarchy to build the training school, slaves which came from everywhere with very specialised skills, the structure finally came to life. Future gladiators arrived. Some were slaves, others volunteers. Fifty in all, and that was only the beginning, I was told.

I was supplied with guards. And Marius came to oversee everything. Finally the men were lined up in front of me. "These are yours to mould as you wish," Marius announced.

It was with a sincere amount of regret that I stepped forward, ran my gaze over all the expressionless faces and said, "Welcome to the House of Nicolaus."

About the Author

I write not only for my own pleasure, but for the pleasure of my readers. I can't remember a time in my life when I haven't written and told stories. When I'm not writing, I'm dreaming about writing. Eroticism between consenting adults, in all its many forms is the icing on the cake of life but one does not live by sex alone. The story of how two people find love in spite of the odds is what really turns me on.

D.J. Manly loves to hear from readers. You can find her contact information, website details and author profile page at http://www.total-e-bound.com.

Total-E-Bound Publishing

www.total-e-bound.com

Take a look at our exciting range of literagasmic™
erotic romance titles and discover pure quality
at Total-E-Bound.